CONTENTS

The Girl Who Cried Monster

I love scaring my little brother, Randy. I tell him scary stories about monsters until he begs me to stop. And I'm always teasing him by pretending to see monsters everywhere.

I suppose that's why no one believed me the day I saw a *real* monster.

I suppose that's why no one believed me until it was too late, and the monster was right in my own house.

But I'd better not tell the ending of my story at the beginning.

My name is Lucy Dark. I'm twelve. I live with my brother, Randy, who is six, and my parents in a medium-sized house in a medium-sized town called Timberland Falls.

I don't know why it's called Timberland Falls. There are a few forests outside town, but no one cuts the trees down for timber. And there aren't any waterfalls.

So, why Timberland Falls?

It's a mystery.

We have a redbrick house at the end of our street. There's a tall, overgrown hedge that runs along the side of our house and separates our garden from the Killeens' garden next door. Dad's always talking about how he should trim the hedge, but he never does.

We have a small front garden and a pretty big back garden with a lot of tall, old trees in it. There's an old sassafras tree in the middle of the garden. It's cool and shady under the tree. That's where I like sitting with Randy when there's nothing better to do, and see if I can scare the socks off him!

It isn't very hard. Randy gets scared easily.

He looks a lot like me, even though he's a boy. He's got straight black hair just like mine, only I wear mine longer. He's short for his age, like me, and just a little bit chubby.

He has a round face, rounder than mine, and big black eyes, which really stand out since we both have such pale skin.

Mum says Randy has longer eyelashes than mine, which makes me kind of jealous. But my nose is straighter, and my teeth don't stick out as much when I smile. So I suppose I shouldn't complain.

Anyway, on a hot afternoon a couple of weeks ago, Randy and I were sitting under the old

4

sassafras tree, and I was getting ready to scare him to death.

I really didn't have anything better to do. As soon as summer came around this year and school finished, most of my really good friends went away for the summer. I was stuck at home, and so I got pretty lonely.

Randy is usually a total pain. But at least he is somebody to talk to. And someone I can *scare*.

I have a really good imagination. I can dream up the most amazing monsters. And I can make them sound really real.

Mum says with my imagination, maybe I'll be a writer when I grow up.

I really don't know about that.

I *do* know that it doesn't take a whole lot of imagination to frighten Randy.

Usually all I have to do is tell him there's a monster trying on his clothes upstairs in his wardrobe, and Randy turns even whiter than normal and starts shaking all over.

The poor kid. I can even make his teeth chatter. It's unbelievable.

I leaned back against the smooth part of the tree trunk and rested my hands on the grass, and closed my eyes. I was dreaming up a good story to tell my brother.

The grass felt soft and moist against my bare feet. I dug my toes into the earth.

Randy was wearing denim shorts and a plain white sleeveless T-shirt. He was lying on his side, pulling up blades of grass with one hand.

"Did you ever hear about the Timberland Falls toe-biter?" I asked him, brushing a spider off my white tennis shorts.

"Huh?" He kept pulling up blades of grass one by one, making a little pile.

"There was this monster called the Timberland Falls toe-biter," I told Randy.

"Aw, please, Lucy," he whined. "You said you wouldn't make up any more monster stories."

"No, I'm not!" I told him. "This story isn't made up. It's true."

He looked up at me and made a face. "Yeah. Of course."

"No. Really," I insisted, staring hard into his round, black eyes so he'd know I was sincere. "This is a true story. It really happened. Here. In Timberland Falls."

Randy pulled himself up to a sitting position. "I think I'll go inside and read some comics," he said, tossing down a handful of grass.

Randy has a big comic collection. But they're all Disney comics and *Archie* comics because the superhero comics are too scary for him.

"The toe-biter showed up one day right next door," I told Randy. I knew once I started the story, he wouldn't leave.

6

"At the Killeens'?" he asked, his eyes growing wider.

"Yeah. He arrived in the middle of the afternoon. The toe-biter isn't a night monster, you see. He's a day monster. He strikes when the sun is high in the sky. Just like now."

I pointed up through the shimmering tree leaves to the sun, which was high overhead in a clear summer-blue sky.

"A d-day monster?" Randy asked. He turned his head to look at the Killeens' house rising up on the other side of the hedge.

"Don't be scared. It happened a couple of summers ago," I continued. "Becky and Lilah were over there. They were swimming. You know. In that plastic pool that their mum inflates for them. The one that half the water always spills out of."

"And a monster came?" Randy asked.

"A toe-biter," I told him, keeping my expression very serious and lowering my voice nearly to a whisper. "A toe-biter came crawling across their back garden."

"Where'd he come from?" Randy asked, leaning forward.

I shrugged. "No one knows. You see, the thing about toe-biters is they're very hard to see when they crawl across grass. Because they make themselves the exact colour of the grass."

"You mean they're green?" Randy asked, rubbing his pudgy nose.

I shook my head. "They're only green when they creep and crawl over the grass," I replied. "They change their colour to match what they're walking on. So you can't see them."

"Well, how big is it?" Randy asked thoughtfully.

"Big," I said. "Bigger than a dog." I watched an ant crawl up my leg, then flicked it off. "No one really knows how big because this monster blends in so well."

"So what happened?" Randy asked, sounding a bit breathless. "I mean to Becky and Lilah." Again he glanced over at the Killeens' grey-tiled house.

"Well, they were in their little plastic pool," I continued. "You know. Splashing around. And I think Becky was lying on her back and had her feet hanging over the side of the pool. And the monster scampered over the grass, nearly invisible. And it saw Becky's toes dangling in the air."

"And—and Becky didn't see the monster?" Randy asked.

I could see he was starting to get really pale and trembly.

"Toe-biters are just so hard to see," I said, keeping my eyes locked on Randy's, keeping my face very straight and solemn.

8

I took a deep breath and let it out slowly. Just to build up suspense. Then I continued the story.

"Becky didn't notice anything at first. Then she felt a kind of *tickling* feeling. She thought it was the dog licking at her toes. She kicked a little and told the dog to go away.

"But then it didn't tickle so much. It started to hurt. Becky shouted for the dog to stop. But the hurting got even worse. It felt as if the dog was chewing on her toes, with very sharp teeth.

"It started to hurt a lot. So Becky sat up and pulled her feet into the pool. And . . . when she looked down at her left foot, she saw it."

I stopped and waited for Randy to ask.

"Wh-what?" he asked finally, in a shaky voice. "What did she see?"

I leaned forward and brought my mouth close to his ear. "All the toes were missing from her left foot," I whispered.

"No!" Randy screamed. He jumped to his feet. He was as pale as a ghost, and he looked really scared. "That's not true!"

I shook my head solemnly. I forced myself not to crack a smile. "Ask Becky to take off her left shoe," I told him. "You'll see."

"No! You're lying!" Randy wailed.

"Ask her," I said softly.

And then I glanced down at my feet, and my

9

eyes popped wide with horror. "R-R-Randy—look!" I stammered and pointed with a trembling hand down to my feet.

Randy uttered a deafening scream when he saw what I was pointing at.

All the toes on my left foot were missing.

"Waaaaiiiii!"

Randy let out another terrified wail. Then he took off, running full speed to the house, crying for Mum.

I took off after him. I didn't want to get into trouble for scaring him again.

"Randy—wait! Wait! I'm okay!" I shouted, laughing.

Of course I had my toes buried in the earth.

He should've been able to work that out.

But he was too scared to think straight.

"Wait!" I called after him. "I didn't get to show you the monster in the tree!"

He heard that. He stopped and turned round, his face still all twisted with fright. "Huh?"

"There's a monster up in the tree," I said, pointing to the sassafras tree we'd just been sitting under. "A tree monster. I saw it!"

"No way!" he screamed, and started running again to the house.

11

"I'll show it to you!" I called, cupping my hands around my mouth so he'd hear me.

He didn't look back. I watched him stumble up the steps to the back door and disappear into the house. The screen door slammed hard behind him.

I stood staring at the back of the house, waiting for Randy to poke his frightened head out again. But he didn't.

I burst out laughing. I mean, the toe-biter was one of my best creations. And then digging my toes into the earth and pretending the monster had got me, too—*what a riot!*

Poor Randy. He was just too easy a victim.

And now he was probably in the kitchen, squealing on me to Mum. That meant that really soon I'd be in for another lecture about how it wasn't nice to scare my little brother and fill him full of scary monster stories.

But what else was there to do?

I stood there staring at the house, waiting for one of them to call me in. Suddenly a hand grabbed my shoulder hard from behind. "*Gotcha!*" a voice growled.

"Oh!" I cried out and nearly jumped out of my skin.

A monster!

I spun round—and stared at the laughing face of my friend Aaron Messer.

12

Aaron giggled his high-pitched giggle till he had tears in his eyes.

I shook my head, frowning. "You didn't scare me," I insisted.

"Oh. Sure," he replied, rolling his blue eyes. "That's why you screamed for help!"

"I *didn't* scream for help," I protested. "I just cried out a little. In surprise. That's all."

Aaron chuckled. "You thought it was a monster. Admit it."

"A monster?" I said, sneering. "Why would I think that?"

"Because that's all you think about," he said smugly. "You're obsessed."

"Oooh. Big word!" I teased him.

He made a face at me. Aaron is my only friend who stuck around this summer. His parents are taking him somewhere out west in a few months. But in the meantime he's stuck like me, just hanging around, trying to fill in the time.

Aaron is about a foot taller than me. But who isn't? He has curly red hair and freckles all over his face. He's very skinny, and he wears long, baggy shorts that make him look even skinnier.

"I just saw Randy run into the house. Why was he crying like that?" Aaron asked, glancing at the house.

I could see Randy at the kitchen window, staring out at us.

"I think he saw a monster," I told Aaron.

"Huh? Not monsters again!" Aaron cried. He gave me a playful shove. "Get out of here, Lucy!"

"There's one up in that tree," I said seriously, pointing.

Aaron turned around to look. "You're so stupid," he said, grinning.

"No. Really," I insisted. "There's a really ugly monster. I think it's trapped up there in that tree."

"Lucy, stop it," Aaron said.

"That's what Randy saw," I continued. "That's what made him run screaming into the house."

"You see monsters everywhere," Aaron said. "Don't you ever get tired of it?"

"I'm not kidding this time," I told him. My chin trembled, and my expression turned to outright fear as I gazed over Aaron's shoulder at the broad, leafy sassafras tree. "I'll prove it to you."

"Yeah. Of course," Aaron replied with his usual sarcasm.

"Really. Go and get that broom." I motioned to the broom leaning against the back of the house.

"Huh? What for?" Aaron asked.

"Go and get the broom," I insisted. "We'll see if we can get the monster down from the tree."

14

"Uh . . . why do we want to do *that*?" Aaron asked. He sounded very hesitant. I could see that he was starting to wonder if I was being serious or not.

"So you'll believe me," I said seriously.

"I don't *believe* in monsters," Aaron replied. "You know that, Lucy. Save your monster stories for Randy. He's just a kid."

"Will you believe me if one drops out of that tree?" I asked.

"Nothing is going to drop out of that tree. Except maybe some leaves," Aaron said.

"Go and get the broom and we'll see," I said.

"Okay. Fine." He went trotting towards the house.

I grabbed the broom out of his hand when he brought it over. "Come on," I said, leading the way to the tree. "I hope the monster hasn't climbed away."

Aaron rolled his eyes. "I can't believe I'm going along with this, Lucy. I must be *really* bored!"

"You won't be bored soon," I promised. "If the tree monster is still up there."

We stepped into the shade of the tree. I moved close to the trunk and gazed up into its leafy green branches. "Whoa. Stay right there." I put my hand on Aaron's chest, holding him back. "It could be dangerous."

"Give me a break," he muttered under his breath.

"I'll try to shake the branch and bring it down," I said.

"Let me get this straight," Aaron said. "You expect me to believe that you're going to take the broom, shake a tree branch, and a monster is going to come tumbling down from up there?"

"Uh-huh." I could see that the broom handle wasn't quite long enough to reach. "I'm going to have to climb up a little," I told Aaron. "Just watch out, okay?"

"Ooh, I'm shaking. I'm *sooo* scared!" Aaron cried, making fun of me.

I shinned up the trunk and pulled myself onto the lowest limb. It took me a while because I had the broom in one hand.

"See any scary monsters up there?" Aaron asked smugly.

"It's up there," I called down, fear creeping into my voice. "It's trapped up there. It's ... very angry, I think."

Aaron sniggered. "You're so stupid."

I pulled myself up to a kneeling position on the limb. Then I raised the broom in front of me.

I lifted it up to the next branch. Higher. Higher.

Then, holding on tightly to the trunk with my free hand, I raised the broom as far as it would go—and pushed it against the tree limb.

Success!

I lowered my eyes immediately to watch Aaron.

He let out a deafening shriek of horror as the monster toppled from the tree and landed right on his chest.

Well, actually it wasn't a monster that landed with a soft, crackly thud on Aaron's chest.

It was a ratty old bird's nest that some blue jays had built two springs ago.

But Aaron wasn't expecting it. So it gave him a really good scare.

"Gotcha!" I proclaimed after climbing down from the tree.

He scowled at me. His face was a little purple, which made his freckles look really weird. "You and your monsters," he muttered.

That's exactly what my mum said about ten minutes later. Aaron had gone home, and I'd come into the kitchen and pulled a carton of juice out of the fridge.

Sure enough, Mum appeared in the doorway, her eyes hard and steely, her expression grim. I could see straight away that she was ready to give her "Don't Scare Randy" lecture.

I leaned back against the counter and pretended to listen. The basic idea of the lecture was that my stories were doing permanent harm to my delicate little brother. That I should be encouraging Randy to be brave instead of making him terrified that monsters lurked in every corner.

"But Mum—I saw a *real* monster under the hedge this morning!" I said.

I don't really know why I said that. I suppose I just wanted to interrupt the lecture.

Mum got really exasperated. She threw up her hands and sighed. She has straight, shiny black hair, like Randy and me, and she has green eyes, cat eyes, and a small, feline nose. Whenever Mum starts in on me with one of her lectures, I always picture her as a cat about to pounce.

Don't get me wrong. She's very pretty. And she's a good mum, too.

"I'm going to discuss this with your dad tonight," she said. "Your dad thinks this monster obsession is just a phase you're going through. But I'm not so sure."

"*Life* is just a phase I'm going through," I said softly.

I thought it was pretty clever. But she just glared at me.

Then she reminded me that if I didn't hurry, I'd be late for my Reading Rangers meeting.

I glanced at the clock. She was right. My appointment was for four o'clock.

Reading Rangers is a summer reading course at the town library that Mum and Dad made me enrol in. They said they didn't want me to waste the whole summer. And if I joined this thing at the library, at least I'd read some good books.

The way Reading Rangers works is, I have to go and see Mr Mortman, the librarian, once a week. And I have to give a short report and answer some questions about the book I read that week. I get a gold star for every book I report on.

If I get six gold stars, I get a prize. I think the prize is a book. Big deal, right? But it's just a way to make you read.

I thought I'd read some of the scary mystery novels that all my friends are reading. But no way. Mr Mortman insists on everyone reading "classics". He means *old* books.

"I'm going to skate over," I told my mum, and hurried to my room to get my Rollerblades.

"You'd better *fly* over!" my mum called up to me. "Hey," she added a few seconds later, "it looks like rain!"

She was always giving me weather reports.

I passed by Randy's room. He was in there in the dark, no lights, the blinds pulled down. Playing Super Nintendo, as usual.

By the time I got my Rollerblades laced and tied, I had only five minutes to get to the library. Luckily, it was only six or seven blocks away.

I was in big trouble anyway. I had managed to read only four chapters of *Huckleberry Finn*, my book for the week. That meant I was going to have to fake it with Mr Mortman.

I picked the book up from my shelf. It was a new paperback. I wrinkled up some of the pages near the back to make it look as if I'd read that far. I tucked it into my rucksack, along with a pair of trainers. Then I made my way down the stairs—not easy in Rollerblades—and headed for the Timberland Falls town library.

The library was in a ramshackle old house on the edge of the Timberland woods. The house had belonged to some eccentric old hermit. And when he died, he had no family, so he donated the house to the town. They turned it into a library.

Some kids said the house had been haunted. But kids say that about *every* creepy old house. The library *did* look like a perfect haunted house, though.

It was three storeys tall, dark-tiled, with a dark, pointy roof between two stone turrets. The house was set back in the trees, as if hiding there. It was always in the shade, always dark and cold inside.

Inside, the old floorboards creaked beneath the thin carpet the town council had put down. The high windows let in very little light. And the old wooden bookcases reached nearly to the ceiling. When I edged my way through the narrow aisles between the tall, dark shelves, I always felt as if they were about to close in on me.

I had this frightening feeling that the shelves would lean in on me, cover me up, and I'd be buried there in the darkness forever. Buried under a thousand pounds of dusty, mildewy old books.

But of course that's silly.

It was just a very old house. Very dark and damp. Very creaky. Not as clean as a library should be. Lots of cobwebs and dust.

Mr Mortman did his best, I suppose. But he was pretty creepy, too.

The thing all us kids hated the most about him was that his hands always seemed to be clammy. He would smile at you with those beady little black eyes of his lighting up on his plump, bald head. He would reach out and shake your hand. And his hand was always *sopping wet*!

When he turned the pages of books, he'd leave clammy fingerprints on the corners. His desktop always had small puddles on the top, moist handprints on the leather desk protector.

He was short and round. With that shiny, bald head and those tiny black eyes, he looked a lot like a mole. A wet-pawed mole.

He spoke in a high, scratchy voice. Nearly always whispered. He wasn't a bad man, really. He seemed to like kids. He wasn't unkind or anything. And he *really* liked books.

He was just weird, that's all. He sat on a tall wooden stool that made him hover over his enormous desk. He kept a deep aluminium pan on the side of his desk. Inside the pan were several little turtles, moving around in a couple of centimetres of water. "My timid friends," I heard him call them once.

Sometimes he'd pick up one of them and hold it in his pudgy fingers, high in the air, until it tucked itself into its shell. Then he'd gently put it down, a pleased smile on his pale, flabby face.

He certainly loved his turtles. I suppose they were okay as pets. But they were pretty smelly. I always tried to sit on the other side of the desk, as far away from the turtle pan as I could get.

Well, I skated to the library as fast as I could. I was only a few minutes late when I skated into the cool shade of the library drive. The sky was clouding over. I sat down on the stone steps and pulled off the Rollerblades. Then I quickly slid into my trainers and, carrying my Rollerblades, I walked through the front door.

Making my way through the stacks—the tall, narrow shelves at the back of the main reading room—I dropped the skates against the wall. Then I walked quickly through the aisles to Mr Mortman's desk against the back wall.

He heard my footsteps and immediately glanced up from the pile of books he was stamping with a big rubber stamp. The ceiling light made his bald head shine like a lamp. He smiled. "Hi, Lucy," he said in his squeaky voice. "Be right with you."

I said hi and sat down on the folding chair in front of his desk. I watched him stamp the books. He was wearing a grey poloneck sweater, which made him look a lot like his pet turtles.

Finally, after glancing at the big, loudly ticking clock on the wall, he turned to me.

"And what did you read for Reading Rangers this week, Lucy?" He leaned over the desk towards me. I could see wet fingerprints on the dark desktop.

"Uh . . . *Huckleberry Finn*." I pulled the book from my rucksack and dropped it into my lap.

"Yes, yes. A wonderful book," Mr Mortman said, glancing at the paperback in my lap. "Don't you agree?"

"Yes," I said quickly. "I really enjoyed it. I . . . couldn't put it down."

24

That was sort of true. I'd never picked it up—
so how could I put it down?

"What did you like best about *Huckleberry Finn*?" Mr Mortman asked, smiling at me expectantly.

"Uh . . . the description," I told him.

I had my Reading Rangers gold star in my T-shirt pocket. And I had a new book in my rucksack—*Frankenstein*, by Mary Shelley.

Maybe I'll read *Frankenstein* out loud to Randy, I thought evilly.

That would probably make his teeth chatter forever!

The late afternoon sun was hidden behind spreading rain clouds. I had walked nearly all the way home when I realized I had forgotten my Rollerblades.

So I turned round and went back. I wasn't sure how late the library stayed open. Mr Mortman had seemed to be entirely alone in there. I hoped he hadn't decided to shut up shop early. I really didn't want to leave my new Rollerblades in there overnight.

I stopped and stared up at the old library. Deep in the shade, it seemed to stare back at me, its dark windows like black, unblinking eyes.

I climbed the stone steps, then hesitated with my hand on the door. I felt a sudden chill.

Was it just from stepping into the deep shade?

No. It was something else.

I had a funny feeling. A bad feeling.

I get those sometimes. A signal. A moment of unease.

As if something bad is about to happen.

Shaking it off, I pushed open the creaking old door and stepped into the musty darkness of the library.

Shadows danced across the wall as I made my way to the main room. A tree branch tapped noisily against the dust-covered pane of a high window.

The library was silent except for the creaking floorboards beneath my trainers. As I entered the main room, I could hear the steady *tick-tick-tick* of the wall clock.

The lights had all been turned off.

I thought I felt something scamper across my shoe.

A mouse?

I stopped short and glanced down.

Just a dustball clinging to the base of a bookshelf.

Whoa, Lucy, I scolded myself. It's just a dusty old library. Nothing to get spooked about. Don't let your wild imagination take off and lead you into trouble.

Trouble?

I still had that strange feeling. A gentle but insistent gnawing at my stomach. A tug at my chest.

Something isn't right. Something bad is about to happen.

People call them *premonitions*. It's a good word for what I was feeling right then.

I found my Rollerblades where I had left them, against the wall at the back of the stacks. I grabbed them, eager to get out of that dark, creepy place.

I headed quickly back towards the entrance, tiptoeing for some reason. But a sound made me stop.

I held my breath. And listened.

It was just a cough.

Peering down the narrow aisle, I could see Mr Mortman hovering over his desk. Well, actually, I could just see part of him—one arm, and some of his face when he leaned to the left.

I was still holding my breath.

The clock *tick-tick-ticked* noisily from across the room. Behind his desk, Mr Mortman's face moved in and out of blue-purple shadows.

The Rollerblades suddenly felt heavy. I lowered them silently to the floor. Then my curiosity got the better of me, and I took a few steps towards the front.

Mr Mortman began humming to himself. I didn't recognize the song.

The shadows grew deeper as I approached. Peering down the dark aisle, I saw him holding a large glass jar between his pudgy hands. I was close enough to see that he had a pleasant smile on his face.

Keeping in the shadows, I moved closer.

I like spying on people. It's kind of thrilling, even when they don't do anything very interesting.

Just knowing that you're watching them and they don't know they're being watched is exciting.

Humming to himself, Mr Mortman held the jar in front of his chest and started to unscrew the top. "Some juicy flies, my timid friends," he announced in his high-pitched voice.

So. The jar was filled with flies.

Suddenly, the room grew much darker as clouds rolled over the late afternoon sun. The light from the window dimmed. Grey shadows rolled over Mr Mortman and his enormous desk, as if blanketing him in darkness.

From my hidden perch among the shelves, I watched him prepare to feed his turtles.

But wait.

Something was wrong.

My premonition was coming true.

Something *weird* was happening!

As he struggled to unscrew the jar lid, Mr Mortman's face began to change. His head floated up from his poloneck and started to expand, like a balloon being inflated.

I uttered a silent gasp as I saw his tiny eyes poke out of his head. The eyes bulged bigger and bigger, until they were as big as doorknobs.

The light from the window grew even dimmer.

The entire room was cast in heavy shadows. The shadows swung and shifted.

I couldn't see well at all. It was as if I was watching everything through a dark fog.

Mr Mortman continued to hum, even as his head bobbed and throbbed above his shoulders and his eyes bulged out as if on stems, poking straight up like insect antennae.

And then his mouth began to twist and grow. It opened wide, like a gaping black hole on the enormous, bobbing head.

Mr Mortman sang louder now. An eerie, frightening sound, more like an animal howling than singing.

He pulled the lid off the jar and let it fall to the desk. It clanged loudly as it hit the desktop.

I leaned forward, struggling to see. Squinting hard, I saw Mr Mortman dip his fat hand into the jar. I could hear loud buzzing from the jar. He pulled out a handful of flies.

I could see his eyes bulge even wider.

I could see the gaping black hole that was his mouth.

He held his hand briefly over the turtle cage. I

30

could see the flies, black dots all over his hand. In his palm. On his short, stubby fingers.

I thought he was going to lower his hand to the aluminium pan. I thought he was going to feed the turtles.

But, instead, he jammed the flies into his own mouth.

I shut my eyes and held my hand over my mouth to keep from throwing up.

Or screaming.

I held my breath, but my heart kept racing.

The shadows lurched and jumped. The darkness seemed to float around me.

I opened my eyes. He was eating another handful of flies, shoving them into his gaping mouth with his fingers, swallowing them whole.

I wanted to shout. I wanted to run.

Mr Mortman, I realized, was a monster.

The shadows seemed to pull away. The sky outside the window brightened, and a grey triangle of light fell over Mr Mortman's desk.

Opening my eyes, I realized I'd been holding my breath. My chest felt as if it were about to burst. I let the air out slowly and took another deep breath.

Then, without glancing again at the front of the room, I turned and ran. My trainers thudded over the creaky floors, but I didn't care.

I had to get out of there as fast as I could.

I bolted out of the front door of the library onto the stone steps, then down the gravel drive. I ran as fast as I could, my arms flying wildly at my sides, my black hair blowing behind me.

I didn't stop until I was a block away.

Then I dropped to the kerb and waited for my heart to stop pounding like a bass drum.

Heavy rain clouds rolled over the sun again. The sky became an eerie yellow-black. An estate car rolled past. Some kids in the back of it called to me, but I didn't raise my head.

I kept seeing the shadowy scene in the library again and again.

Mr Mortman is a monster.

The words echoed nonstop in my mind.

It can't be, I thought, gazing up at the black clouds so low overhead.

I was seeing things. That had to be it.

All the shadows in the dark library. All the swirling darkness.

It was an optical illusion.

It was my wild imagination.

It was a daydream, a silly fantasy.

No! a loud voice in my head cried.

No, Lucy, you *saw* Mr Mortman's head bulge. You *saw* his eyes pop out and grow like hideous toadstools on his ballooning face.

You saw him reach into the fly jar. You heard him humming so happily, so . . . hungrily.

You saw him jam the flies into his mouth. Not one handful, but two.

And maybe he's still in there, eating his fill.

It was dark, Lucy. There were shadows. But you saw what you saw. You saw it all.

Mr Mortman is a monster.

I climbed to my feet. I felt a cold drop of rain on top of my head.

"Mr Mortman is a monster." I said it out loud.

I knew I had to tell Mum and Dad as fast as I

could. "The librarian is a monster." That's what I'd tell them.

Of course, they'll be shocked. Who *wouldn't* be?

Feeling another raindrop on my head, then one on my shoulder, I started jogging for home. I had gone about half a block when I stopped.

The stupid Rollerblades! I had left them in the library again.

I turned back. A gust of wind blew my hair over my face. I pushed it back with both hands. I was thinking hard, trying to work out what to do.

Rain pattered softly on the pavement. The cold raindrops felt good on my hot forehead.

I decided to go back to the library and get my skates. This time, I'd make a lot of noise. Make sure Mr Mortman knew someone was there.

If he heard me coming, I decided, he'd act normally. He wouldn't eat flies in front of me. He wouldn't let his eyes bulge and his head grow like that.

Would he?

I stopped as the library came back into view. I hesitated, staring through the drizzling rain at the old building.

Maybe I should wait and come back tomorrow with my dad.

Wouldn't that be a better plan?

No. I decided I wanted my skates. And I was going to get them.

I've always been pretty brave.

The time a bat flew into our house, *I* was the one who yelled and screamed at it and chased it out with a butterfly net.

I'm not afraid of bats. Or snakes. Or bugs.

"Or monsters," I said out loud.

As I walked up to the front of the library, rain pattering softly all around me, I kept telling myself to make a lot of noise. Make sure Mr Mortman knows you're there, Lucy. Call out to him. Tell him you came back because you left your skates.

He won't let you see that he's a monster if he knows you're there.

He won't hurt you or anything if you give him some warning.

I kept reassuring myself all the way up to the dark, old building. I climbed the stone steps hesitantly.

Then, taking a deep breath, I grabbed the doorknob and started to go in.

I turned the knob and pushed, but the door refused to open. I tried again. It took me a while to realize that it was locked.

The library was closed.

The rain pattered softly on the grass as I walked around to the front window. It was high off the ground. I had to pull myself up on the window ledge to look inside.

Darkness. Total darkness.

I felt relieved and disappointed at the same time.

I wanted my skates, but I didn't really want to go back in there. "I'll get them tomorrow," I said out loud.

I lowered myself to the ground. The rain was starting to come down harder, and the wind was picking up, blowing the rain in sheets.

I started to run, my trainers squelching over the wet grass. I ran all the way home. I was totally drenched by the time I came through the front door. My hair was matted down on my head. My T-shirt was soaked through.

"Mum! Dad? Are you home?" I cried.

I ran through the hallway, nearly slipping on the smooth floor, and burst into the kitchen. "A monster!" I cried.

"Huh?" Randy was seated at the kitchen table, snapping a big pile of string beans for Mum. He was the only one who looked up.

Mum and Dad were standing at the kitchen units, rolling little meatballs in their hands. They didn't even turn round.

"A monster!" I screamed again.

"Where?" Randy cried.

"Did you get caught in the rain?" Mum asked.

"Don't you say hi?" Dad asked. "Do you just explode into a room yelling? Don't I get a 'Hi, Dad,' or anything?"

"Hi, Dad," I cried breathlessly. "There's a monster in the library!"

"Lucy, please—" Mum started impatiently.

"What kind of monster?" Randy asked. He had stopped snapping the ends off the beans and was staring hard at me.

Mum finally turned round. "You're soaked!" she cried. "You're dripping all over the floor. Get upstairs and change into some dry clothes."

Dad turned, too, a frown on his face. "Your mother has just washed the floor," he muttered.

"*I'm trying to tell you something!*" I shouted, raising my fists in the air.

"No need to scream," Mum scolded. "Get changed. Then tell us."

"But Mr Mortman is a *monster!*" I cried.

"Can't you save the monster stuff till later? I've just got home, and I've got an awful headache," Dad complained. His eyes stared down at the kitchen floor. Small puddles were forming around me on the white linoleum.

"I'm serious!" I insisted. "Mr Mortman—he's really a monster!"

Randy laughed. "He's funny-looking."

"Randy, it's not nice to make fun of people's looks," Mum said crossly. She turned back to me. "See what you're teaching your little brother? Can't you set a good example?"

"But, Mum!"

"Lucy, please get into some dry clothes," Dad pleaded. "Then come down and lay the table, okay?"

I was so frustrated! I tilted my head back and let out an angry growl. "Doesn't anyone here *believe* me?" I cried.

"This really isn't the time for your monster stories," Mum said, turning back to her meatballs. "Larry, you're making them too big," she scolded my father. "They're supposed to be small and delicate."

"But I like *big* meatballs," Dad insisted.

No one was paying any attention to me. I turned and stomped angrily out of the kitchen.

"Is Mr Mortman *really* a monster?" Randy called after me.

"I don't know, and I don't care—about *anything*!" I screamed back. I was just so angry and upset.

They didn't have to ignore me like that.

All they cared about was their stupid meatballs.

Up in my room, I pulled off my wet clothes and tossed them to the floor. I changed into jeans and a tank top.

Is Mr Mortman really a monster?

Randy's question echoed in my head.

Did I imagine the whole thing? Do I just have monsters on the brain?

It had been so dark and shadowy in the library with all the lights turned off. Maybe Mr Mortman didn't eat the flies. Maybe he pulled them out of the jar and fed them to his pet turtles.

Maybe I just imagined that he ate them.

Maybe his head didn't swell up like a balloon. Maybe his eyes didn't pop out. Maybe that was just a trick of the darkness, the dancing shadows, the dim grey light.

Maybe I need glasses.

Maybe I'm crazy and weird.

"Lucy—hurry down and set the table," my dad called up the stairs.

"Okay. Coming." As I made my way downstairs, I felt all mixed up.

I didn't mention Mr Mortman at dinner. Actually, Mum brought him up. "What book did you choose to read this week?" she asked.

"*Frankenstein*," I told her.

Dad groaned. "More monsters!" he cried, shaking his head. "Don't you ever get *enough* monsters? You *see* them wherever you go! Do you have to *read* about monsters, too?"

Dad has a big booming voice. Everything about my dad is big. He looks very tough, with a broad chest and powerful-looking arms. When he shouts, the whole house shakes.

"Randy, you did a great job with the string beans," Mum said, quickly changing the subject.

After dinner, I helped Dad with the dishes. Then I went upstairs to my room to start reading *Frankenstein*. I'd seen the old film of *Frankenstein* on TV, so I knew what it was about. It was about a scientist who builds a monster, and the monster comes to life.

It sounded like my kind of story.

I wondered if it was true.

To my surprise, I found Randy in my room, sitting on my bed, waiting for me. "What do you want?" I asked. I really don't like him messing around in my room.

"Tell me about Mr Mortman," he said. I could

tell by his face that he was scared and excited at the same time.

I sat down on the edge of the bed. I realized I was eager to tell someone about what had happened in the library. So I told Randy the whole story, starting with how I had to go back there because I'd left my Rollerblades behind.

Randy was squeezing my pillow against his chest and breathing really hard. The story got him pretty scared, I suppose.

I was just finishing the part where Mr Mortman stuffed a handful of flies into his mouth. Randy gasped. He looked ill.

"Lucy!" My dad burst angrily into the room. "What is your *problem*?"

"Nothing, Dad, I—"

"How many times do we have to tell you not to frighten Randy with your silly monster stories?"

"Silly?" I shrieked. "But, Dad—this one is *true!*"

He made a disgusted face and stood there glaring at me. I expected fire to come shooting out of his nostrils at any minute.

"I—I'm not scared. Really!" Randy protested, coming to my defence. But my poor brother was as white as the pillow he was holding, and trembling all over.

"This is your last warning," Dad said. "I mean it, Lucy. I'm *really* angry." He disappeared back downstairs.

I stared at the doorway where he'd been standing.

I'm really angry, too, I thought.

I'm really angry that no one in this family believes me when I'm being serious.

I knew at that moment that I had no choice.

I had to prove that I wasn't a liar. I had to prove that I wasn't making it all up.

I had to *prove* to Mum and Dad that Mr Mortman was a monster.

"What's that?" I asked Aaron.

It was a week later. I had to pass his house to get to the library for my Reading Rangers meeting. I stopped when I saw Aaron in the front garden. He was tossing a blue disc, then catching it when it snapped back at him.

"It's like a Frisbee on a long rubber band," he said. He tossed the disc and it snapped back fast. He missed it and it flew behind him, then snapped back again—and hit him on the back of the head.

"That's not how it's supposed to work exactly," he said, blushing. He started to untangle a knot in the thick rubber band.

"Can I play with you?" I asked.

He shook his head. "No. It's for one person, see?"

"It's a one-person Frisbee?" I asked.

"Yeah. Haven't you seen the adverts on TV?

You play it by yourself. You throw it and then you catch it."

"But what if someone wants to play *with* you?" I demanded.

"You can't," Aaron answered. "It doesn't work that way."

I thought it was pretty stupid. But Aaron seemed to be having a good time. So I said goodbye and continued on to the library.

It was a beautiful, sunny day. Everything seemed bright and cheerful, golden and summer green.

The library, as usual, was bathed in blue shadows. I'd only been back once since that day. Once *very* quickly, to get my Rollerblades. I stopped at the kerb, staring up at it. I felt a sudden chill.

The whole world seemed to grow darker here. Darker and colder.

Just my imagination?

We'll see, I thought. We'll see today what's real and what isn't.

I pulled my rucksack off my shoulders and, swinging it by the straps, made my way to the front door. Taking a deep breath, I pushed open the door and stepped inside.

Perched over his desk in the main reading room, Mr Mortman was just finishing with another Reading Rangers member. It was a girl I knew from school, Ellen Borders.

I watched from the end of a long row of books. Mr Mortman was saying goodbye. He handed her a gold star. Then he shook Ellen's hand, and I could see her try not to make a disgusted face. His hand was probably sopping wet, as usual.

She said something, and they both laughed. Very jolly.

Ellen said goodbye and headed towards the doorway. I stepped out to greet her. "What book did you get?" I asked after we had said our hellos.

She held it up for me. "It's called *White Fang*," she said.

"It's about a monster?" I guessed.

She laughed. "No, Lucy. It's about a dog."

I thought I saw Mr Mortman's head lift up when I said the word *monster*.

But I might've imagined that.

I chatted a short while longer with Ellen, who was three books ahead of me this summer. She had only one more to read to get her prize. What a show-off.

I heard the front door close behind her as I took my seat next to Mr Mortman's desk and pulled *Frankenstein* from my bookbag.

"Did you enjoy it?" Mr Mortman asked. He had been studying his turtles, but he turned to face me, a friendly smile on his face.

He was wearing another poloneck, a bright yellow one this time. I noticed that he wore a big, purple ring on one of his pudgy pink fingers. He twirled the ring as he smiled at me.

"It was quite hard," I said. "But I liked it."

I had read more than half of this one. I would have finished it if it didn't have such tiny type.

"Did you enjoy the description in this book, too?" Mr Mortman asked, leaning closer to me over the desk.

My eye caught the big jar of flies on the shelf behind him. It was very full.

"Well, yeah," I said. "I sort of expected more action though."

"What was your favourite part of the book?" Mr Mortman asked.

"The monster!" I answered instantly.

I watched his face to see if he reacted to that word. But he didn't even blink. His tiny black eyes remained locked on mine.

"The monster was really great," I said. I decided to test him. "Wouldn't it be cool if there were *real* monsters, Mr Mortman?"

Again he didn't blink. "Most people wouldn't be very happy about that," he said quietly, twirling his purple ring. "Most people like to get their scares in books or in films. They don't want their scares to be in real life." He chuckled.

I forced myself to chuckle, too.

I took a deep breath and continued my little test. I was trying to catch him out, to reveal that he wasn't really human. "Do you believe that real monsters exist?" I asked.

Not very subtle. I admit it.

But he didn't seem to notice.

"Do I believe that a scientist such as Dr Frankenstein could build a living monster?" Mr Mortman asked. He shook his round, bald head. "We can build robots, but not living creatures."

That wasn't what I meant.

Some other people came into the library. A little girl with her white-haired grandmother. The little girl went skipping to the children's book section. The grandmother picked up a newspaper and carried it to an armchair across the room.

I was very unhappy to see them. I knew that the librarian wouldn't change into a monster while they were here. I was sure he only ate flies when the library was empty. I was going to have to hide somewhere and wait for them to leave.

Mr Mortman reached into his desk drawer, pulled out a gold star, and handed it to me. I thought he was going to shake my hand, but he didn't. "Have you read *Anne of Green Gables*?" he asked, picking up a book from the pile on his desk.

"No," I said. "Does it have monsters in it?"

He threw back his head and laughed, his chins quivering.

47

I thought I caught a flash of recognition in his eyes. A question. A tiny moment of hesitation.

I thought my question brought something strange to his eyes.

But, of course, again it could have been my imagination.

"I don't think you'll find any monsters in this one," he said, still chuckling. He stamped it with his rubber stamp and handed it to me. The cover was moist from where his fingers had been.

I made an appointment for the same time next week. Then I walked out of the main reading room and pretended to leave the library.

I pulled open the front door and let it slam, but I didn't go out. Instead, I crept back, keeping in the shadows. I stopped at the back wall, hidden by a long row of bookshelves.

Where to hide?

I had to find a safe hiding place. Safe from Mr Mortman's beady eyes. And safe from anyone else who might enter the library.

What was my plan?

Well, I'd been thinking about it all week. But I really didn't have much of a plan. I just wanted to catch him in the act, that's all.

I wanted to see clearly. I wanted to erase all doubts from my mind.

My plan was to hide until the library was empty, to spy on Mr Mortman, to watch him change into a monster and eat flies again.

Then I'd know I wasn't crazy. Then I'd know my eyes hadn't been playing tricks on me.

On the other side of the room, I could hear the little girl's grandmother calling to Mr Mortman. "Do you have any spelling books? Samantha only likes picture books. But I want her to learn to spell."

"Grandma, whisper!" Samantha called harshly. "This is a library, remember! Whisper!"

My eyes searched the long, dark shelves for a hiding place. And there it was. A low bookshelf along the floor near the back was empty. It formed a narrow cave that I could crawl into.

Trying to be as quiet as I could, I got down on my knees, sat down on the shelf, turned, slid my body back, and tucked myself in.

It wasn't really large enough to stretch out. I had to keep my legs folded. My head was pressed hard against the upright board. Not very comfortable. I knew I couldn't stay like this forever.

But it was late afternoon. Maybe Samantha and her grandmother would leave soon. Maybe I wouldn't have to stay tucked on the shelf like a mouldy old book for very long.

My heart was pounding. I could hear Mr Mortman talking softly to Samantha. I could hear the rustle of the old lady's newspaper. I could hear the *tick-tick-tick* of the big wall clock on the front wall.

I could hear every sound, every creak and groan.

I suddenly had to sneeze. My nose tickled like crazy! There was so much dust down here.

I reached up and squeezed my nose hard between my thumb and forefinger. Somehow I managed to stop the sneeze.

My heart was pounding even harder. I could hear it over the *tick-tick-tick* of the clock.

Please leave, I thought, wishing Samantha and her grandmother *out* of there.

Please leave. Please leave. Please leave.

I don't know how long I can stay tucked on this dusty shelf.

My neck was already starting to hurt from being pressed against the shelf. And I felt another sneeze coming on.

"This book is too hard. I need an easier one," Samantha was saying to Mr Mortman.

I heard Mr Mortman mutter something. I heard shuffling feet. Footsteps.

Were they coming this way?

Were they going to see me?

No. They turned and headed back to the children's section on the side.

"I've already read this one," I heard Samantha complain.

Please leave. Please leave. Please leave.

It must have been only a few minutes later

when Samantha and her grandmother left, but it seemed like hours to me.

My neck was stiff. My back ached. My legs were tingling, both asleep.

I heard the front door close behind them.

The library was empty now. Except for Mr Mortman and me.

I waited. And listened.

I heard the scrape of his tall stool against the floor. Then I heard his footsteps. He coughed.

It suddenly grew darker. He was turning off the lights.

It's show time! I thought.

He's closing up. Now's the time. Now's the time he'll turn into a monster before my eyes.

I rolled silently off the shelf, onto the floor. Then I pulled myself up to a standing position. Holding onto a higher shelf, I raised one leg, then the other, trying to get the circulation back.

As the overhead lights went out, most of the library was blanketed in darkness. The only light came from the late afternoon sunlight flooding through the window at the front of the room.

Where was Mr Mortman?

I heard him cough again. Then he began to hum to himself.

He was closing up.

Holding my breath, I tiptoed closer to his desk.

I leaned my side against the shelves as I moved, keeping in the shadows.

Whoa.

I suddenly realized Mr Mortman wasn't at his desk.

I heard his footsteps behind me, at the back of the main reading room. Then I heard his shoes thud across the floor of the front entrance.

I froze in place, listening hard, still holding my breath.

Was he leaving?

No.

I heard a loud *click*.

The sound of a lock being turned.

He had locked the front door!

I hadn't planned on that. No way. That was definitely *not* part of my plan.

Frozen in the dark aisle, I realized that I was *locked in* with him!

Now what?

Maybe my plan wasn't exactly the best plan in the world.

Maybe the whole idea was stupid.

You can bet I had plenty of doubts racing through my mind as I heard Mr Mortman return to the main reading room.

My plan, of course, was to prove to myself that I was right, that he was a monster. And then—to run out of the library!

The plan wasn't to be locked in that dark, creepy building with him, unable to escape.

But here I was.

So far, I was okay. He had no idea that anyone else was here with him. No idea that he was being spied on.

Pressed against the tall shelves, I crept along the narrow aisle until I was as close as I dared to go. I could see his entire desk, caught in a deep orange rectangle of light from the high window.

Mr Mortman stepped behind his desk, humming softly to himself. He straightened a pile of books, then shoved it to a corner of the desk.

He pulled open his desk drawer and shuffled things around, searching for something in there.

I crept a little closer. I could see very clearly now. The afternoon sunlight made everything orangey-red.

Mr Mortman tugged at the neck of his polo-neck. He rolled some pencils off the desktop into the open desk drawer. Then he shut the drawer.

This is boring, I thought.

This is boring. And normal.

I must have been wrong last week. I must have imagined the whole thing.

Mr Mortman is just a funny little man. He isn't a monster at all.

I sank against the tall shelf, disappointed.

I'd wasted all this time, hiding on that filthy shelf—for nothing.

And now here I was locked in the library after closing time, watching the librarian clear up his desk.

What a thrill!

I've got to get out of here, I thought. I've been really stupid.

But then I saw Mr Mortman reach for the fly jar on the shelf behind him.

I swallowed hard. My heart gave a sudden lurch.

A smile crossed Mr Mortman's pudgy face as he put the big glass jar down in front of him. Then he reached across the desk and, with both hands, pulled the rectangular turtle pan closer.

"Dinnertime, my timid friends," he said in his high, scratchy voice. He grinned down at the turtles. He reached into the pan and splashed the water a bit. "Dinnertime, friends," he repeated.

And, then, as I stared without blinking, stared with my jaw dropping lower and lower in disbelief, his face began to change again.

His round head began to swell up.

His black eyes bulged.

His mouth grew until it became an open black pit.

The enormous head bobbed above the yellow poloneck. The eyes swam in front of the head. The mouth twisted, opening and closing like an enormous fish mouth.

I was right! I realized.

Mr Mortman is a monster!

I knew I was right! But no one would believe me.

They'll have to believe me now, I told myself. I'm seeing this so clearly. It's all so bright in the red-orange light.

I'm seeing it. I'm not imagining it.

They'll have to believe me now.

And as I gaped openmouthed at the gross creature the librarian had become, he reached into the fly jar, removed a handful of flies, and shovelled them hungrily into his mouth.

"Dinnertime," he rasped, talking as he chewed.

I could hear the buzz of the flies inside the jar.

They were *alive*! The flies were alive, and he was gobbling them up as if they were chocolates.

I raised my hands and pressed them against the sides of my face as I stared.

"Dinnertime!"

Another handful of flies.

Some of them had escaped. They buzzed loudly around his swollen, bobbing head.

As he chewed and swallowed, Mr Mortman grabbed at the flies in the air, his tiny hands surprisingly quick. He pulled flies out of the air—one, another, another—and popped them into his enormous gorge of a mouth.

Mr Mortman's eyes swam out in front of his face.

For a short, terrifying moment, the eyes stopped. They were staring right at me!

I realized I had leaned too far into the aisle.

Had he spotted me?

I jumped back with a gasp of panic.

The bulging black eyes, like undulating toad-stools, remained in place for another second or two. Then they continued rolling and swimming about.

After a third handful of flies, Mr Mortman closed the jar, licking his lips with a snake-like, pencil-thin tongue.

The buzzing stopped.

The room was silent again except for the ticking clock and my thundering heartbeats.

Now what? I thought.

Is that it?

No.

"Dinnertime, my timid friends," the librarian said in a thin, trembling voice, the voice seeming to bob along with the enormous head.

He reached a hand into the pan and picked up one of the little green-shelled turtles. I could see the turtle's legs racing.

Is he going to feed some flies to the turtles now? I wondered.

Mr Mortman held the turtle higher, studying it with his bulging, rolling eyes. He held it up to the sunlight. The turtle's legs continued to move.

Then he popped the turtle into his mouth.

I heard the crack of the shell as Mr Mortman bit down.

He chewed noisily, several times, making a loud *crunch* with each chew. Then I saw him swallow once, twice, till he got it down.

I'd seen enough.

More than enough.

I turned away. I began to make my way blindly back through the dark aisle. I jogged quickly. I didn't really care if he heard me or not.

I just had to get out of there.

Out into the sunlight and fresh air.

Away from the crunching sound that kept echoing in my ears. The crunch of the turtle shell as Mr Mortman chewed it and chewed it.

Chewed it alive.

I ran from the main reading room, my heart thudding, my legs feeling heavy as stone.

I was gasping for breath when I reached the front entrance. I ran to the door and grabbed the handle.

And then remembered.

The door was locked.

I couldn't get out.

I was locked in.

And, then, as I stood staring straight ahead at the closed door, my hand gripping the brass knob, I heard footsteps. Behind me. Rapid footsteps.

Mr Mortman had heard me.

I was trapped.

I froze in panic, staring at the door until it became a dark blur in front of me.

Mr Mortman's footsteps grew louder behind me.

Help! I uttered a silent plea. *Somebody—help me!*

The librarian would burst into the front entrance any second. And there I'd be. Trapped at the door.

Trapped like a rat. Or like a turtle!

And then what?

Would he grab me up like one of his pets?

Would he crunch me between his teeth?

There had to be a way out of there. There *had* to be!

And, then, staring at the blur of the door, it suddenly came clear to me. It all came back in focus. And I realized that maybe—just maybe—I wasn't trapped at all.

Mr Mortman had locked the door from the inside.

The *inside*.

That meant that maybe I could unlock it and open the door.

If the door locked with a key, then I was stuck.

But if it was just an ordinary lock that you turned . . .

"Hey, is someone out there?" Mr Mortman's raspy voice burst into my thoughts.

My eyes frantically searched the door. I found the lock under the brass knob.

I reached for it.

Please turn. Please turn. Please turn.

The lock turned in my hand with a soft click. The prettiest sound I ever heard!

In a second, I had pulled open the door. In another second, I was out on the stone steps. Then, I was running as fast as I could, running across the front lawn, cutting through some shrubs, diving through a hedge—running for my life!

Gasping for air, I turned halfway down the road. I could see Mr Mortman, a shadowy figure in the library door. He was standing in the doorway, staring out, not moving. Just standing there.

Had he seen me?

Did he know it was me spying on him?

I didn't want to know. I just wanted to get away.

The late afternoon sun was ducking behind the trees, making the shadows long and dark. I lowered my head and ran into the long, blue shadows, my trainers thudding hard against the pavement.

I was out. I was okay. I had seen the monster, but he hadn't seen me. I hoped.

I ran until I got to Aaron's house. He was still in the front garden. He was sitting on the stump of an old tree his parents had removed. I could see the blue frisbee-type thing in his lap. He was struggling to untangle the long rubber band.

Aaron had his head down, concentrating on undoing the knots, and didn't see me at first.

"Aaron—Mr Mortman is a monster!" I cried breathlessly.

"Huh?" He looked up, startled.

"Mr Mortman—he's a monster!" I repeated, panting like a dog. I put my hands on my knees and leaned forward, trying to catch my breath.

"Lucy, what's your problem?" Aaron muttered, returning his attention to the rubber band.

"Listen to me!" I screamed impatiently. I didn't sound like myself. I didn't recognize my shrill, panicky voice.

"This thing stinks," Aaron muttered. "It's totally tangled."

"Aaron, *please!*" I pleaded. "I was in the library. I saw him. He changed into a monster. He ate one of his turtles!"

Aaron laughed. "Yum!" he said. "Did you bring *me* one?"

"Aaron, it isn't funny!" I cried, still out of breath. "I—I was so scared. He's a monster. He really is. I thought I was locked in with him. I thought—"

"Tell you what," Aaron said, still picking at the knots in the rubber band. He held the blue plastic disc up to me. "If you can untangle this big knot, I'll let you play with it."

"Aaaaaagh!" I let out an angry scream. "*Why don't you listen to me?*"

"Lucy, give me a break," Aaron said, still holding the disc up to me. "I don't want to talk about monsters now. It's babyish, you know?"

"But, Aaron!"

"Why don't you save that stuff for Randy?" Aaron suggested. He waved the blue disc. "Do you want to help me with this or not?"

"*Not!*" I screamed. Then I added: "You're a *lousy* friend!"

He looked a little surprised.

I didn't wait for him to say anything else. I took off again, heading for home.

I was really angry. What was *his* problem, anyway? You're supposed to take a friend seriously. You're not supposed to think automatically that your friend is just making up a story.

Couldn't Aaron see how frightened and upset I was? Couldn't he see that it wasn't a joke?

He's a total jerk, I decided, as my house finally came into view. I'm never speaking to him again.

I ran up the drive, pulled open the screen door, and burst into the house. "Mum! Dad!" My heart was pounding so hard, my mouth was so dry, my cry was a hoarse whisper.

"Mum—where are you?"

I ran through the house until I found Randy in the study. He was lying on the floor, his face five centimetres from the TV, watching a Bugs Bunny cartoon.

"Where are Mum and Dad?" I cried breathlessly.

He ignored me. Just stared at his cartoon. The colours from the TV danced over his face.

"Randy—where *are* they?" I repeated frantically.

"Grocery shopping," he muttered without turning around.

"But I have to talk to them!" I said. "When did they leave? When will they be back?"

He shrugged without taking his eyes off the screen. "I don't know."

"But, Randy!"

"Leave me alone," he whined. "I'm watching a cartoon."

"But I saw a monster!" I screamed. "A real one!"

His eyes went wide. His mouth dropped open. "A real monster?" he stammered.

"Yes!" I cried.

"Did he follow you home?" Randy asked, turning pale.

"I hope not!" I exclaimed. I wheeled around and ran out of the study. I glanced out of the living room window as I hurried past. No sign of my parents' car.

So I ran up to my room.

I was so upset. So angry and upset.

I took two steps into my room, then stopped.

There in my bed, under the covers, lay a big, hairy monster, its gnarled brown head on my pillow, its gaping, toothless mouth twisted in an evil grin.

I grabbed the top of my dressing table and
uttered a loud gasp of shock.

The monster stared at me, one round eye
bigger than the other. It didn't move off my
pillow.

It uttered a high-pitched giggle.

I mean, I *thought* it giggled. It took me a short
while to realize that the giggling was coming
from behind me.

I spun around to see Randy just outside the
door. When he saw the terrified look on my face,
his giggle became a roar of laughter.

"Like it?" he asked, stepping past me into the
room and walking up to my bed. "I made it in art
class."

"Huh?"

Randy picked up the lumpy brown monster
head. As soon as he picked it up, I saw that the
hair was brown wool, and that the face was
painted on.

"It's papier-mâché," Randy announced proudly. "Good, huh?"

I let out a long sigh and slumped onto the edge of the bed. "Yeah. Great," I muttered unhappily.

"I put the pillows under your covers to make it look like he had a body," Randy continued, grinning. His grin looked a lot like the grin on the monster head.

"Very clever," I said bitterly. "Listen, Randy, I've just had a really scary experience. And I'm really not in the mood for jokes."

His grin grew wider. He tossed the brown monster head at me.

I caught it and held it in my lap. He motioned for me to toss it back, but I didn't.

"Didn't you hear me?" I cried. "I'm very upset. I saw a monster. A real one. In the library."

"You're just embarrassed because my monster head fooled you," Randy said. "You're annoyed because I really scared you."

"Mr Mortman is a monster," I told him, bouncing the monster head on my lap. "I saw him change into a monster. His head grew big, and his eyes popped out, and his mouth twisted open."

"Stop it!" Randy cried, starting to look scared.

"I saw him eat flies," I continued. "Handfuls of flies."

"Flies?" Randy asked. "Yuck!"

"And then I saw him pick up one of his pet

turtles. You know. The ones he keeps in that pan on his desk. I saw him pop it in his mouth and eat it."

Randy shuddered. He stared at me thoughtfully. For a moment, I thought maybe he believed me. But then his expression changed, and he shook his head.

"No way, Lucy. You're just annoyed because I scared you for once. So now you're trying to scare me. But it isn't going to work."

Randy grabbed the monster head from my lap and started out of the door. "I don't believe you about Mr Mortman."

"But it's true!" I protested shrilly.

"I'm missing my cartoons," he said.

Just then, I heard a knock at the front door.

"Mum!" I cried. I leapt off the bed and went tearing to the stairs. I shoved Randy out of my way, and practically flew down the steps, taking them three at a time.

"Mum! Dad—you're home! I have to tell you—"

I froze in front of the screen door.

It wasn't my parents.

It was Mr Mortman.

My first thought was to *run*.

My next thought was to slam the front door.

My next thought was to run back upstairs and hide in my room.

But it was too late to hide. Mr Mortman had already seen me. He was staring at me through the screen door with those beady black eyes, an evil, thin-lipped smile on his pale, round face.

He saw me, I realized.

He saw me spying on him in the library.

He saw me running away.

He knows that I know his secret. He knows that I know he's a monster.

And he's come to get me.

He's come to get rid of me, to make sure his secret is safe.

"Lucy?" he called.

I stared at him through the screen.

I could see in his eyes that he knew it had been me in the library.

68

The sun had nearly gone down. The sky behind him was sunset-purple. His face looked even paler than usual in the evening light.

"Lucy, hi. It's me," he said.

He was waiting for me to say something. But I was frozen there in panic, trying to decide whether to run or scream. Or both.

Randy had stopped halfway down the stairs. "Who is it?" he asked.

"It's Mr Mortman," I replied softly.

"Oh," said my little brother. He came the rest of the way down, then walked past me on his way back to the study.

"Hi, Mr Mortman," I managed to say, not moving any closer to the door. Then I blurted out, "My parents aren't at home."

I knew instantly that it was a stupid thing to say.

Now the monster knew that Randy and I were here alone.

Why did I say that? I asked myself. *How could I be so stupid?*

"I didn't come to see your parents," Mr Mortman said softly. "I came to see you, Lucy."

He knows! I thought. *He really knows! I'm dead meat!*

I swallowed hard. I didn't know what to say. My eyes searched the front hall for a weapon, something to hit him with when he broke through the screen door and came after me.

Mr Mortman's eyes narrowed. His smile faded.

This is it! I thought.

There was nothing around that I could use to fight him off. A little glass flower vase. That's all I could see. I didn't think it would be too effective against a roaring monster.

"Lucy, I believe this belongs to you," Mr Mortman said. He held up my blue canvas rucksack.

"Huh?"

"I found it at the back of the stacks," Mr Mortman said, his smile returning. "I didn't know who had left it. But I found your name and address on the tag here."

"You—you mean—?" I stammered.

"I always walk home after I close the library, so I thought I'd bring it to you," he said.

Was this a trap?

I studied his face warily. I couldn't tell *what* he was thinking.

I had no choice. I pushed open the screen door, and he handed me the rucksack. "Wow. Thanks," I said. "That was really nice of you."

He straightened the sleeves of his yellow poloneck. "Well, I thought you'd probably want to get started on *Anne of Green Gables* tonight," he said.

"Yeah. Of course," I replied uncertainly.

"I think you must have run out of the library

pretty quickly," Mr Mortman said, staring into my eyes.

"Uh . . . yeah. I had to get home," I told him, glancing back to the study. The cartoon music floated into the hall.

"So you didn't wait around or anything after our appointment?" he asked.

Does he know? I wondered.

Or is he just trying to find out if it was me or not?

"No," I said, trying to keep my voice from shaking. "I ran straight out. I was in a hurry. I—I suppose that's why I forgot my bag."

"Oh, I see," Mr Mortman replied thoughtfully, rubbing his chins.

"Why?" I blurted out.

The question seemed to surprise him. "Oh, it's nothing, really," he said. "I think someone was playing a trick on me. Staying in the library after closing."

"Really?" I asked, opening my eyes wide and trying to sound as innocent as possible. "Why would they do that?"

"To scare me," Mr Mortman answered, chuckling. "Some kids don't have anything better to do than try to scare the kindly old librarian."

But you're *not* a kindly old librarian, I thought. You're a *monster*!

"I got up to look around," Mr Mortman

continued, "and whoever it was had legged it."
He chuckled again.

"I wouldn't want to be locked in there overnight," I said, studying his face, hoping my innocent act was working.

"Neither would I!" he exclaimed. "It's a pretty creepy old building! Sometimes I get so scared from all the strange creaks and groans."

Yeah. Sure! I thought sarcastically.

Behind him, I saw my parents' car turn into the drive. I breathed a silent sigh of relief. Thank *goodness* they were finally home!

"I suppose I'll say good night," Mr Mortman said pleasantly. He turned and watched as my parents rolled past him up the drive, heading for the back of the house.

"Thanks for bringing the bag," I said, eager to go and meet Mum and Dad.

"No problem. See you next week." He hurried away.

I went running through to the kitchen. Mum was just coming in through the kitchen door, carrying a brown grocery bag. "Wasn't that Mr Mortman at the front door?" she asked, surprised.

"Yeah," I answered eagerly. "I'm so glad to see you, Mum. I have to tell you—"

"What did he want?" Mum interrupted.

"He...uh...returned my rucksack. I left it at

the library. I have to tell you about him, Mum. He—"

"That was really nice of him," Mum said, setting the grocery bag down on the worktop. "How come you forgot it, Lucy?"

"I ran out of there really fast, Mum. You see—"

"Well, that was really nice of Mr Mortman," she interrupted again. She started to remove things from the grocery bag. "He doesn't live in this direction. I think he lives right over on the north side of town."

"Mum, I'm *trying* to tell you something!" I cried impatiently. My hands were clenched into tight fists. My heart was pounding. "Mr Mortman is a monster!"

"Huh?" She turned away from the worktop and stared at me.

"He's a monster, Mum! A real one!" I cried.

"Lucy, Lucy." She shook her head. "You and your monsters."

"Mum!"

"Stop it, Lucy. Stop being silly, now. I hope you were polite to Mr Mortman."

"Mu-um!"

"Enough. Go outside and help your father bring in the rest of the groceries."

So, once again my wonderful parents refused to believe me.

I tried to describe what I had seen from my hiding place in the library. But Mum just shook her head. Dad said I had a great imagination. Even Randy refused to be scared. He told Mum and Dad how he had scared me with his stupid papier-mâché monster head.

I practically begged them to believe me.

But Mum said I was just lazy. She said I was making up the story about Mr Mortman so I could get out of the Reading Rangers course and wouldn't have to read any more books this summer.

When she said that, I got really insulted, of course. I shouted something back. And it ended up with all of us growling and snapping at each other, followed by me storming up to my room.

Slumped unhappily on my bed, I thought hard about my predicament.

I could see that they were never going to
believe me.

I had told too many monster stories, played
too many monster jokes.

So, I realized, I needed someone else to tell my
parents about Mr Mortman. I needed someone
else to see Mr Mortman become a monster. I
needed someone else to *believe* the truth with
me.

Aaron.

If Aaron came along with me and hid in the
library and saw Mr Mortman eating flies and
turtles with his bulging head—then Aaron could
tell my parents.

And they'd believe Aaron.

They had no reason *not* to believe Aaron. He
was a serious, no-nonsense type. My most
serious, no-nonsense friend.

Aaron was definitely the answer to my
problem.

Aaron would finally make my parents realize
the truth about Mr Mortman.

I phoned him immediately.

I told him I needed him to come and hide in the
library and spy on Mr Mortman with me.

"When?" he asked. "At your next Reading
Rangers meeting?"

"No. I can't wait a whole week," I said,
whispering into the phone, even though my
parents were downstairs and there was no one

around. "How about tomorrow afternoon? Just before closing time. Around five."

"It's too stupid," Aaron insisted. "I don't think I want to."

"I'll *pay* you!" I blurted out.

"How much?" he asked.

What a friend!

"Five dollars," I said reluctantly. I never save much of my pocket money. I wondered if I still had five dollars in my drawer.

"Well, okay," Aaron agreed. "Five dollars. In advance."

"And you'll hide with me and then tell my parents everything you see?" I asked.

"Yeah. Okay. But I still think it's pretty stupid." He was silent for a moment. "And what if we get caught?" he asked after a while.

"We'll be careful," I said, feeling a little chill of fear.

I spent most of the next day hanging around,
teasing Randy. I couldn't wait for the afternoon
to come round.

I was so excited. And nervous.

I had it all worked out. Aaron and I would
sneak into the main reading room without
Mr Mortman knowing anyone had come in.
We'd hide in the dark shelves, just as I had
done.

Then, when the librarian turned off the lights
and closed up the library, we'd sneak up the
aisle, keeping in the shadows, and watch him
become a monster.

We wouldn't run out the way I had done.
That was far too risky. We would go back to our
hiding places in the low shelves and wait for
Mr Mortman to leave. Once he was gone, Aaron
and I would let ourselves out of the library and
hurry to my house to tell my parents what we
had seen.

Easy. Nothing to it, I kept telling myself.

But I was so nervous, so eager to get it over with, I arrived at Aaron's house an hour early. I rang the bell.

No answer.

I rang it again.

Finally, after a long wait, Aaron's teenage brother, Burt, pulled open the door. He had on blue denim shorts and no shirt. "Hi," he said, scratching his chest. "You looking for Aaron?"

"Yeah." I nodded.

"He isn't here."

"Huh?" I practically fell off the porch. "Where is he? I mean, when will he be back?"

"Don't know. He went to the dentist," Burt said, gazing past me to the street.

"He did?"

"Yeah. He had an appointment. With the orthodontist. He's getting a brace. Didn't he tell you?"

"No," I said glumly. I could feel my heart sink to my knees. "I was supposed to meet him."

"Suppose he forgot," Bart said with a shrug. "You know Aaron. He never remembers things like that."

"Well. Thanks," I muttered unhappily. I said goodbye and trudged back down to the pavement.

That dirty traitor.

I felt really betrayed.

I had waited all day. I was so *psyched up* for spying on Mr Mortman.

I had counted on Aaron. And all the while, he had a stupid orthodontist appointment.

"I hope your brace really hurts!" I shouted out loud.

I kicked a small stone across the pavement. I felt like kicking a *lot* of stones. I felt like kicking Aaron.

I turned and headed for home, thinking all kinds of ugly thoughts. I was at the bottom of my drive when an idea popped into my head.

I didn't need Aaron, I suddenly realized.

I had a camera.

My parents had given me a really good camera last Christmas.

If I sneaked into the library with the camera and took a few snapshots of Mr Mortman after he became a monster, the photos would be all the proof I needed.

My parents would *have* to believe actual colour photographs.

Forgetting my disappointment about Aaron, I hurried up to my room and pulled the camera off the shelf. It already had film in it. I had taken a lot of photos at Randy's birthday party just before school had finished for the summer.

I examined it carefully. There were still eight or nine shots left on the roll.

That should be plenty to capture Mr Mortman at his ugliest.

I glanced at the clock on my desk. It was still early. Just after four-thirty. I had half an hour before the library closed.

"This has *got* to work," I said out loud, crossing my fingers on both hands.

Then I strapped the camera around my neck and headed for the library.

I entered the library silently and crept to the doorway of the main reading room. My plan was to sneak into the low shelf where I had hidden before. But I quickly saw that it wasn't going to be as easy as I thought.

The library was very crowded. There were several kids in the children's book section. There were people thumbing through the magazines. One of the microfiche machines was being used against one wall. And several aisles, including the one with my special hiding place, had people in them, browsing and searching the shelves.

I'll just have to hang around until they've all gone, I decided, turning and pretending to search on one of the back shelves.

I could see Mr Mortman standing behind his desk. He was checking out a pile of books for a young woman, opening the covers, stamping the card, then slamming the covers shut.

It was nearly five o'clock. Just about closing time.

I crept along the back wall, searching for another hiding place. Near the corner, I spotted a large wooden cabinet. I recognized it as I stepped behind it and lowered myself from view. It was the long, tall cabinet that held the card catalogue.

It will hide me quite nicely, I thought.

I hunched down behind the old cabinet and waited. Time dragged by. Every second seemed like an hour.

At five-fifteen, Mr Mortman was still checking out books for people. He announced closing time, but some of the magazine readers seemed very reluctant to leave.

I felt myself getting more and more nervous. My hands were ice cold. The camera suddenly seemed to weigh a thousand pounds, like a dead weight around my neck. I removed it and dropped it to my lap.

It will be worth it, I kept repeating to myself.

It will be worth it if I get a good, clear shot of the monster.

I leaned against the back of the cabinet and waited, my hand gripping the camera in my lap.

Finally, the room emptied out.

I climbed to my knees, suddenly very alert, as I heard the librarian go to lock the front door. A few seconds later, I heard him return to his desk.

I stood up and peered around the side of the cabinet. He was busily shuffling papers, straightening his desk for the night.

In a few minutes, I hoped, it would be feeding time.

Monster time.

Taking a deep breath, I gripped the camera tightly in one hand and, feeling my heart start to pound, began to make my way silently towards Mr Mortman's desk at the front of the room.

Everything seemed to be taking so long today.

Was time really in slow motion? Or did everything seem so slow because my pulse was racing so fast?

I was so eager to get my proof—and get out of there!

But Mr Mortman was certainly taking his time. He shuffled through a pile of papers, reading some of them, folding some of them in half, and tossing them in the wastepaper basket beside his desk.

He hummed to himself as he read through the entire pile. Finally, he got to the bottom of the pile and tossed the last sheet away.

Now! I thought. *Now you'll start your monster routine, won't you, Mr Mortman!*

But no.

He lifted a pile of books from his desk and carried them to the shelves. Humming loudly, he started returning the books to their places.

I pressed myself into the shadows, hoping he wouldn't come to my row. I was near the far wall in front of the row of microfiche machines.

Please, let's get on with it! I begged silently.

But when he'd finished with the first pile, Mr Mortman returned to his desk and hoisted up another pile of books to replace.

I'm going to be late for dinner, I realized with a growing sense of dread. My parents are going to *kill* me!

The thought made me chuckle. Here I was locked inside this creepy old library with a monster, and I was worried about getting scolded for being late for dinner!

I could hear Mr Mortman, but I couldn't see him. He was somewhere among the rows of shelves, replacing books.

Suddenly his humming grew louder.

I realized he was in the next aisle. I could see him over the tops of the books on the shelf to my right.

And that meant *he* could see *me*!

Gripped with panic, I ducked and dropped to the floor.

Had he heard me? Had he seen me?

I didn't move. I didn't breathe.

He continued to hum to himself. The sound grew fainter as he moved in the other direction.

Letting out a silent sigh of relief, I climbed back to my feet. Gripping the camera tightly in my right hand, I peered around the side of the shelf.

I heard his shoes shuffling along the floor. He reappeared, his bald head shiny in the late afternoon sunlight from the window, and made his way slowly to his desk.

The clock on the wall ticked noisily.

My hand gripping the camera was cold and clammy.

Watching him shuffle things around inside his desk drawer, I suddenly lost my nerve.

This is stupid, I thought. A really bad idea.

I'm going to get caught.

As soon as I step out to take the picture, he'll see me.

He'll chase after me. He won't let me get out of the library with this camera.

He won't let me get out of here *alive*.

Turn and run! a voice inside my head commanded.

Quick, while you have the chance—turn and run!

Then another voice interrupted that one. *He isn't going to turn into a monster tonight, Lucy,* the voice said. *You're wasting your time. You're getting yourself all nervous and scared for no reason.*

My mind was spinning, whirring with voices and frightening thoughts. I leaned hard against the wooden shelf, steadying myself. I closed my eyes for a moment, trying to clear my head.

How many shots can you take? A voice in my head asked. *Can you shoot off three or four before he realizes what is happening?*

You only need one good shot, another voice told me. *One good clear shot will be the proof you need.*

You'd better hope he's humming very loudly, another voice said. *Otherwise, he'll hear your camera shutter click.*

Turn and run! another voice repeated. *Turn and run!*

You only need one good shot.

Don't let him hear your shutter click.

I stepped forward and peered round the shelf.

Mr Mortman, humming happily away, was reaching for the fly jar.

Yes! I cried silently. *Finally.*

"Dinnertime, my timid friends," I heard him say in a pleasant singsong. And as he started to unscrew the jar lid, his head began to grow.

His eyes bulged. His mouth twisted open and enlarged.

In a few seconds, his monstrous head was bobbing above his shirt. His snakelike tongue flicked out of his black mouth as he removed the jar lid and pulled out a handful of flies.

"Dinnertime, my timid friends!"

Picture time! I thought, gathering my courage.

I raised the camera to my eye with a trembling hand. I gripped it tightly with both hands to keep it from shaking.

Then, holding my breath, I leaned as far forward as I could.

Mr Mortman was downing his first handful of flies, chewing noisily, humming as he chewed.

I struggled to centre him in the viewfinder.

I was so nervous, the camera was shaking all over the place!

I'm so glad he's humming, I thought, raising my finger to the shutter button.

He won't hear the camera click.

I'll be able to take more than one shot.

Okay. Okay . . .

He was still enjoying his first batch of tender flies.

Now! I told myself.

I was about to push the button—when Mr Mortman suddenly turned away.

With a gasp, I stopped myself just in time.

My pulse was pounding at my temples so hard, I could barely see straight.

What was he doing?

He was reaching for another jar. He put it down on his desk and unscrewed the lid.

I raised the camera again and squinted at him through the viewfinder.

What did he have in this jar? Something was

fluttering in there. It took me a while to realize they were moths. White moths.

He closed his fist around one and shoved it hungrily into his mouth. Another moth fluttered out of the jar before he could close the lid.

Mr Mortman's eyes bulged like toadstools growing out of his balloonlike head. His mouth twisted and coiled as he chewed the moth.

Taking another deep breath and holding it, I leaned forward as far as I could, steadied the camera in front of my eye—and snapped the shutter.

15

The FLASH!

I had forgotten about the flash!

I was so worried about the click of the shutter I had totally forgotten that my camera had automatic flash!

The instant flash of white light made Mr Mortman cry out angrily. Startled, he raised his hands to cover his bulging eyes.

I stood frozen in the aisle, frozen by carelessness, frozen by my stupidity!

"*Who's* there?" he growled, still covering his eyes.

I realized he hadn't seen me yet. Those big eyes must have been very sensitive to light. The flash had momentarily blinded him.

He let out a monstrous roar that echoed off the four walls of the vast room.

Somehow I revived my senses enough to pull myself back, out of view.

"Who's there?" he repeated, his voice a

rasping snarl. "You won't get away!"

I saw him lumbering in my direction. As he lurched towards me, his body swayed awkwardly, as if his eyes were still blinded.

I gaped in horror as he approached.

He seemed steadier with each step. His bulging eyes searched the rows of shelves. He was breathing hard, each breath a furious growl.

"Who's there? Who's there?"

Get going! I told myself, still gripping the camera in both hands. *Get going! What are you waiting for?*

"You won't get away!" the monster cried.

Oh, yes, I will!

He was three rows away, his eyes peering down the dark aisles. Searching. Searching.

He hadn't seen me, I knew. The light of the flash had startled him, then blinded him.

He didn't know it was me.

Now all I had to do was run. All I had to do was get out of there with the proof safely in my hands.

So what was I waiting for?

He lumbered closer. He was only a row away.

Run! I ordered my paralysed legs. *Run! Don't just stand there!*

I spun round, clumsily bumping into a shelf of books. Several books toppled to the floor.

Run! Don't stop!

It was taking me so long to move. I was weighed down by my fear.

Run, Lucy! He's right behind you!

Finally, my legs started to cooperate.

Holding the camera in one hand, I began to run through the dark aisle towards the back of the room.

"You won't get away!" the monster bellowed from the next aisle. "I hear you! I know where you are!"

Uttering an animal cry of terror, I ran blindly to the end of the aisle, turned towards the doorway—and crashed into a low book trolley.

The trolley toppled over as I fell on top of it.

I landed hard on my stomach and knees. The camera bounced from my hand and slid across the floor.

"I've got you now!" the monster growled, moving quickly from the next aisle.

I scrambled to get up, but my leg was caught in the trolley.

The monster lumbered towards me, panting loudly.

Once again, my fear tried to paralyse me. I tried to push myself up with both hands, but my body felt as if it weighed a thousand pounds.

I'm dead meat! I thought.

Finally, I pushed myself up and freed myself from the trolley.

Dead meat. Dead meat.

The panting, growling monster was only a few metres away now, lurching out of a row of shelves.

I grabbed the camera and stumbled to the door, my knee throbbing, my head whirring.

I'll never make it. Never.

And then I heard the loud electronic ringing.

At first, I thought it was an alarm.

But then I realized it was the telephone.

I pulled myself into the doorway and turned.

The monster hesitated at the end of the aisle. His bulbous, black eyes floated up above his face. His gaping mouth, drooling green liquid, twisted into an O of surprise.

He stopped short, startled by the sudden interruption.

Saved by the bell! I thought happily. I pulled open the heavy front door and burst out to freedom.

I ran for two blocks, my trainers slapping the pavement, my heart refusing to slow its frantic beat. I closed my eyes as I ran, enjoying the feel of the warm, fresh air on my face, the warmth of the late afternoon sun, the sweep of my hair flying behind me as I ran. Feeling *free*. Free and safe!

When I opened my eyes and slowed my pace, I realized that I was gripping the camera so tightly, my hands hurt.

My proof. I had my proof.

One snapshot. One snapshot that nearly cost me my life. But I had it in the camera, my proof that Mr Mortman was a monster.

"I have to get it developed," I said out loud. "Fast."

I jogged the rest of the way home, cradling the camera under my arm.

As my house came into view, I had a chilling

feeling that Mr Mortman would be waiting there. That he would be waiting beside the front porch, waiting to grab the camera from me, to rob me of my proof.

I hesitated at the bottom of the drive.

No one there.

Was he hiding in the bushes? Around the side of the house?

I walked up the front lawn slowly. *You're being stupid*, I scolded myself. *How could Mr Mortman get here before you?*

Besides, I wasn't even sure he had recognized me.

The lights were out in the library. The room was dark. The closest he had come was the aisle next to mine. And he was blinded for a long while by the camera flash.

I started to breathe a little easier. Yes, it was possible that the librarian didn't know who he was chasing. It was possible that he never got a good look at me at all.

My dad's car pulled up the drive as I reached the front porch. I went tearing after him, running around the side of the house to the back.

"Dad! Hi!" I called as he climbed out of the car.

"Hey, how's it going?" he asked. His suit was rumpled. His hair was dishevelled. He looked tired.

"Dad, can we get this film developed—straight away?" I demanded, shoving the camera towards him.

"Whoa!" he cried. "I've just got home. Let's talk about it at dinner, okay?"

"No, Dad—really!" I insisted. "I have to get this developed. There's something very important on it."

He walked past me towards the house, his shoes crunching over the gravel drive.

I followed right behind, still holding my camera up high. "Please, Dad? It's really important. Really really important!"

He turned, chuckling. "What have you got? A picture of that boy who's moved in across the street?"

"No," I replied angrily. "I'm serious, Dad. Can't you take me to the shopping centre? There's that one-hour developing place there."

"What's so important?" he asked, his smile fading. He ran a hand over his head, smoothing down his thick, black hair.

I had the urge to tell him I had a photo of the monster in there. But I stopped myself.

I knew he wouldn't believe me. I knew he wouldn't take me seriously.

And then he wouldn't drive me to the shopping centre to get my film developed. No way.

"I'll show it to you when it's developed," I said.

He held open the screen door. We walked into the kitchen. Dad sniffed the air a couple of times, expecting the aroma of cooking food.

Mum came bursting in from the hall to greet us. "Don't sniff," she told my dad. "There's nothing cooking. We're eating out tonight."

"Great!" I cried. "Can we eat at the shopping centre? At that Chinese restaurant you like?" I turned to my dad. "Please? Please? Then I could get my film developed while we eat."

"I could go for Chinese food," Mum said, thoughtfully. Then she turned her gaze on me. "Why so eager to get your film developed?"

"It's a secret," Dad said before I could reply. "She won't tell."

I couldn't hold it any longer. "It's a picture I snapped of Mr Mortman," I told her excitedly. "It's my proof that he's a monster."

Mum rolled her eyes. Dad shook his head.

"It's proof!" I insisted. "Maybe when you see the photo, you'll finally believe me."

"You're right," Dad said sarcastically. "I'll believe it when I see it."

"Randy! Hurry downstairs," Mum shouted into the hallway. "We're going to the shopping centre for Chinese food!"

"Aw, do we *have* to have Chinese food?" my brother called down unhappily. His standard reply.

"I'll get you the plain *lo mein* noodles you

like," Mum called up to him. "Just hurry. We're all hungry."

I pushed the button on my camera to rewind the roll of film. "I'm going to drop this at the one-hour developing place before dinner," I told them. "Then we can pick it up after dinner."

"No monster talk at dinner tonight— promise?" Mum said sternly. "I don't want you scaring your brother."

"Promise," I said, pulling the film roll out of the camera, squeezing it between my fingers.

After dinner, I told myself, *I won't have to talk about monsters—I'll show you one!*

Dinner seemed to take forever.

Randy didn't stop complaining the whole time. He said his noodles tasted funny. He said the spareribs were too greasy, and the soup was too hot. He spilled his glass of water all over the table.

I barely paid any attention to what anyone said. I was thinking about my snapshot. I couldn't wait to see it—and to show it to Mum and Dad.

I could just imagine the looks on their faces when they saw that I was right, that I hadn't been making it up—that Mr Mortman really was a monster.

I imagined both my parents apologizing to me, promising they'd never doubt me again.

97

"I feel so bad," I imagined my dad saying, "I'm going to buy you that computer you've been asking for."

"And a new bike," I imagined Mum saying. "Please forgive us for doubting you."

"And I'm sorry, too," I imagined Randy saying. "I know I've been a real jerk."

"And you can stay up till midnight every night from now on, even on school nights," I imagined Dad saying.

Suddenly, my mum's voice broke into my daydreams. "Lucy, I don't think you heard a word I said," she scolded.

"No . . . I . . . uh . . . was thinking about something," I admitted. I picked up my chopsticks and raised a chunk of rice to my mouth.

"She was thinking about *monsters*!" Randy cried, raising both hands up over the table, curling his fingers as if he were a monster about to attack me.

"No monster talk!" Mum insisted sharply.

"Don't look at me!" I cried. "He said it—not me!" I pointed an accusing finger at Randy.

"Just finish your dinner," Dad said quietly. He had sparerib grease all over his chin.

Finally, we were opening our fortune cookies. Mine said something about waiting for sunshine when the clouds part. I never get those fortunes.

Dad paid the bill. Randy nearly spilled another glass of water as we were standing up. I went running out of the restaurant. I was so excited, so eager, I couldn't wait another second.

The little photo shop was on the upper level. I leapt onto the escalator, grabbed the rail, and travelled to the top. Then I tore into the shop, up to the counter, and called breathlessly to the young woman at the developing machine, "Are my photos ready yet?"

She turned, startled by my loud voice. "I think so. What's your name?"

I told her. She walked over to a rack of yellow envelopes and began slowly shuffling through them.

I tapped my fingers nervously on the counter, staring at the stack of yellow envelopes. *Couldn't she hurry it up a little?*

She shuffled all the way through the stack, then turned back to me. "What did you say your name was again?"

Trying not to sound too exasperated, I told her my name again. I leaned eagerly on the counter, my heart pounding, and stared at her as she began once again to shuffle through the yellow envelopes, moving her lips as she read the names.

Finally, she pulled one out and handed it to me.

I grabbed it and started to tear it open.

"That comes to fourteen dollars," she said.

I realized I didn't have any money. "I'll have

to get my dad," I told her, not letting go of the precious package.

I turned, and Dad appeared in the doorway. Mum and Randy waited outside.

He paid.

I carried the envelope of photos out of the shop. My hands were shaking as I pulled it open and removed the snapshots.

"Lucy, calm down," Mum said, sounding worried.

I stared down at the snapshots. All photos of Randy's birthday party.

I sifted through them quickly, staring at the grinning faces of Randy's stupid friends.

Where is it? Where is it? Where is it?

Of course, it was the very last photo, the one on the bottom of the pile.

"Here it is!" I cried.

Mum and Dad leaned forward to see over my shoulder.

The other photos fell from my hand and scattered over the floor as I raised the photo to my face—

—and gasped.

The photo was clear and sharp.

Mr Mortman's large desk stood in the centre in a burst of bright light. I could see papers on the desk, the pan of turtles at the far corner, a low pile of books.

Behind the desk, I could see the top of Mr Mortman's tall wooden stool. And behind the stool, the shelves were in clear focus, even the glass jar of flies on the lower shelf.

But there was no monster.

No Mr Mortman.

No one.

No one in the photograph at all.

"He—he was standing right there!" I cried. "Beside the desk!"

"The room looks empty," Dad said, staring down over my shoulder at the photo in my quivering hand.

"There's no one there," Mum said, turning her gaze on me.

"He was there," I insisted, unable to take my eyes off the photo. "Right there." I pointed to where the monster had stood.

Randy laughed. "Let me see." He pulled the photo from my hand and examined it. "I see him!" he declared. "He's invisible!"

"It isn't funny," I said weakly. I pulled the photo away from him. I sighed unhappily. I felt so bad. I wanted to sink into a hole in the floor and never come out.

"He's invisible!" Randy repeated gleefully, enjoying his own joke.

Mum and Dad were staring at me, looks of concern on their faces.

"Don't you see?" I cried, waving the photo in one hand. "Don't you see? This *proves* it! This proves he's a monster. He doesn't show up in photographs!"

Dad shook his head and frowned. "Lucy, haven't you carried this joke far enough?"

Mum put a hand on my shoulder. "I'm starting to get worried about you," she said softly. "I think you're really starting to believe in your own monster joke."

"Can we get some ice cream?" asked Randy.

"I can't believe we're doing this," Aaron complained.

"Just shut up. You *owe* me one!" I snapped.

It was the next evening. We were crouched

down, hiding behind the low hedge at the side of the library.

It was a crisp, cool day. The sun was already lowering itself behind the trees. The shadows stretched long and blue over the library lawn.

"I owe you one?" Aaron protested. "Are you crazy?"

"You owe me one," I repeated. "You were supposed to come to the library with me yesterday, remember? You let me down."

He brushed an insect off his freckled nose. "Can I help it if I had an orthodontist appointment?" He sounded funny. His words were coming out all sticky. He wasn't used to his new brace yet.

"Yes," I insisted. "I counted on you, and you let me down—and you got me into all kinds of trouble."

"What kind of trouble?" He dropped to the ground and sat cross-legged, keeping his head low behind the hedge.

"My parents said I'm never allowed to mention Mr Mortman again, or the fact that he's a monster," I told him.

"Good," Aaron said.

"Not good. It means I really need you, Aaron. I need you to see that I'm telling the truth, and tell my parents." My voice broke. "They think I'm crazy. They really do!"

He started to reply, but he could see I was really upset. So he stopped himself.

A cool breeze swept past, making the trees all seem to whisper at us.

I kept my eyes trained on the library door. It was five-twenty. Past closing time. Mr Mortman should be coming out any second.

"So we're going to follow Mr Mortman home?" Aaron asked, scratching the back of his neck. "And spy on him at his house? Why don't we just watch him through the library window?"

"The window is too high," I replied. "We have to follow him. He told me he walks home every evening. I want you to see him turn into a monster," I said, staring straight ahead over the top of the bush. "I want you to believe me."

"What if I just *say* I believe you?" Aaron asked, grinning. "Then could we just go home?"

"Ssshhh!" I pressed a hand over Aaron's mouth.

The library door was opening. Mr Mortman appeared on the front steps.

Aaron and I ducked down lower.

I peered through the branches of the hedge. The librarian turned to lock the front door. He was wearing a red-and-white-striped short-sleeved sports shirt and baggy grey trousers. He had a red baseball cap on his bald head.

"Stay far behind," I whispered to Aaron. "Don't let him see you."

"Good advice," Aaron said sarcastically.

We both shifted onto our knees and waited for Mr Mortman to head down the pavement. He hesitated on the steps, replacing the keys in his trouser pocket. Then, humming to himself, he walked down the drive and turned away from us.

"What's he humming about?" Aaron whispered.

"He always hums," I whispered back. Mr Mortman was more than half a block away. "Let's go," I said, climbing quickly to my feet.

Keeping in the shadows of the trees and shrubs, I began following the librarian. Aaron followed just behind me.

"Do you know where he lives?" Aaron asked.

I turned back to him, frowning. "If I knew where he lived, we wouldn't have to follow him—would we!"

"Oh. Right."

Following someone was a lot harder than I'd thought. We had to cut through front gardens. Some of them had barking dogs. Some had lawn sprinklers going. Some had thick hedges we somehow had to duck through.

At every street corner, Mr Mortman would stop and look both ways for oncoming cars. Each time, I was certain he was going to look over his shoulder, too, and see Aaron and me creeping along behind him.

He lived farther from the library than I had realized. After several blocks, the houses ended, and a bare, flat field spread in front of us.

Mr Mortman cut through the field, walking quickly, swinging his stubby arms rhythmically with each step. We had no choice but to follow him across the field. There were no hiding places. No shrubs to duck behind. No hedges to shield us.

We were completely out in the open. We just had to pray that he didn't turn around in the middle of the field and see us.

A block of small, older houses stood beyond the field. Most of the houses were brick, set close to the street on tiny front gardens.

Mr Mortman turned onto a block of these houses. Aaron and I crouched behind a postbox and watched him walk up to a house near the middle of the block. He stepped onto the small front step, and fiddled in his pocket for the keys.

"We're here," I whispered to Aaron. "We made it."

"My friend Ralph lives on this block, I think," Aaron said.

"Who cares?" I snapped. "Keep your mind on the job, okay?"

We waited until Mr Mortman had disappeared through the front door of his house, then crept closer.

His house was white weatherboard, badly in need of a paint job. He had a small rectangle of a front garden, with recently cut grass bordered by a single row of tall, yellow tiger lilies.

Aaron and I made our way quickly to the side of the house where there was a narrow strip of grass that led to the back. The window near the front of the house was high enough for us to stand under and not be seen.

A light came on in the window. "That must be his living room," I whispered.

Aaron had a frightened expression. His freckles seemed a lot paler than usual. "I don't like this," he said.

"The hard part was following him," I assured Aaron. "This part is easy. We just watch him through the window."

"But the window is too high," Aaron pointed out. "We can't see anything."

He was right. Staring up from beneath the window, all I could see was the living room ceiling.

"We'll have to stand on something," I said.

"Huh? What?"

I could see Aaron was going to be no help. He was so frightened, his nose was twitching like a bunny rabbit's. I decided if I could keep him busy, maybe I could keep him from totally freaking out and running away.

"Go round the back. See if there's a ladder or something," I whispered, motioning towards the back of the house.

Another light came on, this one in a back window. Probably the kitchen, I thought. It was also too high to see into.

"Wait. What about that?" Aaron asked. I followed his gaze to a wheelbarrow, tilted against the side of the house.

"Yeah. Maybe," I said. "Bring it over. I'll try to stand on it."

Keeping his head and shoulders bent low, Aaron scampered over to the wheelbarrow. He lifted it away from the house by the handles, then pushed it under the front window.

"Hold it steady," I said.

He grabbed the wooden handles, gazing up at me fearfully. "You sure about this?"

"I'll give it a try," I said, glancing up at the high window.

Holding onto Aaron's shoulder, I gave myself a boost onto the wheelbarrow. He held on firmly to the handles as I struggled to find my balance inside the metal basket part.

"It—it's kind of tilty," I whispered, pressing one hand against the side of the house to steady myself.

"I'm doing the best I can," Aaron grumbled.

"There. I think I can stand," I said. I wasn't very high off the ground, but I wasn't at all

108

comfortable. A wheelbarrow is a difficult thing to stand on.

Somewhere down the road a dog barked. I hoped he wasn't barking because of Aaron and me.

Another dog, closer to us, quickly joined in, and it became a barking conversation.

"Are you high enough? Can you see anything?" Aaron asked.

One hand still pressed against the side of the house, I raised my head and peered into the house through the bottom of the window.

"Yeah. I can see a bit," I called down. "There's a big aquarium in front of the window, but I can see most of the living room."

And just as I said that, Mr Mortman's face loomed inches from mine.

He was staring right at me!

I gasped and lost my balance.

I toppled to the ground, knocking over the wheelbarrow, landing hard on my knees and elbows. "Ow!"

"What happened?" Aaron cried, alarmed.

"He saw me!" I choked out, waiting for the pain to stop throbbing.

"Huh?" Aaron's mouth dropped open.

We both gazed up at the window. I expected to see Mr Mortman staring down at us.

But no. No sign of him.

I climbed quickly to my feet. "Maybe he was looking at his aquarium," I whispered, motioning for Aaron to set up the wheelbarrow. "Maybe he didn't see me."

"Wh-what are you going to do?" Aaron stammered.

"Get back up, of course," I told him. My legs were shaking as I climbed back onto the wheelbarrow. I grabbed the window ledge and pulled myself up.

The sun had nearly gone down. The darkness outside made it easier to see inside the house. And, I hoped, harder for Mr Mortman to see out.

I didn't have the best view in the world, I quickly realized. The aquarium, crowded with colourful tropical fish, blocked my view of most of the room.

If only I were a little higher, I thought, I could see over it. But if I *had* been higher, I realized, Mr Mortman would have seen me.

"What's he doing?" Aaron asked in a trembling whisper.

"Nothing. He's . . . wait!"

Mr Mortman was staring down at the fish. He stood only a few feet from me, on the other side of the aquarium.

I froze, pressing my hands against the side of the house.

He gazed down into his aquarium, and a smile formed on his pudgy face. He had removed the red baseball cap. His bald head looked yellow in the living room lamplight.

His mouth moved. He was saying something to the tropical fish in the aquarium. I couldn't hear him through the glass.

Then, as he smiled down at his fish, he began to change.

"He's doing it," I whispered to Aaron. "He's turning into a monster."

As I watched Mr Mortman's head inflate and his eyes bulge out, I was filled with all kinds of strange feelings. I was terrified. And I was fascinated. It was exciting to be so close, inches away from a real monster.

And I felt so happy and relieved that Aaron would finally see for himself that I was telling the truth.

Then, as Mr Mortman's mouth grew wider and began to gyrate, a twisting black hole on his swollen, yellow face, fear overtook me. I froze there, my face pressed against the window, not blinking, not moving.

I stared as he reached a hand into the aquarium.

His fat fingers wrapped around a slender blue fish. He pulled it up and flipped it into his mouth. I could see long, yellow teeth inside the enormous mouth, biting down, chewing the wriggling fish.

Then, as I gaped in growing terror, Mr Mortman pulled a black snail off the side of the aquarium glass. Holding its shell between his fingertips, he stuffed the snail into his mouth. His teeth crunched down hard on the shell, cracking it—a crack so loud, I could hear it through the window glass.

My stomach churned. I felt sick.

He swallowed the snail, then reached to pull another one off the aquarium glass.

"I think I'm going to throw up my lunch," I whispered down to Aaron.

Aaron.

I had forgotten all about him.

I was so fascinated by the monster, so excited, so terrified to watch him close up, I had forgotten the whole purpose of being here.

"Aaron, help me down," I whispered. "Quick."

Still staring through the window, I reached a hand down for Aaron to take it.

"Aaron—hurry! Help me down so you can climb up here. You have to see this! You have to see the monster!"

He didn't reply.

"Aaron? Aaron?"

I lowered my eyes from the window.

Aaron had disappeared.

I felt a stab of panic in my chest.

My whole body convulsed in a tremor of cold fear.

Where was he?

Had he run away?

Was Aaron so frightened that he just ran off without telling me?

Or had something happened to him? Something really bad?

"Aaron? Aaron?" In my panic, I forgot that I was centimetres away from a monster, and started to shout. "Aaron? Where *are* you?"

"Ssh," I heard a whisper from the back of the house. Aaron appeared, making his way quickly towards me along the narrow strip of grass. "I'm right here, Lucy."

"Huh? Where'd you go?"

He pointed to the back of the house. "I thought maybe I could find a ladder or something. You know. So I could see, too."

"You scared me half to death!" I cried.

I returned my glance to the window. Mr Mortman was sucking a slithering eel into his mouth like a strand of spaghetti.

"Quick, Aaron—help me down," I instructed, still feeling shaken from the scare of his disappearance. "You have to see this. You have to. Before he changes back."

"He—he's really a monster?" Aaron's mouth dropped open. "You're not joking?"

"Just get up here!" I cried impatiently.

But as I tried to lower myself to the ground, the wheelbarrow slid out from under me.

It toppled onto its side, the handles scraping the side of the house.

My hands shot up to grab the windowsill. I missed and fell heavily on top of the wheelbarrow. "Ow!" I cried out as sharp pain cut through my side.

Glancing up, I saw the monster's startled face, goggling down at me through the glass.

I scrambled to get up. But the throbbing pain in my side took my breath away.

"Aaron—help me!"

But he was already running to the street, his trainers scraping the grass, his arms stretched straight out in front of him as if trying to grab onto safety.

Ignoring the pain in my side, I scrambled to my feet.

I took an unsteady step, then another. I shook my head, trying to shake away my dizziness.

Then I sucked in a deep breath and started to run, following Aaron towards the street.

I had gone about four or five steps when I felt Mr Mortman's surprisingly strong hands grab my shoulders from behind.

I tried to scream, but no sound came out.

He held firmly onto my shoulders. I could feel his hot, clammy hands through my T-shirt.

I tried to pull away, but he was too strong.

He spun round.

His face was back to normal.

He squinted at me with those little black eyes, as if he couldn't believe what he was seeing. "Lucy!" he exclaimed in his scratchy voice.

He let go of my shoulders and stepped back.

I was panting loudly. I was so frightened, my chest felt about to explode.

How had he changed back from his monster form so quickly?

What was he going to do to me?

"Lucy, good heavens. I thought you were a burglar," he said, shaking his head. He removed a white handkerchief from his back pocket and wiped his perspiring forehead.

"S-sorry," I stammered. My voice came out in a choked whisper.

He rolled up the handkerchief between his fat hands and jammed it back into his pocket. "What are you doing here?"

"Well . . ." My heart was pounding so hard, I could feel the blood pulsing in my temples. My side still ached from where I had fallen on the wheelbarrow.

I struggled to clear my mind. I had to think of an answer to his question. I *had* to.

"Well . . ." I started again, thinking desperately. "I . . . uh . . . came to tell you that I'll . . . uh . . . be a little late for my Reading Rangers appointment tomorrow."

He narrowed his eyes and stared at me thoughtfully. "But why were you looking through my window?" he demanded.

"Well . . . I just . . ."

Think, Lucy—think!

"I didn't know if you were at home or not. I was just trying to see if you were there. I mean. So I could tell you. About the appointment tomorrow."

Staring into his face, trying to sound sincere, I took a step back, in case I had to make a run for it.

Did he believe me?

Was he buying it?

I couldn't tell. He continued to stare at me thoughtfully.

He rubbed his chins. "You really didn't have to come all the way out here," he said softly. "Did you ride your bike?" His eyes darted over the small front lawn.

"No. I ... uh ... walked. I like to walk," I replied awkwardly.

"It's getting dark," he said. "Maybe you should phone your mum or dad to come and pick you up. Why don't you come inside and use the phone?"

Come inside?

Come inside the monster's house?

No way!

"Uh . . . no thanks, Mr Mortman," I said, taking another step backwards towards the street. "My parents don't mind if I walk home. It isn't that far. Really."

"No. I insist," he said, an odd grin starting across his molelike face. He motioned towards the house. "Come on in, Lucy. The phone is in the living room," he urged. "Come on. I won't bite."

I shuddered.

I'd just seen him bite snails. And eels.

There was no way I was going into that house. I knew that if I went in, chances are I'd never come out.

"I—I've got to go," I said, giving him a wave of

one hand. I could feel the fear creeping up my back, running over my body. I knew if I didn't get away from there—*that moment*—I'd be frozen by my terror, unable to escape.

"Lucy—" Mr Mortman insisted.

"No. Really. Bye, Mr Mortman." I waved again, turned, and started jogging to the street.

"You really shouldn't have come all this way!" he called after me in his high, scratchy voice. "Really. You shouldn't have!"

I know! I thought. *I know I shouldn't have.*

I trotted along the street, turned the corner, and continued down the next street.

Was I really getting away?

Was he really letting me go?

I couldn't believe he'd bought my pathetic excuse.

Why was he letting me get away?

I slowed to a walk. My side still ached. I suddenly had a throbbing headache.

Night had fallen. Passing cars had their headlights on. A slender trail of dark cloud drifted over a pale half-moon still low in the purple-grey sky.

I was about to cross the street onto the broad, empty field when hands grabbed my shoulders again.

I cried out, more of a *yelp* than a scream, and spun round, expecting to see the monster.

"Aaron!" I cried. I swallowed hard, trying to force down my fear. "Where—?"

"I waited for you," he said. His voice trembled. His hands were knotted into fists. He looked about ready to burst into tears.

"Aaron—"

"I've been waiting all this time," he said shrilly. "Where've you been? I've been so scared."

"I was . . . back there," I told him.

"I was ready to call the police or something," Aaron said. "I was hiding down the road. I—"

"You saw him?" I asked eagerly, suddenly remembering why we had risked our lives tonight. "You saw Mr Mortman?"

Aaron shook his head. "No, I didn't. I was too far away."

"But earlier," I said. "Through the window. When he was a monster. Didn't you see him then? Didn't you see him eat the snails and the eels?"

Aaron shook his head again. "I didn't see anything, Lucy," he said softly. "I'm sorry. I wish I had."

Big help, I thought bitterly.

Now what was I going to do?

121

"Mum—you don't understand. I *can't* go!"

"Lucy, I'm not giving you a choice. You're going, and that's that."

It was the next afternoon, a stormy, grey day, and Mum and I were in the kitchen, arguing. I was trying to tell her there was no way I could go to my Reading Rangers meeting at the library. And she was insisting that I had to go.

"Mum, you've got to believe me," I pleaded. I was trying not to whine, but my voice kept creeping higher and higher. "Mr Mortman is a monster. I can't go to the library any more."

Mum made a disgusted face and threw down the teatowel she'd been folding. "Lucy, your father and I have had it up to here with your silly monster stories."

She turned to face me. Her expression was angry. "The fact is, Lucy dear, that you are lazy. You never stick with anything. You're really lazy. That's your problem."

"Mr Mortman is a monster," I interrupted. "*That's* my problem."

"Well, I don't care," Mum replied sharply. "I don't care if he turns into a drooling werewolf at night. You're not giving up Reading Rangers. You're going to your appointment this afternoon if I have to take you by the hand and walk you there myself."

"Really—would you?" I asked.

The idea flashed into my head that Mum could hide in the stacks and see for herself when Mr Mortman turned into a monster.

But I think she thought I was being sarcastic. She just scowled and walked out of the kitchen.

And so, an hour later, I was trudging up the stone steps to the old library. It was raining hard, but I didn't take an umbrella. I didn't care if I got drenched.

My hair was soaked and matted on my head. I shook my head hard as I stepped into the entrance, sending drops of water flying in all directions.

I shivered, more from my fear, from being back in this frightening place, than from the cold. I pulled off my rucksack. It was dripping wet, too.

How can I face Mr Mortman? I wondered as I made my way reluctantly into the main reading room. How can I face him after last night?

He must surely suspect that I know his secret.

123

He *couldn't* have believed me last night, could he?

I was so furious with my mum for forcing me to come here.

I hope he turns into a monster and chews me to bits! I thought bitterly. That will really teach Mum a lesson.

I pictured Mum and Dad and Randy, sitting mournfully in our living room, crying their eyes out, wailing. "If only we had believed her! If only we had listened!"

Holding my wet rucksack in front of me like a shield, I made my way slowly past the long rows of books to the front of the room.

To my relief, there were several people in the library. I saw two little kids with their mothers and a couple of other women browsing in the mystery book section.

Great! I thought, starting to feel slightly calmer. Mr Mortman won't dare do anything while the library is filled with people.

The librarian was dressed in a green poloneck today, which really made him look like a big, round turtle. He was stamping a pile of books and didn't look up as I stepped close to the desk.

I cleared my throat nervously. "Mr Mortman?"

It took him a long while to look up. When he finally did, a warm smile formed above his chins. "Hi, Lucy. Give me a few minutes, okay?"

"Okay," I said. "I'll go and dry off."

He seems very friendly, I thought, heading over to a chair at one of the long tables. He doesn't seem angry at all.

Maybe he really did believe my story last night.

Maybe he really doesn't know that I've seen him turn into a monster.

Maybe I'll get out of here alive. . . .

I sat down at the table and shook some more water from my hair. I stared at the big, round wall clock, nervously waiting for him to call me up for our meeting. The clock ticked noisily. Each second seemed to take a minute.

The kids with their mothers checked out some books and left. I turned to the mystery section and saw that the two women had also cleared out. The librarian and I were the only ones left.

Mr Mortman shoved a pile of books across his desk and stood up. "I'll be right back, Lucy," he said, another friendly, reassuring smile on his face. "Then we'll have our meeting."

He stepped away from his desk and, walking briskly, headed for the back of the reading room. I supposed he was going to the toilet or something.

A jagged flash of white lightning flickered across the dark sky outside the window. It was followed by a drumroll of thunder.

I stood up from the table and, carrying my wet

125

rucksack by the straps, started towards Mr Mortman's desk.

I was halfway to the desk when I heard the loud click.

I knew at once that he had locked the front door.

A few seconds later, he returned, walking briskly, still smiling. He was rubbing his pudgy white hands together as he walked.

"Shall we talk about your book?" he asked, stepping up to me.

"Mr Mortman—you've locked the front door," I said, swallowing hard.

His smile didn't fade.

His dark little eyes locked on mine.

"Yes. Of course," he said softly, studying my face. His hands were still clasped together in front of him.

"But—why?" I stammered.

He brought his face close to mine, and his smile faded. "I know why you were at my house last night," he growled into my ear. "I know everything."

"But, Mr Mortman, I—"

"I'm sorry," he said in his throaty growl. "But I can't let you leave, Lucy. I can't let you leave the library."

"Ohhh." The sound escaped my lips, a moan of total terror.

I stared at him without moving. I suppose I wanted to see if he was serious or not. If he really meant what he said.

His eyes told me he did.

And as I stared at him, his head began to inflate. His tiny, round eyes shot out of their sockets and grew into throbbing, black bulbs.

"Ohhh."

Again, the terrified sound escaped my lips. My whole body convulsed in a shudder of terror.

His head was throbbing now, throbbing like a heart. His mouth opened into a gaping, gruesome leer, and green spittle ran down his quivering chin.

Move! I told myself. *Move, Lucy! DO something!*

His disgusting grin grew wider. His enormous head bobbed and throbbed excitedly.

He uttered a low growl of attack. And reached out both arms to grab me.

"No!" I shrieked.

I leaned back and, with all my might, swung the rucksack into his flabby stomach.

It caught him by surprise.

He gasped as it took his breath away.

I let go of the rucksack, spun round, and started to run.

He was right behind me. I could hear his panting breath and low, menacing growls.

I ran through a narrow aisle between two tall shelves.

A rumble of thunder from outside seemed to shake the room.

He was still behind me. Close. Closer.

He was going to catch me, going to grab me from behind.

I reached the end of the row. I hesitated. I didn't know which way to turn. I couldn't think.

He roared, a monstrous animal sound.

I turned left and started to run along the back wall of the room.

Another rumble of thunder.

"Ohh!" I realized to my horror that I'd made a mistake.

A fatal mistake.

I was running right into the corner.

There was no exit here. No escape.

He roared again, so loud that it drowned out the thunder.

I was trapped.

I knew it.

Trapped.

With a desperate cry, I ran blindly—headlong into the card catalogue.

Behind me, I heard the monster's roar of laughter.

He knew he had won.

The card catalogue toppled over. Drawers came sliding out. Cards spilled at my feet, scattering over the floor.

"Noooo!" the monster howled. At first I thought it was a victory cry. But then I realized it was an angry cry of protest.

With a moan of horror, he stooped to the floor and began gathering up the cards.

Staring in disbelief, I plunged past him, running frantically, my arms thrashing wildly at my sides.

In that moment of terror, I remembered the one thing that librarians hate most: having cards from the card catalogue spilled on the floor!

Mr Mortman was a monster—but he was also a librarian.

He couldn't bear to have those cards in disorder. He had to try to replace them before chasing after me.

It took only a few seconds to run into the front entrance, turn the lock, pull open the door, and flee out into the rain.

My trainers slapped the pavement as I ran, sending up splashes of rainwater.

I made my way to the street and was halfway up the block when I realized he was chasing after me.

A flash of lightning crackled to my left.

I cried out, startled, as a deafening burst of thunder shook the ground.

I glanced back to see how close the monster was.

And stopped.

With trembling hands, I frantically brushed a glaze of rainwater from my eyes.

"Aaron!" I cried. "What are *you* doing here?"

He ran up to me, hunching against the cold rain. He was breathing hard. His eyes were wide and frightened. "I—I was in the library," he stammered, struggling to catch his breath. "Hiding. I saw it. I saw the monster. I saw everything."

"You *did*?" I was so happy. I wanted to hug him.

A sheet of rain swept over us, driven by a gust of wind.

"Let's get to my house!" I cried. "You can tell my parents. Now maybe they'll finally believe it!"

Aaron and I burst into the study. Mum looked up from the sofa, lowering the newspaper to her lap. "You're dripping on the rug," she said.

"Where's Dad? Is he home yet?" I asked, rainwater running down my forehead. Aaron and I were soaked from head to foot.

"Here I am." He appeared behind us. He had changed out of his work clothes. "What's all the excitement?"

"It's about the monster!" I blurted out. "Mr Mortman—he—"

Mum shook her head and started to raise a hand to stop me.

But Aaron quickly came to my rescue. "I saw him, too!" Aaron exclaimed. "Lucy didn't make it up. It's true!"

Mum and Dad listened to Aaron. I knew they would.

He told them what he had seen in the library. He told them how the librarian had turned into a monster and chased me into the corner.

Mum listened intently to Aaron's story, shaking her head. "I suppose Lucy's story is true," she said when Aaron had finished.

"Yeah, I suppose it is," Dad said, putting a hand gently on my shoulder.

"Well, now that you *finally* believe me—what are you going to do, Dad?" I demanded.

He gazed at me thoughtfully. "We'll invite Mr Mortman to dinner," he said.

"Huh?" I goggled at him, rainwater running down my face. "You'll *what*? He tried to gobble me up! You *can't* invite him here!" I protested. "You can't!"

"Lucy, we have no choice," Dad insisted. "We'll invite him to dinner."

Mr Mortman arrived a few evenings later,
carrying a bouquet of flowers. He was wearing
lime-green trousers and a bright yellow, short-
sleeved sports shirt.

Mum accepted the flowers from him and led
him into the living room where Dad, Randy,
and I were waiting. I gripped the back of a
chair tightly as he entered. My legs felt rubbery,
and my stomach felt as if I'd swallowed a heavy
rock.

I *still* couldn't believe that Dad had invited Mr
Mortman into our house!

Dad stepped forward to shake hands with the
librarian. "We've been meaning to invite you for
quite a while," Dad told him, smiling. "We want
to thank you for the excellent reading course at
the library."

"Yes," Mum joined in. "It's really meant a lot
to Lucy."

Mr Mortman glanced at me uncertainly. I

could see that he was studying my expression. "I'm glad," he said, forcing a tight-lipped smile.

Mr Mortman lowered himself onto the sofa. Mum offered him a tray of crackers with cheese on them. He took one and chewed on it delicately.

Randy sat down on the rug. I was still standing behind the armchair, gripping the back of it so tightly, my hands ached. I had never been so nervous in all my life.

Mr Mortman seemed nervous, too. When Dad handed him a glass of iced tea, Mr Mortman spilled a little on his trousers. "It's such a humid day," he said. "This iced tea hits the spot."

"Being a librarian must be interesting work," Mum said, taking a seat beside Mr Mortman on the sofa.

Dad was standing at the side of the sofa.

They chatted for a while. As they talked, Mr Mortman kept darting glances at me. Randy, sitting cross-legged on the floor, drummed his fingers on the carpet.

Mum and Dad seemed calm and perfectly at ease. Mr Mortman seemed a little uncomfortable. He had glistening beads of perspiration on his shiny, round forehead.

My stomach growled loudly, more from nervousness than from hunger. No one seemed to hear it.

The three adults chatted for a while longer. Mr Mortman sipped his iced tea.

He leaned back on the sofa and smiled at my mother. "It was so kind of you to invite me. I don't get very many home-cooked meals. What's for dinner?" he asked.

"*You* are!" my Dad told him, stepping in front of the sofa.

"What?" Mr Mortman raised a hand behind his ear. "I didn't hear you correctly. What is for dinner?"

"*You* are!" Dad repeated.

"Ulllp!" Mr Mortman let out a little cry and turned bright red. He struggled to raise himself from the low sofa.

But Mum and Dad were too fast for him.

They both pounced on him. Their fangs popped down. And they gobbled the librarian up in less than a minute, bones and all.

Randy laughed gleefully.

I had a big smile on my face.

My brother and I haven't got our fangs yet. That's why we couldn't join in.

"Well, that's that," Mum said, standing up and straightening the sofa cushion. Then she turned to Randy and me. "That's the first monster to come to Timberland Falls in nearly twenty years," she told us. "That's why it took us so long to believe you, Lucy."

"You certainly gobbled him up fast!" I exclaimed.

"In a few years, you'll get your fangs," Mum said.

"Me, too!" Randy declared. "Then maybe I won't be afraid of monsters any more!"

Mum and Dad chuckled. Then Mum's expression turned serious. "You both understand why we had to do that, don't you? We can't allow any *other* monsters in town. It would frighten the whole community. And we don't *want* people to get frightened and chase us away. We like it here!"

Dad burped loudly. "Pardon me," he said, covering his mouth

Later that night, I was upstairs in Randy's room. He was all tucked in, and I was telling him a bedtime story.

". . . And so the librarian hid behind the tall bookshelf," I said in a low, whispery voice. "And when the little boy named Randy reached up to pull a book down from the shelf, the librarian stuck his long arms through the shelf and *grabbed* the boy, and—"

"Lucy, how many times do I have to tell you?"

I glanced up to see Mum standing in the doorway, a frown on her face.

"I don't want you frightening your little brother before bedtime," Mum scolded. "You'll give him nightmares. Now, come on, Lucy—no more monster stories!"

Welcome to Camp Nightmare

I stared out of the dusty window as the camp bus bounced over the narrow, winding road. I could see sloping red hills in the distance beneath a bright yellow sky.

Stumpy white trees lined the road like fence posts. We were way out in the wilderness. We hadn't passed a house or a farm for nearly an hour.

The bus seats were made of hard blue plastic. When the bus hit a bump, we all bounced up off our seats. Everyone laughed and shouted. The driver kept growling at us, shouting at us to pipe down.

There were twenty-two kids going to camp on the bus. I was sitting in the back row on the aisle, so I could count them all.

There were eighteen boys and only four girls. I guessed that the boys were all going to Camp Nightmoon, which is where I was going. The girls were going to a girls' camp nearby.

The girls sat together in the front rows and talked quietly to each other. Every once in a while, they'd glance back quickly to sneak a look at the boys.

The boys were a lot louder than the girls, cracking jokes, laughing, making funny noises, shouting out stupid things. It was a long bus ride, but we were having a good time.

The boy next to me was called Mike. He had the window seat. Mike looked a bit like a bulldog. He was chubby, with a round face and pudgy arms and legs. He had short, spiky black hair, which he scratched a lot. He was wearing baggy brown shorts and a sleeveless green T-shirt.

We had been sitting together the whole trip, but Mike didn't say much. I thought he must be shy, or maybe very nervous. He told me this was his first time at a camp.

It was my first time, too. And I have to admit that, as the bus took me further and further from home, I was already starting to miss my mum and dad just a little.

I'm twelve, but I've never really stayed away from home before. Even though the long bus ride was fun, I had this sad kind of feeling. And I think Mike was feeling the same way.

He pressed his chubby face against the window and stared out at the red hills rolling past in the distance.

"Are you okay, Mike?" I asked.

"Yeah. Of course, Billy," he replied quickly without turning round.

I thought about my mum and dad. Back at the bus station, they had seemed so serious. I suppose they were nervous, too, about me going off to camp for the first time.

"We'll write every day," Dad said.

"Do your best," Mum said, hugging me harder than usual.

What a weird thing to say. Why didn't she say, "Have a good time"? Why did she say, "Do your best"?

As you can tell, I'm a bit of a worrier.

The only other boys I'd met so far were the two in the seat in front of us. One was called Colin. He had long brown hair down to his collar, and he wore silver sunglasses so you couldn't see his eyes. He acted pretty tough, and he wore a red bandanna on his forehead. He kept tying and untying the bandanna.

Sitting next to him in the seat on the aisle was a big, loud kid called Jay. Jay talked a lot about sports and kept bragging about what a good athlete he was. He liked showing off his big, muscular arms, especially when one of the girls turned round to check us out.

Jay teased Colin a lot and kept wrestling with him, gripping his head in a headlock and messing up his bandanna. You know. Just kidding around.

Jay had wild, bushy red hair that looked as if it had never been brushed. He had big blue eyes. He never stopped grinning and horsing around. He spent the whole trip telling terrible jokes and shouting things at the girls.

"Hey—what's your name?" Jay called to a blonde-haired girl who sat at the front by the window.

She ignored him for a long time. But the fourth time Jay called out the question, she turned round, her green eyes flashing. "Dawn," she replied. Then she pointed to the red-haired girl next to her. "And this is my friend Dori."

"Hey—that's amazing! My name is Dawn, too!" joked Jay.

A lot of the other boys laughed, but Dawn didn't crack a smile. "Nice to meet you, Dawn," she called back to him. Then she turned back to the front.

The bus bounced over a hole in the road, and we all bounced with it.

"Hey, look, Billy," Mike said suddenly, pointing out of the window.

Mike hadn't said anything for a long time. I leaned towards the window, trying to see what he was pointing at.

"I think I saw a wildcat," he said, still staring hard.

"Huh? Really?" I saw a clump of low, white trees and a lot of jagged, red rocks. But I couldn't see any wildcats.

"It went behind those rocks," Mike said, still pointing. Then he turned towards me. "Have you seen any towns or anything?"

I shook my head. "Just desert."

"But isn't the camp supposed to be near a town?" Mike looked worried.

"I don't think so," I told him. "My dad told me that Camp Nightmoon is past the desert, right out in the woods."

Mike thought about this for a while, frowning. "Well, what if we want to phone home or something?" he asked.

"They probably have phones at the camp," I told him.

I glanced up in time to see Jay toss something up towards the girls at the front. It looked like a green ball. It hit Dawn on the back of the head and stuck in her blonde hair.

"Hey!" Dawn cried out angrily. She pulled the sticky, green ball from her hair. "What *is* this?" She turned to glare at Jay.

Jay giggled his high-pitched giggle. "I don't know. I found it stuck under the seat!" he called to her.

Dawn scowled at him and heaved the green ball back. It missed Jay and hit the rear window, where it stuck with a loud *plop*.

Everyone laughed. Dawn and her friend Dori made faces at Jay.

Colin fiddled with his red bandanna. Jay slumped down low and raised his knees against the seat in front of him.

A few rows ahead of me, two grinning boys were singing a song we all knew, but with really gross words replacing the original words.

A few other kids began to sing along.

Suddenly, without warning, the bus squealed to a stop, the tyres skidding loudly over the road.

We all cried out in surprise. I bounced off my seat, and my chest hit the seat in front of me.

"Ugh!" That hurt.

As I slid back in the seat, my heart still pounding, the bus driver stood up and turned to us, leaning heavily into the aisle.

"Ohh!" Several loud gasps filled the small bus as we saw the driver's face.

His head was enormous and pink, topped with a mop of wild, bright blue hair that stood straight up. He had long, pointed ears. His huge red eyeballs bulged out of their dark sockets, bouncing in front of his snoutlike nose. Sharp white fangs drooped from his gaping mouth. A green liquid oozed over his heavy black lips.

As we goggled in silent horror, the driver lifted back his monstrous head and uttered an animal roar.

The driver roared so loudly that the bus windows rattled.

Several kids shrieked in fright.

Mike and I both ducked down low, hiding behind the seat in front of us.

"He's turned into a *monster*!" Mike whispered, his eyes wide with fear.

Then we heard laughter at the front of the bus.

I raised myself up in time to see the bus driver reach one hand up to his bright blue hair. He tugged—and his face slid right off!

"Ohhh!" Several kids shrieked in horror.

But we quickly realized that the face dangling from the driver's hand was a mask. He had been wearing a rubber monster mask.

His real face was perfectly normal, I saw with relief. He had pale skin, short, thinning black hair, and tiny blue eyes. He laughed, shaking his head, enjoying his joke.

"This fools 'em every time!" he declared, holding up the ugly mask.

A few kids laughed along with him. But most of us were too surprised and confused to think it was funny.

Suddenly, his expression changed. "Everybody out!" he ordered gruffly.

He pulled a lever and the door slid open with a *whoosh*.

"Where are we?" someone called out.

But the driver ignored the question. He tossed the mask onto the driver's seat. Then, lowering his head so he wouldn't bump the roof, he quickly made his way out of the door.

I leaned across Mike and stared out of the window, but I couldn't see much. Just mile after mile of flat, yellow ground, broken occasionally by clumps of red rock. It looked like a desert.

"Why are we getting out here?" Mike asked, turning to me. I could see he was really worried.

"Maybe this is the camp," I joked. Mike didn't think that was very funny.

We were all confused as we pushed and shoved our way off the bus. Mike and I were the last ones off since we'd been sitting at the back.

As I stepped onto the hard ground, I shielded my eyes against the bright sunlight, high in the afternoon sky. We were in a flat, open area. The bus was parked beside a concrete platform, about the size of a tennis court.

"It must be some kind of bus station or something," I told Mike. "You know. A drop-off point."

He had his hands shoved into the pockets of his shorts. He kicked at the ground, but didn't say anything.

On the other side of the platform, Jay was in a shoving match with a boy I hadn't met yet. Colin was leaning against the side of the bus, being cool. The four girls were standing in a circle near the front of the platform, talking quietly about something.

I watched the driver walk over to the side of the bus and pull open the luggage compartment. He began pulling out bags and suitcases and carrying them to the concrete platform.

A couple of boys had sat down on the edge of the platform to watch the driver work. On the other side of the platform, Jay and some other boys were having competitions, tossing little red pebbles as far as they could.

Mike, his hands still buried in his pockets, stepped up behind the sweating bus driver. "Hey, where are we? Why are we stopping here?" Mike asked him nervously.

The driver slid a heavy black case from the back of the luggage compartment. He completely ignored Mike's questions. Mike asked them again. And again the driver pretended Mike wasn't there.

Mike made his way back to where I was standing, walking slowly, dragging his shoes across the hard ground. He looked really worried.

I was confused, but I wasn't worried. I mean, the bus driver was calmly going about his business, unloading the bus. He knew what he was doing.

"Why won't he answer me? Why won't he tell us anything?" Mike demanded.

I felt bad that Mike was so nervous. But I didn't want to hear any more of his questions. He was starting to make me nervous, too.

I wandered away from him, making my way along the side of the platform to where the four girls were standing. Across the platform, Jay and his buddies were still having their stone-throwing contest.

Dawn smiled at me as I came closer. Then she glanced away quickly. She's really pretty, I thought. Her blonde hair gleamed in the bright sunlight.

"Are you from Center City?" her friend Dori asked, squinting at me, her freckled face twisted against the sun.

"No," I told her. "I'm from Midlands. It's north of Center City. Near Outreach Bay."

"I *know* where Midlands is!" Dori snapped snottily. The other three girls laughed.

I could feel myself blushing.

"What's your name?" Dawn asked, staring at me with her green eyes.

"Billy," I told her.

"My bird's name is Billy!" she exclaimed, and the girls all laughed again.

"Where are you girls going?" I asked quickly, eager to change the subject. "I mean, what camp?"

"Camp Nightmoon. There's one for boys and one for girls," Dori answered. "This is an all-Camp Nightmoon bus."

"Is your camp near ours?" I asked. I didn't even know there was a Camp Nightmoon for girls.

Dori shrugged. "We don't know," Dawn replied. "This is our first year."

"All of us," Dori added.

"Me, too," I told them. "I wonder why we've stopped here."

The girls all shrugged.

I saw that Mike was lingering behind me, looking even more scared. I turned and made my way back to him.

"Look. The driver has finished carrying out our stuff," he said, pointing.

I turned in time to see the driver slam the luggage compartment door shut.

"What's happening?" Mike cried. "Is someone picking us up here? Why did he unload all our stuff?"

151

"I'll go and find out," I said quietly. I started to jog over to the driver. He was standing in front of the open bus door, mopping his perspiring forehead with the short sleeve of his tan driver's uniform.

He saw me coming—and quickly climbed into the bus. He slid into the driver's seat, pulling a green sun visor down over his forehead as I walked up to the door.

"Is someone coming for us?" I called in to him.

To my surprise, he pulled the lever, and the bus door slammed shut in my face.

The engine started up with a roar and a burst of grey exhaust fumes.

"Hey—!" I screamed and pounded angrily on the glass door.

I had to leap back as the bus squealed away, its tyres spinning noisily on the hard ground. "Hey!" I shouted. "You don't have to run me over!"

I stared angrily as the bus bounced onto the road and roared away. Then I turned back to Mike. He was standing beside the four girls. They were all looking upset now.

"He—he's left," Mike stammered as I approached them. "He's just *left* us here in the middle of nowhere."

We gazed down the road at the bus until it disappeared over the darkening horizon. We all grew very quiet.

A few seconds later, we heard the frightening animal cries.

Very close. And getting closer.

"Wh-what's that?" stammered Mike.

We turned in the direction of the shrill cries.

They seemed to be coming from across the platform. At first, I thought that Jay and Colin and their friends were playing a joke on us, making the animal cries to frighten us.

But then I saw the scared, wide-eyed expressions on their faces. Jay, Colin, and the others had frozen in place. They weren't making the noises.

The cries grew louder. Closer.

Shrill warnings.

And then, staring into the distance beyond the platform, I saw them. Small, dark creatures, keeping low, rolling rapidly along the flat ground, tossing their heads back and uttering excited shrieks as they came towards us.

"What are *they*?" Mike cried, moving closer to me.

"Are they wolves?" Dori asked in a trembling voice.

"I hope not!" one of the girls called out.

We all climbed onto the concrete platform and were huddled behind our cases and bags.

The animal cries grew louder as the creatures drew nearer. I could see dozens of them. They scurried towards us over the flat ground as if being blown by the wind.

"Help! Somebody *help* us!" I heard Mike scream.

Next to me, Jay still had two of the red pebbles from his stone-throwing competition in his hand. "Pick up stones!" he was shouting frantically. "Maybe we can scare them away!"

The creatures stopped a few metres from the concrete platform and raised themselves up menacingly on their hind legs.

Huddled between Mike and Jay, I could see them clearly now. They were wolves or wildcats of some sort. Standing upright, they were nearly three feet tall.

They had slender, almost scrawny bodies, covered with spotty red-brown fur. Their paws had long, silvery nails growing out of them. Their heads were nearly as slender as their bodies. Tiny red weasel eyes stared hungrily at us. Their long mouths snapped open and shut, revealing double rows of silvery, daggerlike teeth.

155

"No! No! Help!" Mike dropped to his knees. His whole body convulsed in a shudder of terror.

Some of the kids were crying. Others gaped at the advancing creatures in stunned silence.

I was too scared to cry out or move or do *anything*.

I stared at the row of creatures, my heart thudding, my mouth as dry as cotton wool.

The creatures grew silent. Standing a few metres from the platform, they eyed us, snapping their jaws loudly, hungrily. White froth began to drip from their mouths.

"They—they're going to attack!" a boy yelled.

"They look hungry!" I heard one of the girls say.

The white froth poured thickly over their pointed teeth. They continued to snap their jaws. It sounded like a dozen steel traps being snapped shut.

Suddenly, one of them leapt onto the edge of the platform.

"No!" several kids cried out in unison.

We huddled closer together, trying to stay behind the pile of cases and bags.

Another creature climbed onto the platform. Then three more.

I took a step back.

I saw Jay pull back his arm and heave a red stone at one of the creatures. The stone hit the platform with a *crack* and bounced away.

The creatures weren't frightened. They arched their backs, preparing to attack.

They started making a high-pitched chattering sound.

And moved nearer. Nearer.

Jay threw another stone.

This one hit one of the advancing creatures on the side. It uttered a shrill *eek* of surprise. But it kept moving steadily forward, its red eyes trained on Jay, its jaws snapping hungrily.

"Go away!" Dori cried in a trembling voice. "Go home! Go away! Go *away!*"

But her shouts had no effect.

The creatures advanced.

"Run!" I urged. "Run!"

"We can't outrun *them!*" someone shouted.

The shrill chittering grew louder. Deafening. Until it seemed as if we were surrounded by a wall of sound.

The ugly creatures lowered themselves, ready to pounce.

"Run!" I repeated. "Come on—run!"

My legs wouldn't cooperate. They felt rubbery and weak.

Trying to back away from the attacking creatures, I toppled over backwards off the platform.

I saw flashing stars as the back of my head hit the hard ground.

They're going to get me, I realized.

I can't get away.

I heard the sirenlike attack cry.

I heard the scrape of the creatures' long toenails over the concrete platform.

I heard the screams and cries of the frightened campers.

Then, as I struggled frantically to pull myself up, I heard the deafening roar.

At first I thought it was an explosion.

I thought the platform had blown up.

But then I turned and saw the rifle.

Another explosion of gunfire. White smoke filled the air.

The creatures spun round and darted away, silent now, their scraggly fur scraping the ground as they kept low, their tails between their furry legs.

"Ha-ha! Look at 'em run!" The man kept the rifle poised on his shoulder as he watched the creatures retreat.

Behind him stood a long green bus.

I pulled myself up and brushed myself off.

Everyone was laughing now, jumping up and down joyfully, celebrating the narrow escape.

I was still too shaken up to celebrate.

"They're running like jackrabbits!" the man declared in a booming voice. He lowered the rifle.

It took me a while to realize he had come out of the camp bus to rescue us. We didn't hear or see the bus pull up because of the attack cries of the animals.

"Are you okay, Mike?" I asked, walking over to my frightened-looking new friend.

"I think so," he replied uncertainly. "I think I'm okay now."

Dawn slapped me on the back, grinning. "We're okay!" she cried. "We're all okay!"

We gathered in front of the man with the rifle.

He was big and red-faced, mostly bald except for a fringe of curly yellow hair around his head. He had a blond moustache under an enormous beak of a nose, and tiny black bird eyes beneath bushy blond eyebrows.

"Hi, kids! I'm Uncle Al. I'm your friendly camp director. I hope you enjoyed that welcome to Camp Nightmoon!" he boomed in a deep voice.

I heard muttered replies.

He leaned the rifle against the bus and took a few steps towards us, studying our faces. He was wearing white shorts and a bright green camp

159

T-shirt that stretched over his big belly. Two young men, also in green and white, stepped out of the bus, serious expressions on their faces.

"Let's load up," Uncle Al instructed them in his deep voice.

He didn't apologize for being late.

He didn't explain about the weird animals. And he didn't ask if we were okay after that scare.

The two counsellors began dragging the camp trunks and shoving them into the luggage compartment on the bus.

"Looks like a good group this year," Uncle Al shouted. "We'll drop you girls off first across the river. Then we'll get you boys settled in."

"What *were* those awful animals?" Dori called to Uncle Al.

He didn't seem to hear her.

We began climbing onto the bus. I looked for Mike and found him near the end of the line. His face was pale, and he still looked really shaken. "I—I was really scared," he admitted.

"But we're okay," I reassured him. "Now we can relax and have some fun."

"I'm so hungry," Mike complained. "I haven't eaten all day."

One of the counsellors overheard him. "You won't be hungry when you taste the camp food," he told Mike.

We piled into the bus. I sat next to Mike. I could

hear the poor kid's stomach growling. I suddenly realized I was starving, too. And I was really eager to see what Camp Nightmoon looked like. I hoped it wouldn't be a long bus ride to get there.

"How far away is our camp?" I called to Uncle Al, who had slid into the driver's seat.

He didn't seem to hear me.

"Hey, Mike, we're on our way!" I said happily as the bus pulled onto the road.

Mike forced a smile. "I'm so glad to get *away* from there!"

To my surprise, the bus ride took less than five minutes.

We all muttered our shock at what a short trip it was. Why hadn't the first bus taken us all the way?

A big wooden sign proclaiming CAMP NIGHT-MOON came into view, and Uncle Al turned the bus onto a gravel road that led through a patch of short trees into the camp.

We followed the narrow, winding road across the small, brown river. Several small cabins came into view. "Girls' camp," Uncle Al announced. The bus stopped to let the four girls off. Dawn waved to me as she climbed down.

A few minutes later, we pulled into the boys' camp. Through the bus window I could see a row of small, white cabins. On top of a gently sloping hill stood a large, white-tiled building, probably a meeting lodge or refectory.

At the edge of a field, three counsellors, all dressed in white shorts and green T-shirts, were working to start a fire in a large stone barbecue pit.

"Hey, we're going to have a barbecue!" I exclaimed to Mike. I was starting to feel really excited.

Mike smiled, too. He was practically drooling at the thought of food!

The bus came to an abrupt stop at the end of the row of small cabins. Uncle Al pulled himself up quickly from the driver's seat and turned to us. "Welcome to beautiful Camp Nightmoon!" he bellowed. "Step down and line up for your cabin allotments. Once you get unpacked and have dinner, I'll see you at the campfire."

We pushed our way noisily out of the bus. I saw Jay enthusiastically slapping another boy on the back. I think we were all feeling a lot better, forgetting about our earlier experience.

I stepped down and took a deep breath. The cool air smelled really sweet and fresh. I saw a long row of short evergreen trees behind the white lodge on the hill.

As I took my place in the queue, I searched for the riverbank. I could hear the soft rush of the river behind a thick row of evergreens, but I couldn't see it.

Mike, Jay, Colin, and I were assigned to the same cabin. It was Cabin 4. I thought the cabin should have a more interesting name. But it just had a number. Cabin 4.

It was really small, with a low ceiling and windows on both sides. It was just big enough for six campers. There were bunk beds against three walls and tall shelves on the fourth wall, with a little square of space in the middle.

There was no bathroom. I decided it must be in another building.

As the four of us entered the cabin, we saw that one of the beds had already been claimed. It had been carefully made, the green blanket tucked in neatly, some sports magazines and a tape player resting on top.

"That must belong to our counsellor," Jay said, inspecting the tape player.

"Hope we don't have to wear those ugly green T-shirts," Colin said, grinning. He was still wearing his silver sunglasses, even though the sun was nearly down and it was just about as dark as night in the cabin.

Jay claimed a top bunk, and Colin took the bed beneath his.

"Can I have a lower one?" Mike asked me. "I roll around a lot at night. I'm afraid I might fall out of a top one."

"Yeah. Sure. No problem," I replied. I wanted the top bunk anyway. It would be a lot more fun.

"Hope you lot don't snore," Colin said.

"We're not going to sleep in here anyway," Jay

said. "We're going to party all night!" He slapped Mike on the back playfully, but hard enough that Mike went sprawling into the chest of drawers.

"Hey!" Mike whined. "That hurt!"

"Sorry. Suppose I don't know my own strength," Jay replied, grinning at Colin.

The cabin door opened, and a red-haired man with dark freckles all over his face walked in, carrying a big grey plastic bag. He was tall and very skinny and was wearing white shorts and a green camp T-shirt.

"Hey, kids," he said, and dropped the large bag on the cabin floor with a groan. He looked over, then pointed to the bag. "There's your bed stuff," he said. "Make your beds. Try to make them as neat as mine." He pointed to the bunk against the window with the tape player on it.

"Are you our counsellor?" I asked.

He nodded. "Yeah. I'm the lucky one." He turned and started to walk out.

"What's your name?" Jay called after him.

"Larry," he said, pushing open the cabin door. "Your cases will be here in a few minutes," he told us. "You can fight it out over drawer space. Two of the drawers are stuck shut."

He started to leave, then turned back to us. "Keep away from my stuff." The door slammed hard behind him.

Peering out of the window, I watched him lope away, taking long, fast strides, bobbing his head as he walked.

"Great guy," Colin muttered sarcastically.

"Really friendly," Jay added, shaking his head.

Then we dived into the plastic bag and pulled out sheets and blankets. Jay and Colin got into a wrestling match over a blanket they claimed was softer than the others.

I tossed a sheet onto my mattress and started to climb up to tuck it in.

I was halfway up the ladder when I heard Mike scream.

S Mike was right beneath me, making his bed. He screamed so loud, I cried out and nearly fell off the ladder.

I leapt off the ladder, my heart pounding, and landed beside him.

Staring straight ahead, his mouth wide open in horror, Mike backed away from his bed.

"Mike—what's wrong?" I asked. "What *is* it?"

"S-snakes!" Mike stammered, staring straight ahead at his unmade bed as he backed away.

"Huh?" I followed his gaze. It was too dark to see anything.

Colin laughed. "Not *that* old joke!" he cried.

"Larry put rubber snakes in your bed," Jay said, grinning as he stepped up beside us.

"They're not rubber! They're real!" Mike insisted, his voice trembling.

Jay laughed and shook his head. "I can't believe you fell for that old gag." He took a few steps towards the bed—then stopped. "Hey—!"

I moved close, and the two snakes came into focus. Raising themselves from the shadows, they arched their slender heads, pulling back as if preparing to attack.

"They're real!" Jay cried, turning back to Colin. "Two of them!"

"Probably not poisonous," Colin said, venturing closer.

The snakes let out angry hisses, raising themselves high off the bed. They were very long and skinny. Their heads were wider than their bodies. Their tongues flicked from side to side as they arched themselves menacingly.

"I'm scared of snakes," Mike uttered in a soft voice.

"They're probably scared of you!" Jay joked, slapping Mike on the back.

Mike winced. He was in no mood for Jay's horseplay. "We've got to get Larry or somebody," Mike said.

"No way!" Jay insisted. "You can handle 'em, Mike. There's only two of them!"

Jay gave Mike a playful shove towards the bed. He only meant to give him a scare.

But Mike stumbled—and fell onto the bed.

The snakes darted in unison.

I saw one of them clamp its teeth into Mike's hand.

Mike rose to his feet. He didn't react at first. Then he uttered a high-pitched shriek.

Two drops of blood appeared on the back of his right hand. He stared down at them, then grabbed the hand.

"It *bit* me!" he shrieked.

"Oh, no!" I cried.

"Did it puncture the skin?" Colin asked. "Is it bleeding?"

Jay rushed forward and grabbed Mike's shoulder. "Hey, man—I'm really sorry," he said. "I didn't mean to—"

Mike groaned in pain. "It—really hurts," he whispered. He was breathing really hard, his chest heaving, making weird noises as he breathed.

The snakes, coiled in the middle of his lower bunk, began to hiss again.

"You'd better hurry to the nurse," Jay said, his hand still on Mike's shoulder. "I'll come with you."

"N-no," Mike stammered. His face was as pale as a ghost. He held his hand tightly. "I'll go and find her!" He burst out of the cabin, running at full speed. The door slammed behind him.

"Hey—I didn't mean to push him, you know," Jay explained to us. I could see he was really upset. "I was just joking, just trying to scare him a little. I didn't mean him to fall or anything. . . ." His voice trailed off.

"What are we going to do about *them*?" I asked, pointing at the two coiled snakes.

"I'll get Larry," Colin offered. He started towards the door.

"No, wait." I called him back. "Look. They're sitting on Mike's sheet, right?"

Jay and Colin followed my gaze to the bed. The snakes arched themselves high, preparing to bite again.

"So?" Jay asked, scratching his dishevelled hair.

"So we can wrap them up in the sheet and carry them outside," I said.

Jay stared at me. "Wish I'd thought of that. Let's do it, man!"

"You'll get bitten," Colin warned.

I stared at the snakes. They seemed to be studying me, too. "They can't bite us through the sheet," I said.

"They can try!" Colin exclaimed, hanging back.

"If we're fast enough," I said, taking a cautious step towards the bed, "we can wrap them up before they know what's happening."

The snakes hissed out a warning, drawing themselves higher.

"How did they get in here, anyway?" Colin asked.

"Maybe the camp is *crawling* with snakes," Jay said, grinning. "Maybe you've got some in *your* bed, too, Colin!" He laughed.

"Let's be serious here," I said sternly, my eyes

locked on the coiled snakes. "Are we going to try this or not?"

"Yeah. Let's do it," Jay answered. "I mean, I owe it to Mike."

Colin remained silent.

"I bet I could grab one by the tail and swing him out through the window," Jay said. "You could grab the tail end of the other one and—"

"Let's try my plan first," I suggested quietly.

We crept over to the snakes, sneaking up on them. It was kind of silly since they were staring right at us.

I pointed to one end of the sheet, which was folded up onto the bed. "Grab it there," I instructed Jay. "Then pull it up."

He hesitated. "What if I miss? Or you miss?"

"Then we're in trouble," I replied grimly. My eyes on the snakes, I reached my hand forward to the other corner of the sheet. "Ready? On three," I whispered.

My heart was in my mouth. I could barely choke out, "One, two, three."

At the count of three, we both grabbed for the ends of the sheet.

"Pull!" I cried in a shrill voice I couldn't believe was coming from me.

We pulled up the sheet and brought the ends together, making a bundle.

At the bottom of the bundle, the snakes wriggled frantically. I heard their jaws snap.

They wriggled so hard, the bottom of the bundle swung back and forth.

"They don't like this," Jay said as we hurried to the door, carrying our wriggling, swaying bundle between us, trying to keep our bodies as far away from it as possible.

I pushed open the door with my shoulder, and we ran out onto the grass.

"Now what?" Jay asked.

"Keep going," I replied. I could see one of the snakes poking its head out. "Hurry!"

We ran past the cabins towards a small clump of bushes. Beyond the bushes stood a patch of low trees. When we reached the trees, we swung the bundle back, then heaved the whole sheet into the trees.

It opened as it fell to the ground. The two snakes slithered out instantly and pulled themselves to shelter under the trees.

Jay and I let out loud sighs of relief. We stood there for a moment, hunched over, hands on our knees, trying to catch our breath.

Crouching down, I looked for the snakes. But they had slithered deep into the safety of the evergreens.

I stood up. "I think we should take back Mike's sheet," I said.

"He probably won't want to sleep on it," Jay said. But he reached down and pulled it up from the grass. He bundled it up and tossed it to me.

"It's probably dripping with snake venom," he said, making a disgusted face.

When we got back to the cabin, Colin had made his bed and was busily unpacking the contents of his suitcase, shoving everything into a drawer. He turned as we entered. "How'd it go?" he asked casually.

"Horrible," Jay replied quickly, his expression grim. "We both got bitten. Twice."

"You're a terrible liar!" Colin told him, laughing. "You shouldn't even try."

Jay laughed, too.

Colin turned to me. "You're a hero," he said.

"Thanks for all your help," Jay told him sarcastically.

Colin started to reply. But the cabin door opened, and Larry poked his freckled face in. "How's it going?" he asked. "You're not settled in yet?"

"We had a little problem," Jay told him.

"Where's the fourth boy? The chubby one?" Larry asked, lowering his head so he wouldn't bump it on the doorframe as he stepped inside.

"Mike got bitten. By a snake," I told him.

"There were two snakes in his bed," Jay added.

Larry's expression didn't change. He didn't seem at all surprised. "So where did Mike go?" he asked casually, swatting a mosquito on his arm.

172

"His hand was bleeding. He went to the nurse to get it taken care of," I told him.

"Huh?" Larry's mouth dropped open.

"He went to find the nurse," I repeated.

Larry tossed back his head and started to laugh. "Nurse?" he cried, laughing hard. "*What* nurse?!"

The door opened and Mike returned, still holding his wounded hand. His face was pale, his expression frightened. "They said there *was* no nurse," he told me.

Then he saw Larry perched on top of his bunk. "Larry—my hand," Mike said. He held the hand up so the counsellor could see it. It was stained with bright red blood.

Larry lowered himself to the floor. "I think I have some bandages," he told Mike. He pulled out a slender black case from beneath his bunk and began to search through it.

Mike stood beside him, holding up his hand. Drops of blood splashed on the cabin floor. "They said the camp doesn't have a nurse," Mike repeated.

Larry shook his head. "If you get hurt in *this* camp," he told Mike seriously, "you're on your own."

"I think my hand is swelling up a little," Mike said.

Larry handed him a roll of bandages. "The washroom is at the end of this row of cabins," he told Mike, closing his case and shoving it back under the bed. "Go and wash the hand and bandage it. Hurry. It's almost suppertime."

Holding the bandages tightly in his good hand, Mike hurried off to follow Larry's instructions.

"By the way, how'd you boys get the snakes out of here?" Larry asked, glancing around the cabin.

"We carried them out in Mike's sheet," Jay told him. He pointed at me. "It was Billy's idea."

Larry stared hard at me. "Hey, I'm impressed, Billy," he said. "That was pretty brave, man."

"Maybe I inherited something from my parents," I told him. "They're scientists. Explorers, sort of. They go off for months at a time, exploring the wildest places."

"Well, Camp Nightmoon is pretty wild," Larry said. "And you boys had better be careful. I'm warning you." His expression turned serious. "There's no nurse at Camp Nightmoon. Uncle Al doesn't believe in mollycoddling you boys."

The hot dogs were all charred black but we were so hungry, we didn't care. I wolfed three of them

175

down in less than five minutes. I don't think I'd ever been so hungry in all my life.

The campfire was in a flat clearing surrounded by a circle of round, white stones. Behind us, the large, white-tiled lodge loomed over the sloping hill. Ahead of us a thick line of evergreen trees formed a fence that hid the river from view.

Through a small gap in the trees, I could see a flickering campfire in the distance on the other side of the river. I wondered if that was the campfire of the girls' camp.

I thought about Dawn and Dori. I wondered if the two camps ever got together, if I'd ever see them again.

Dinner around the big campfire seemed to put everyone in a good mood. Jay was the only one sitting near me who complained about the hot dogs being burned. But I think he put away four or five of them anyway!

Mike had trouble eating because of his bandaged hand. When he dropped his first hot dog, I thought he was going to burst into tears. By the end of dinner, he was in a much better mood. His wounded hand had swelled up just a little. But he said it didn't hurt as much as before.

The counsellors were easy to spot. They all wore identical white shorts and green T-shirts. There were eight or ten of them, all young men, probably sixteen or seventeen. They ate together quietly, away from us campers. I kept looking at Larry, but he never once turned round to look at any of us.

I was thinking about Larry, trying to work out if he was shy or if he just didn't like us campers very much. Suddenly, Uncle Al got to his feet and motioned with both hands for us all to be quiet.

"I want to welcome you boys to Camp Nightmoon," he began. "I hope you've all unpacked and are comfortable in your cabins. I know that most of you are first-time campers."

He was speaking quickly, without any pauses between sentences, as if he was running through this for the thousandth time and wanted to get it over with.

"I'd like to tell you some of our basic rules," he continued. "First, lights out is at nine sharp."

A lot of the boys groaned.

"You might think you can ignore this rule," Uncle Al continued, paying no attention to their reaction. "You might think you can sneak out of your cabins to meet or take a walk by the river. But I'm warning you now that we don't allow it, and we have very good ways of making sure this rule is obeyed."

He paused to clear his throat.

Some boys were giggling about something. Opposite from me, Jay burped loudly, which caused more giggles.

Uncle Al didn't seem to hear any of this. "On the other side of the river is the girls' camp," he continued loudly, motioning to the trees. "You might be able to see their campfire. Well, I want to make it clear that swimming or rowing over to the girls' camp is strictly forbidden."

Several boys groaned loudly. This made everyone laugh. Even some of the counsellors laughed. Uncle Al remained grim-faced.

"The woods around Camp Nightmoon are filled with grizzlies and tree bears," Uncle Al continued. "They come to the river to bathe and to drink. And they're usually hungry."

This caused another big reaction from all of us sitting around the fading campfire. Someone made a loud growling sound. Another kid screamed. Then everyone laughed.

"You won't be laughing if a bear claws your head off," Uncle Al said sternly.

He turned to the group of counsellors outside our circle. "Larry, Kurt, come over here," he ordered.

The two counsellors rose obediently to their feet and made their way to the centre of the circle beside Uncle Al.

"I want you two to demonstrate to the new campers the procedure to follow when—er, I mean, *if* you are attacked by a grizzly bear."

Immediately, the two counsellors dropped to the ground on their stomachs. They lay flat and covered the backs of their heads with their hands.

"That's right. I hope you're all paying close attention," the camp director thundered at us. "Cover your neck and head. Try your best not to move." He motioned to the two counsellors. "Thanks, boys. You can get up."

"Have there ever been any bear attacks here?" I called out, cupping my hands so Uncle Al could hear me.

He turned in my direction. "Two last summer," he replied.

Several boys gasped.

"It wasn't pretty," Uncle Al continued. "It's hard to keep still when a huge bear is pawing you and drooling all over you. But if you move..." His voice trailed off, leaving the rest to our imaginations, I suppose.

I felt a cold shiver run down my back. I didn't want to think about bears and bear attacks.

What kind of camp have Mum and Dad sent me to? I found myself wondering. I couldn't wait to phone them and tell them about everything that had happened already.

Uncle Al waited for everyone to be silent, then pointed off to the side. "Do you see that cabin over there?" he asked.

In the dim, evening light, I could make out a cabin standing halfway up the hill towards the lodge. It appeared a little larger than the other cabins. It seemed to be built on a slant, sort of tipping on its side, as if the wind had tried to blow it over.

"I want you to make sure you see that cabin," Uncle Al warned, his voice thundering out above the crackling of the purple fire. "That is known as the Forbidden Cabin. We don't talk about that cabin—and we don't go near it."

I felt another cold shiver as I stared through the grey evening light at the shadowy, tilted cabin. I felt a sharp sting on the back of my neck and slapped a mosquito, too late to keep it from biting me.

"I'm going to repeat what I just said," Uncle Al shouted, still pointing to the dark cabin on the hill. "That is known as the Forbidden Cabin. It has been closed and boarded up for many years. No one is to go near that cabin. *No one.*"

This started everyone talking and laughing. Nervous laughter, I think.

"Why is the Forbidden Cabin forbidden?" someone called out.

"We never talk about it," Uncle Al replied sharply.

Jay leaned over and whispered in my ear, "Let's go and check it out."

I laughed. Then I turned back to Jay uncertainly. "You're kidding—right?"

He grinned in reply and didn't say anything.

I turned back towards the fire. Uncle Al was

wishing us all a good stay and saying how much he was looking forward to camp this year. "And one more rule—" he called out. "You must write to your parents every day. Every day! We want them to know what a great time you're having at Camp Nightmoon."

I saw Mike holding his wounded hand gingerly. "It's starting to throb," he told me, sounding very frightened.

"Maybe Larry has something to put on it," I said. "Let's go and ask him."

Uncle Al dismissed us. We all climbed to our feet, scratching and yawning, and started to make our way in small groups back to the cabins.

Mike and I lingered behind, hoping to talk to Larry. We saw him talking to the other counsellors. He was at least a head taller than all of them.

"Hey, Larry—" Mike called.

But by the time we had pushed our way through the groups of kids heading the other way, Larry had disappeared.

"Maybe he's going to our cabin to make sure we obey lights out," I suggested.

"Let's go and see," Mike replied anxiously.

We walked quickly past the dying campfire. It had stopped crackling but still glowed a deep purple-red. Then we headed along the curve of the hill towards Cabin 4.

"My hand really hurts," Mike groaned, holding it tenderly in front of him. "I'm not just complaining. It's throbbing and it's swelling up. And I'm starting to get the shivers."

"Larry will know what to do," I replied, trying to sound reassuring.

"I hope so," Mike said shakily.

We both stopped when we heard the howls.

Hideous howls. Like an animal in pain. But too human to be from an animal.

Long, shrill howls that cut through the air and echoed down the hill.

Mike uttered a quiet gasp. He turned to me. Even in the darkness, I could see the fright on his face.

"Those cries," he whispered. "They're coming from . . . the Forbidden Cabin!"

A few minutes later, Mike and I trudged into the
cabin. Jay and Colin were sitting tensely on
their beds. "Where's Larry?" Mike asked, fear
creeping into his voice.

"Not here," Colin replied.

"Where *is* he?" Mike demanded shrilly. "I've
got to find him. My *hand*!"

"He should be here soon," Jay offered.

I could still hear the strange howls through
the open window. "Do you hear that?" I asked,
walking over to the window and listening hard.

"Probably a wildcat," Colin said.

"Wildcats don't howl," Mike told him. "Wildcats screech, but they don't howl."

"How do *you* know?" Colin asked, walking
over to Larry's bunk and sitting down on the
bottom bed.

"We studied them at school," Mike replied.

Another howl made us all stop and listen.

"It sounds like a man," Jay offered, his eyes

lighting up excitedly. "A man who's been locked up in the Forbidden Cabin for years and years."

Mike swallowed hard. "Do you really think so?"

Jay and Colin laughed.

"What should I do about my hand?" Mike asked, holding it up. It was definitely swollen.

"Go and wash it again," I told him. "And put a fresh bandage on it." I peered out of the window into the darkness. "Maybe Larry will turn up soon. He probably knows where to get something to put on it."

"I can't believe there isn't a nurse," Mike whined. "Why would my parents send me to a camp where there's no nurse or anything?"

"Uncle Al doesn't like to mollycoddle us," Colin said, echoing Larry's words.

Jay stood up and broke into an imitation of Uncle Al. "Stay away from the Forbidden Cabin!" he cried in a booming deep voice. He sounded a lot like him. "We don't talk about it and we don't ever go near it!"

We all laughed at Jay's impression. Even Mike.

"We should go there tonight!" Colin said enthusiastically. "We should check it out immediately!"

We heard another long, sorrowful howl roll down the hill from the direction of the Forbidden Cabin.

"I—I don't think we should," Mike said softly, examining his hand. He started for the door. "I'm going to go and wash this." The door slammed behind him.

"He's scared," Jay scoffed.

"I'm a bit scared, too," I admitted. "I mean, those awful howls . . ."

Jay and Colin both laughed. "Every camp has something like the Forbidden Cabin. The camp director makes it up," Colin said.

"Yeah," Jay agreed. "Camp directors love scaring kids. It's the only fun they have."

He puffed out his chest and imitated Uncle Al again. "Don't go out after lights out or you'll never be seen again!" he thundered, then burst out laughing.

"There's nothing in that Forbidden Cabin," Colin said, shaking his head. "It's probably completely empty. It's all just a joke. You know. Like camp ghost stories. Every camp has its own ghost story."

"How do you know?" I asked, dropping down onto Mike's bed. "Have you been to camp before?"

"No," Colin replied. "But I have friends who've told me about *their* camp." He reached up and pulled off his silver sunglasses for the first time. He had bright sky-blue eyes, like big blue marbles.

We suddenly heard the sound of a bugle,

repeating a slow, sad-sounding tune.

"That must be the signal for lights out," I said, yawning. I started to pull off my shoes. I was too tired to change or wash. I planned to sleep in my clothes.

"Let's sneak out and explore the Forbidden Cabin," urged Jay. "Come on. We can be the first ones to do it!"

I yawned again. "I'm really too tired," I told him.

"Me, too," Colin said. He turned to Jay. "How about tomorrow night?"

Jay's face fell in disappointment.

"Tomorrow," Colin insisted, kicking his shoes into the corner and starting to pull off his socks.

"I wouldn't do it if I were you!"

The voice startled all three of us. We turned to the window where Larry's head suddenly appeared from out of the darkness. He grinned in at us. "I'd listen to Uncle Al if I were you," he said.

How long had he been out there listening to us? I wondered. Was he deliberately *spying* on us?

The door opened. Larry lowered his head as he loped in. His grin had faded. "Uncle Al wasn't messing around," he said seriously.

"Yeah. Sure," Colin replied sarcastically. He climbed up to his bed and slid beneath the wool blanket.

"I suppose the camp ghost will get us if we go out after lights out," Jay joked, tossing a towel across the room.

"No. No ghost," Larry said softly. "But Sabre will." He pulled out his drawer and began searching for something inside it.

"Huh? Who's Sabre?" I asked, suddenly wide awake.

"Sabre is an *it*," Larry answered mysteriously.

"Sabre is a red-eyed monster who eats a camper every night," Colin sneered. He stared down at me. "There *is* no Sabre. Larry's just giving us another phony camp story."

Larry stopped searching his drawer and gazed up at Colin. "No, I'm not," he insisted in a low voice. "I'm trying to save you boys some trouble. I'm not trying to scare you."

"Then what is Sabre?" I asked impatiently.

Larry pulled a sweater from the drawer, then pushed the drawer shut. "You don't want to find out," he replied.

"Come on. Tell us what it is," I begged.

"He isn't going to," Colin said.

"I'll tell you boys only one thing. Sabre will rip your heart out," Larry said flatly.

Jay sniggered. "Yeah. Sure."

"I'm serious!" Larry snapped. "I'm not kidding!" He pulled the sweater over his head. "You don't believe me? Go out one night. Go out and meet Sabre." He struggled to get his arm into the sweater sleeve. "But before you do," he warned, "leave me a note with your address so I'll know where to send your belongings."

We had fun the next morning.

We all woke up really early. The sun was just rising over the horizon to the south, and the air was still cool and damp. I could hear birds chirping.

The sound reminded me of home. As I lowered myself to the floor and stretched, I thought of my mum and dad and wished I could phone them and tell them about the camp. But it was only the second day. I'd be too embarrassed to phone them on the second day.

I was definitely homesick. But luckily there wasn't any time to feel sad. After we pulled on fresh clothes, we hurried up to the lodge on the hill, which served as a meeting hall, theatre, and refectory.

Long tables and benches were set up in straight rows in the centre of the enormous room. The floorboards and walls were all dark redwood. Redwood ceiling beams crisscrossed high above our heads. There were no windows, so it felt as if we were in an enormous, dark cave.

The clatter of dishes and cups and cutlery was deafening. Our shouts and laughter rang off the high ceiling, echoed off the hardwood walls. Mike shouted something to me from across the table, but I couldn't hear him because of the racket.

Some boys complained about the food, but I thought it was okay. We had scrambled eggs, bacon strips, fried potatoes, and toast, with tall cups of orange juice. I never eat a breakfast that big at home. But I found that I was really starving, and I gobbled it up.

After breakfast we lined up outside the lodge to form different activity groups. The sun had climbed high in the sky. It was going to be really hot. Our excited voices echoed off the sloping hill. We were all laughing and talking, feeling good.

Larry and two other counsellors, clipboards in hand, stood in front of us, shielding their eyes from the bright sun as they divided us into groups. The first group of about ten boys headed off to the river for a morning swim.

Some people have all the luck, I thought. I was eager to get to the riverbank and see what the river was like.

As I waited for my name to be called, I spotted a pay phone on the wall of the lodge. My parents flashed into my mind again. Maybe I *will* call them later, I decided. I was so eager to describe the camp to them and tell them about my new friends.

"Okay, boys. Follow me to the ball field," Larry instructed us. "We're going to play our first game of scratchball."

About twelve of us, including everyone from my cabin, followed Larry down the hill towards the flat grassy area that formed the playing field.

I jogged to catch up with Larry, who always seemed to walk at top speed, stretching out his long legs as if he were in a terrible hurry. "Are we going to swim after this?" I asked.

Without slowing his pace, he glanced at his clipboard. "Yeah, I suppose so," he replied. "You boys'll need a swim. We're going to work up a sweat."

"You ever play scratchball before?" Jay asked me as we hurried to keep up with Larry.

"Yeah. Of course," I replied. "We play it a lot at school."

Larry stopped at the far corner of the wide, green field, where the bases and batter's square had already been set up. He made us line up and divided us into two teams.

Scratchball is an easy game to learn. The batter throws the ball in the air as high and as far as he can. Then he has to run round the bases

191

before someone on the other team catches the ball, tags him with it, or throws him out.

Larry started calling out names, dividing us into teams. But when he called out Mike's name, Mike stepped up to Larry, holding his bandaged hand tenderly. "I—I don't think I can play, Larry," Mike stammered.

"Come on, Mike. Don't whine," Larry snapped.

"But it really hurts," Mike insisted. "It's throbbing like mad, Larry. The pain is shooting all the way up and down my side. And, look—" he raised the hand to Larry's face—"It's all swollen up!"

Larry pushed the arm away gently with his clipboard. "Go and sit in the shade," he told Mike.

"Shouldn't I get some medicine or something to put on it?" Mike asked shrilly. I could see the poor boy was really in a bad way.

"Just sit over there by that tree," Larry ordered, pointing to a clump of short, leafy trees at the edge of the field. "We'll talk about it later."

Larry turned away from Mike and blew a whistle to start the game. "I'll take Mike's place on the Blue team," he announced, jogging onto the field.

I forgot about Mike as soon as the game got underway. We were having a lot of fun. Most of the boys were pretty good scratchball players, and we played much faster than my friends do back home in the playground.

My first time up at the batter's square, I heaved the ball really high. But it dropped right into a fielder's hands, and I was out. My second time up, I made it to three bases before I was tagged out.

Larry was a great player. When he came up to the batter's square, he tossed the ball harder than I've ever seen anyone toss it. It sailed over the fielders' heads and, as they chased after it, Larry rounded all the bases, his long legs stretching out gracefully as he ran.

By the fourth inning, our team, the Blue team, was ahead twelve to six. We had all played hard and were really hot and sweaty. I was looking forward to that swim at the riverbank.

Colin was on the Red team. I noticed that he was the only player who wasn't enjoying the game. He had been tagged out twice, and he'd missed an easy catch in the field.

I realized that Colin wasn't very athletic. He had long, skinny arms without any muscles, and he also ran awkwardly.

In the third inning Colin got into an argument with a player on my team about whether a toss had been foul or not. A few minutes later, Colin argued angrily with Larry about a ball that he claimed should have been out.

He and Larry shouted at each other for a few

minutes. It was no big deal, a typical sporting argument. Larry finally ordered Colin to shut up and get back to the outfield. Colin grudgingly obeyed, and the game continued.

I didn't think about it again. I mean, that kind of arguing happens all the time in ball games. And there are boys who enjoy the arguments as much as the game.

But then, in the next inning, something strange happened that gave me a really bad feeling and made me stop and wonder just what was going on.

Colin's team came to bat. Colin stepped up to the batter's square and prepared to toss the ball.

Larry was playing the outfield. I was standing nearby, also in the field.

Colin tossed the ball high, but not very far.

Larry and I both came running in to get it.

Larry got there first. He picked up the small, hard ball on the first bounce, drew back his arm—and then I saw his expression change.

I saw his features tighten in anger. I saw his eyes narrow, his copper-coloured eyebrows lower in concentration.

With a loud grunt of effort, Larry heaved the ball as hard as he could.

It struck Colin in the back of the head, making a loud *crack* sound as it hit.

Colin's silver sunglasses went flying through the air.

Colin stopped short and uttered a short, high-pitched cry. His arms flew up as if he'd been shot. Then his knees buckled.

He collapsed in a heap, face-down on the grass. He didn't move.

The ball rolled away over the grass.

I cried out in shock.

Then I saw Larry's expression change again. His eyes opened wide in disbelief. His mouth dropped open in horror.

"No!" he cried. "It slipped! I didn't mean to throw it at him!"

I knew Larry was lying. I had seen the anger on his face before he threw the ball.

I sank down to my knees on the ground as Larry went running towards Colin. I felt dizzy and upset and confused. I had a sick feeling in my stomach.

"The ball slipped!" Larry was yelling. "It just slipped."

Liar, I thought. Liar. Liar. Liar.

I forced myself up on my feet and hurried to join the circle of boys around Colin. When I got there, Larry was kneeling over Colin, raising Colin's head off the ground gently with both hands.

Colin's eyes were open wide. He stared up at Larry groggily, and uttered low moans.

"Give him room," Larry was shouting. "Give him room." He gazed down at Colin.

"The ball slipped. I'm really sorry. The ball slipped."

Colin moaned. His eyes rolled around in his head. Larry pulled off Colin's red bandanna and mopped Colin's forehead with it.

Colin moaned again. His eyes closed.

"Help me carry him to the lodge," Larry instructed two kids from the Red team. "The rest of you boys get changed for your swim. The riverbank counsellor will be waiting for you."

I watched as Larry and the two boys hoisted Colin up and started to carry him towards the lodge. Larry gripped him under the shoulders. The two boys awkwardly took hold of his legs.

The sick feeling in my stomach hadn't gone away. I kept remembering the intense expression of anger on Larry's face as he'd heaved the ball at the back of Colin's head.

I knew it had been deliberate.

I started to follow them. I don't know why. I suppose I was so upset, I wasn't thinking clearly.

They were nearly at the bottom of the hill when I saw Mike catch up with them. He ran alongside Larry, holding his swollen hand.

"Can I come, too?" Mike pleaded. "Someone has to look at my hand. It's really bad, Larry. Please—can I come, too?"

"Yeah. You'd better," I heard Larry reply curtly.

Good, I thought. Finally someone was going to pay some attention to Mike's snakebite wound.

Ignoring the sweat pouring down my forehead, I watched them make their way up the hill to the lodge.

This shouldn't have happened, I thought, suddenly feeling shivery despite the hot sun.

Something is wrong. Something is terribly wrong here.

How was I to know that the horrors were just beginning . . .

Later that afternoon, Jay and I were writing letters to our parents. I was feeling pretty upset about things. I kept seeing the angry expression on Larry's face as he'd heaved the ball at the back of Colin's head.

I wrote about it in my letter, and I also told my mum and dad about how there was no nurse there, and about the Forbidden Cabin.

Jay stopped writing and looked up at me from his bunk. He was really sunburned. His cheeks and forehead were bright red.

He scratched his red hair. "We're dropping like flies," he said, gesturing around the nearly empty cabin.

"Yeah," I agreed wistfully. "I hope Colin and Mike are okay." And then I blurted out, "Larry deliberately hit Colin."

"Huh?" Jay stopped scratching his hair and lowered his hand to the bunk. "He *what*?"

"He deliberately threw the ball at Colin's

head. I *saw* him," I said, my voice shaky. I wasn't going to tell anyone, but now I was glad I had. It made me feel a little bit better to get it out.

But then I saw that Jay didn't believe me. "That's impossible," he said quietly. "Larry's our counsellor. His hand slipped. That's all."

I started to argue when the cabin door opened and Colin entered, with Larry at his side.

"Colin! How *are* you?" I cried. Jay and I both jumped up.

"Not bad," Colin replied. He forced a thin smile. I couldn't see his eyes. They were hidden once again behind his silver sunglasses.

"He's still a little wobbly, but he's okay," Larry said cheerfully, holding Colin's arm.

"I'm sort of seeing double," Colin admitted. "I mean, this cabin looks really crowded to me. There are two of each of you."

Jay and I uttered short, uncomfortable laughs.

Larry helped Colin over to the lower bunk where Jay had been sitting. "He'll be just fine in a day or two," Larry told us.

"Yeah. The headache is a little better already," Colin said, gently rubbing the back of his head, then lying down on top of the bedcovers.

"Did you see a doctor?" I asked.

"No. Just Uncle Al," Colin replied. "He looked it over and said I'd be fine."

I cast a suspicious glance at Larry, but he turned his back on us and crouched down to search for something in the duffel bag he kept under his bed.

"Where's Mike? Is he okay?" Jay asked Larry.

"Uh-huh," Larry answered without turning round. "He's fine."

"But where is he?" I demanded.

Larry shrugged. "Still at the lodge, I suppose. I don't really know."

"But is he coming back?" I insisted.

Larry shoved the bag under his bed and stood up. "Have you two finished your letters?" he asked. "Hurry up and get changed for dinner. You can post your letters at the lodge."

He started for the door. "Hey, don't forget tonight is Tent Night. You boys are sleeping in a tent tonight."

We all groaned. "But, Larry, it's so cold out!" Jay protested.

Larry ignored him and turned away.

"Hey, Larry, do you have anything I can put on this sunburn?" Jay called after him.

"No," Larry replied and disappeared out of the door.

Jay and I helped Colin up to the lodge. He was still seeing double, and his headache was pretty bad.

The three of us sat at the end of the long table nearest the window. A strong breeze blew cool air over the table, which felt good on our sunburned skin.

We had some kind of meat with potatoes and gravy for dinner. It wasn't great, but I was so hungry, it didn't matter. Colin didn't have much appetite. He picked at the edges of his grey meat.

The refectory was as noisy as ever. Kids were laughing and shouting to friends across the long tables. At one table, boys were throwing breadsticks back and forth like javelins.

As usual, the counsellors, dressed in their green and white, ate together at a table in the far corner and ignored us campers completely.

The rumour spread that we were going to learn all of the camp songs after dinner. Boys were groaning and complaining about that.

About halfway through dinner, Jay and the boy across the table, a boy called Roger, started horsing around, trying to wrestle a breadstick from each other. Jay pulled hard and won the breadstick—and spilled his entire cup of grape juice on my shorts.

"Hey!" I jumped up angrily, staring down as the purple stain spread across the front of my shorts.

"Billy had an accident!" Roger cried out. And everyone laughed.

"Yeah. He purpled in his pants!" Jay added.

Everyone thought that was hilarious. Someone threw a breadstick at me. It bounced off my chest and landed on my dinner plate. More laughter.

The food fight lasted only a few minutes. Then two of the counsellors broke it up. I decided I'd better run back to the cabin and change my shorts. As I hurried out, I could hear Jay and Roger calling out jokes about me.

I ran full-speed down the hill towards the cabins. I wanted to get back up to the refectory in time for dessert.

Pushing open the cabin door with my shoulder, I darted across the small room to the chest of drawers and pulled open my drawer.

"Huh?"

To my surprise, I stared into an empty drawer. It had been completely cleaned out.

"What's going on here?" I asked aloud. "Where's my stuff?"

Confused, I took a step back—and realized I had opened the wrong drawer. This wasn't my drawer.

It was Mike's.

I stared for a long time into the empty drawer.

Mike's clothes had all been removed. I turned and looked for his suitcase, which had been stacked on its side behind our bunk.

Mike's suitcase had gone, too.

Mike wasn't coming back.

I was so upset, I ran back to the refectory without changing my shorts.

Panting loudly, I made my way to the counsellors' table and came up behind Larry. He was talking to the counsellor next to him, a fat guy with long, straggly blond hair. "Larry—Mike's gone!" I cried breathlessly.

Larry didn't turn round. He kept talking to the other counsellor as if I weren't there.

I grabbed Larry's shoulder. "Larry—listen!" I cried. "Mike—he's gone!"

Larry turned round slowly, his expression annoyed. "Go back to your table, Billy," he snapped. "This table is for counsellors only."

"But what about Mike?" I insisted shrilly. "His stuff has gone. What's happened to him? Is he okay?"

"How should I know?" Larry replied impatiently.

"Did they send him home?" I asked, refusing to back away until I had some kind of an answer.

"Yeah. Maybe." Larry shrugged and lowered his gaze. "You spilled something on your shorts."

My heart was pounding so hard, I could feel the blood pulsing at my temples. "You really don't know what happened to Mike?" I asked, feeling defeated.

Larry shook his head. "I'm sure he's fine," he replied, turning back to his pals.

"He probably went for a swim," the straggly-haired guy next to him sniggered.

Larry and some of the other counsellors laughed, too.

I didn't think it was funny. I felt pretty sick. And more than a little frightened.

Don't the counsellors at this camp care what happens to us? I asked myself glumly.

I made my way back to the table. They were passing round chocolate pudding for dessert, but I wasn't hungry.

I told Colin, and Jay, and Roger about Mike's drawer being cleaned out, and about how Larry had pretended he didn't know anything about it. They didn't get as upset about it as I was.

"Uncle Al probably had to send Mike home because of his hand," Colin said quietly, spooning up his pudding. "It was pretty swollen."

"But why wouldn't Larry tell me the truth?" I asked, my stomach still feeling as if I had eaten a giant rock for dinner. "Why did he say he didn't know what had happened to Mike?"

"Counsellors don't like to talk about these things," Jay said, slapping the top of his pudding with his spoon. "It might give us poor little kids nightmares." He filled his spoon with pudding, tilted it back, and flung a dark gob of pudding onto Roger's forehead.

"Jay—you're dead meat now!" Roger cried, plunging his spoon into the chocolate goo. He shot a gob of it onto the front of Jay's sleeveless T-shirt.

That started a pudding war that spread down the long table.

There was no more talk about Mike.

After dinner, Uncle Al talked about Tent Night and what a great time we were going to have sleeping in tents tonight. "Just be very quiet so the bears can't find you!" he joked. Some joke!

Then he and the counsellors taught us the camp songs. Uncle Al made us sing them over and over again until we had learned them off by heart.

I didn't feel much like singing. But Jay and Roger began making up really gross words to the songs. And pretty soon, most of us had joined in, singing our own versions of the songs as loudly as we could.

Later, we were all making our way down the hill towards our tents. It was a cool, clear night. A wash of pale stars covered the purple-black sky.

I helped Colin down the hill. He was still seeing double and feeling a little weak.

Jay and Roger walked a few steps ahead of us, shoving each other with their shoulders, first to the left, then to the right.

Suddenly, Jay turned back to Colin and me. "Tonight's the night," he whispered, a devilish grin spreading across his face.

"Huh? Tonight's *what* night?" I demanded.

"Ssshhh." He raised a finger to his lips. "When everyone's asleep, Roger and I are going to go and explore the Forbidden Cabin." He turned to Colin. "You with us?"

Colin shook his head sadly. "I don't think I can, Jay."

Walking backwards in front of us, Jay locked his eyes on mine. "How about you, Billy? You coming?"

"I—I think I'll stay with Colin," I told him.

I heard Roger mutter something about me being a chicken. Jay looked disappointed. "You're going to miss out," he said.

"That's okay. I'm pretty tired," I said. It was true. I felt so weary after this long day, every muscle ached. Even my hair hurt!

Jay and Roger made whispered plans all the way back to the tent.

At the bottom of the hill, I stopped and gazed up at the Forbidden Cabin. It appeared to lean towards me in the pale starlight. I listened for the familiar howls that seemed to come from inside it. But tonight there was only a heavy silence.

The large plastic tents were lined up in the cabin area. I crawled into ours and lay down on top of my sleeping bag. The ground was really hard. I could see this was going to be a long night.

Jay and Colin were messing around with their sleeping bags at the back of the tent. "It seems weird without Mike here," I said, feeling a sudden chill.

"Now you'll have more room to put your stuff," Jay replied casually. He sat hunched against the tent wall, his expression tense, his eyes on the darkness outside the tent door, which was left open a few centimetres.

Larry was nowhere to be seen. Colin sat quietly. He still wasn't feeling right.

I shifted my weight and stretched out, trying to find a comfortable position. I really wanted to go to sleep. But I knew I wouldn't be able to sleep until Jay and Roger had returned from their adventure.

Time moved slowly. It was cold outside, and the air was heavy and wet inside the tent.

I stared up at the dark plastic tent walls. An insect crawled across my forehead. I squashed it with my hand.

I could hear Jay and Colin whispering behind me, but I couldn't make out their words. Jay sniggered nervously.

I must have dozed off. An insistent whispering sound woke me up. It took me a while to realize it was someone whispering outside the tent.

I lifted my head and saw Roger's face peering in. I sat up, alert.

"Wish us luck," Jay whispered.

"Good luck," I whispered back, my voice clogged from sleep.

In the darkness I saw Jay's large, shadowy form crawl quickly to the tent door. He pushed it open, revealing a square of purple sky, then vanished into the darkness.

I shivered. "Let's sneak back to the cabin," I whispered to Colin. "It's too cold out here. And the ground feels like solid rock."

Colin agreed. We both scrambled out of the tent and made our way silently to our nice, warm cabin. Inside, we headed for the window to try to see Jay and Roger.

"They're going to get caught," I whispered. "I just know it."

"They won't get caught," Colin disagreed. "But they won't see anything, either. There's nothing to see up there. It's just a stupid cabin."

Poking my head out of the window, I could hear Jay and Roger giggling quietly out somewhere in the dark. The camp was so silent, so eerily silent. I could hear their whispers, their legs brushing through the tall grass.

"They'd better be quiet," Colin muttered, leaning against the window frame. "They're making too much noise."

"They must be up to the hill by now," I whispered. I stuck my head out as far as I could, but I couldn't see them.

Colin started to reply, but the first scream made him stop.

It was a scream of horror that cut through the silent air.

"Oh!" I cried out and pulled my head in.

"Was that Jay or Roger?" Colin asked, his voice trembling.

The second scream was more terrifying than the first.

Before it had died down, I heard animal snarls. Loud and angry. Like an eruption of thunder.

Then I heard Jay's desperate plea: "Help us! Please—somebody help us!"

My heart thudding in my chest, I lurched to the cabin door and pulled it open. The hideous screams still ringing in my ears, I plunged out into the darkness, the dew-covered ground soaking my bare feet.

"Jay—where are you?" I heard myself calling, but I didn't recognize my shrill, frightened voice.

And then I saw a dark form running towards me, running bent over, arms outstretched.

"Jay!" I cried. "What—*is* it? What *happened*?"

He ran up to me, still bent forward, his face twisted in horror, his eyes wide and unblinking. His bushy hair appeared to stand straight up.

"It—it got Roger," he moaned, his chest heaving as he struggled to straighten up.

"What did?" I demanded.

210

"What was it?" Colin asked, right behind me.

"I—I don't know!" Jay stammered, shutting his eyes tight. "It—it tore Roger to pieces."

Jay uttered a loud sob. Then he opened his eyes and spun around in terror. "Here it comes!" he shrieked. "Now it's coming after *us*!"

In the pale starlight, I saw Jay's eyes roll up in his head. His knees collapsed, and he began to slump to the ground.

I grabbed him before he fell and dragged him into the cabin. Colin slammed the door behind us.

Once inside, Jay recovered slowly. The three of us froze in place and listened hard. I was still holding onto Jay's heaving shoulders. He was as white as a sheet, and his breath came out in short, frightened moans.

We listened.

Silence.

The air hung hot and still.

Nothing moved.

No footsteps. No animal approaching.

Just Jay's frightened moans and the pounding of my heart.

And then, somewhere far in the distance, I heard the howl. Soft and low at first, then rising on the wind. A howl that chilled my blood and made me cry out.

"It's Sabre!"

"Don't let it get me!" Jay shrieked, covering his face with his hands. He dropped to his knees on the cabin floor. "Don't let it get me!"

I raised my eyes to Colin, who was huddled against the wall, away from the window. "We have to get Larry," I managed to choke out. "We have to get help."

"But how?" Colin demanded in a trembling voice.

"Don't let it get me!" Jay repeated, crumpled on the floor.

"It isn't coming here," I told him, trying to sound certain, trying to sound soothing. "We're okay inside the cabin, Jay. It isn't coming here."

"But it got Roger and—" Jay started. His entire body convulsed in a shudder of terror.

Thinking about Roger, I felt a stab of fear in my chest.

Was it really true? Was it true that Roger had been attacked by some kind of creature? That he'd been slashed to pieces?

I'd heard the screams from the hillside. Two bloodcurdling screams.

They'd been so loud, so horrifying. Hadn't anyone else in the camp heard them, too? Hadn't any other kids heard Roger's cries? Hadn't any counsellors heard?

I froze in place and listened.

Silence. The whisper of the breeze rustling the tree leaves.

No voices. No cries of alarm. No hurried footsteps.

I turned back towards the others. Colin had helped Jay to his bunk. "Where can Larry be?" Colin asked. His eyes, for once not hidden behind the silver sunglasses, showed real fear.

"Where can *everyone* be?" I asked, crossing my arms over my chest and starting to pace back and forth in the small space between the beds. "There isn't a sound out there."

I saw Jay's eyes go wide with horror. He was staring at the open window. "The creature—" he cried. "Here it comes! It's coming through the window!"

All three of us gaped in horror at the open window.

But no creature jumped in.

As I stared, frozen in the middle of the cabin, I could see only darkness and a fringe of pale stars.

Outside in the trees, crickets started up a shrill clatter. There was no other sound.

Poor Jay was so frightened and upset, he was seeing things.

Somehow Colin and I got him a little calmed down. We made him take off his shoes and lie down on the lower bed. And we covered him up with three blankets to help him to stop trembling.

Colin and I wanted to run for help. But we were too frightened to go outside.

The three of us were up all night. Larry never appeared.

Except for the crickets and the brush of the

wind through the trees, the camp was silent.

I think I must have finally dozed off just before dawn. I had strange nightmares about fires and people trying to run away.

I was woken by Colin shaking me hard. "Breakfast," he said hoarsely. "Hurry. We're late."

I sat up groggily. "Where's Larry?"

"He never showed up," Colin replied, motioning to Larry's unused bunk.

"We've got to find him! We've got to tell him what happened!" Jay cried, hurrying to the cabin door with his trainers untied.

Colin and I stumbled after him, both of us only half-awake. It was a cool, grey morning. The sun was trying hard to poke through high white clouds.

The three of us stopped halfway up the hill to the refectory. Reluctantly, our eyes searched the ground around the Forbidden Cabin.

I don't know what I expected to see. But there was no sign of Roger.

No sign of any struggle. No dried blood on the ground. The tall grass wasn't bent or matted down.

"Weird," I heard Jay mutter, shaking his head. "That's weird."

I tugged his arm to get him moving, and we hurried the rest of the way up to the lodge.

The refectory was as noisy as ever. Kids were

laughing and shouting to each other. It all seemed perfectly normal. I guessed that no one had made an announcement about Roger yet.

Some kids called to Colin and me. But we ignored them and searched for Roger, moving quickly through the aisles between the tables.

No sign of him.

I had a heavy, queasy feeling in my stomach as we hurried to the counsellors' table in the corner.

Larry glanced up from a big plate of scrambled eggs and bacon as the three of us advanced on him.

"What happened to Roger?"

"Is he okay?"

"Where were you last night?"

"Roger and I were attacked."

"We were afraid to go and find you."

All three of us bombarded Larry at once.

His face was filled with confusion, and he raised both hands to silence us. "Whoa," he said. "Calm down, boys. What are you talking about?"

"About Roger!" Jay screamed, his face turning bright red. "The creature—it jumped on him. And—and—"

Larry glanced at the other counsellors at the table, who looked as confused as he did. "Creature? What creature?" Larry demanded.

"It attacked Roger!" Jay screamed. "It was coming after me and—"

Larry stared up at Jay. "Someone was attacked? I don't think so, Jay." He turned to the counsellor next to him, a pudgy guy called Derek. "Did you hear anything in your area?"

Derek shook his head.

"Isn't Roger in your group?" Larry asked Derek.

Derek shook his head. "Not in *my* group."

"But Roger—!" Jay insisted.

"We didn't get any report about any attack," Larry said, interrupting. "If a camper had been attacked by a bear or anything, we'd hear about it."

"And we'd hear the noise," Derek offered. "You know. Screams or something."

"I heard screams," I told them.

"We both heard screams," Colin added quickly. "And Jay came running back, crying for help."

"Well, why didn't anyone else hear it?" Larry demanded, turning his gaze on Jay. His expression changed. "Where did this happen? When?" he asked suspiciously.

Jay's face darkened to a deeper red. "After lights out," he admitted. "Roger and I went up to the Forbidden Cabin, and—"

"Are you sure it wasn't a bear?" Derek interrupted. "Some bears were spotted downriver yesterday afternoon."

"It was a *creature!*" Jay screamed angrily.

"You shouldn't have been out," Larry said, shaking his head.

"Why won't you listen to me?" Jay screamed. "Roger was attacked. This big thing jumped on him and—"

"We would've heard something," Derek said calmly, glancing at Larry.

"Yeah," Larry agreed. "The counsellors were all up here at the lodge. We would've heard any screams."

"But, Larry—you've got to check it out!" I cried. "Jay isn't making it up. It really happened!"

"Okay, okay," Larry replied, raising his hands as if surrendering. "I'll go and ask Uncle Al about it, okay?"

"Hurry," Jay insisted. "Please!"

"I'll ask Uncle Al after breakfast," Larry said, turning back to his eggs and bacon. "I'll see you boys at morning swim later. I'll report what Uncle Al says."

"But, Larry—" Jay pleaded.

"I'll ask Uncle Al," Larry said firmly. "If anything happened last night, he'll know about it." He raised a piece of bacon to his mouth and chewed on it. "I think you've just had a bad nightmare or something," he continued, eyeing Jay suspiciously. "But I'll let you know what Uncle Al says."

"It wasn't a nightmare!" Jay cried shrilly.

219

Larry turned his back on us and continued eating his breakfast. "Don't you *care*?" Jay screamed at him. "Don't you *care* what happens to us?"

I saw that a lot of kids had stopped eating their breakfast to gawp at us. I pulled Jay away, and tried to get him to go to our table. But he insisted on searching the entire refectory again. "I know Roger *isn't* here," he insisted. "He—he *can't* be!"

For the second time, the three of us made our way up and down the aisles between the tables, studying every face.

One thing was for sure: Roger was nowhere to be seen.

The sun burned through the high clouds just as we reached the riverbank for morning swim. The air was still cool. The thick, leafy bushes along the riverbank glistened wetly in the white glare of sunlight.

I dropped my towel under a bush and turned to the gently flowing green water. "I bet it's cold this morning," I said to Colin, who was retying the string on his swimming trunks.

"I just want to go back to the bunk and go to sleep," Colin said, plucking at a knot. He wasn't seeing double any longer, but he was tired from being up all night.

Several boys were already wading into the river. They were complaining about the cold water, splashing each other, shoving each other forward.

"Where's Larry?" Jay demanded breathlessly, pushing his way through the clump of bushes to get to us. His auburn hair was a mess, half of it standing straight up on the side of his head. His eyes were red-rimmed and bloodshot.

"Where's Larry? He promised he'd be here," Jay said, frantically searching the waterfront.

"Here I am." The three of us spun round as Larry appeared from the bushes behind us. He was wearing baggy green Camp Nightmoon swimming trunks.

"Well?" Jay demanded. "What did Uncle Al say? About Roger?"

Larry's expression was serious. His eyes locked on Jay's. "Uncle Al and I went all around the Forbidden Cabin," he told Jay. "There wasn't any attack there. There couldn't have been."

"But it—it got Roger," Jay cried shrilly. "It slashed him. I saw it!"

Larry shook his head, his eyes still burning into Jay's. "That's the other thing," he said softly. "Uncle Al and I went up to the office and checked the records, Jay. And there *is* no camper here this year called Roger. Not a first name or a middle name. No Roger. No Roger at all."

Jay's mouth dropped open and he uttered a low gasp.

The three of us stared in disbelief at Larry, letting his startling news sink in.

"Someone's made a mistake," Jay said finally, his voice trembling with emotion. "We searched the refectory for him, Larry. And he's gone. Roger isn't here."

"He never *was* here," Larry said without any emotion at all.

"I—I just don't believe this!" Jay cried.

"How about a swim, boys?" Larry said, motioning to the water.

"Well, what do *you* think?" I demanded of Larry. I couldn't believe he was being so calm about this. "What do *you* think happened last night?"

Larry shrugged. "I don't know what to think," he replied, his eyes on a cluster of swimmers farthest from the shore. "Maybe you boys are trying to pull a weird joke on me."

"Huh? Is *that* what you think?" Jay cried. "That it's a *joke*?!"

Larry shrugged again. "Swim time, boys. Get some exercise, okay?"

Jay started to say more, but Larry quickly turned and went running into the green water. He took four or five running steps off the shore, then dived in, pulling himself quickly through the water, taking long, steady strokes.

"I'm not going in," Jay insisted angrily. "I'm going back to the cabin." His face was bright red. His chin was trembling. I could see that he was about to cry. He turned and began running through the bushes, dragging his towel along the ground.

"Hey, wait up!" Colin went running after him.

I stood there trying to decide what to do. I didn't want to follow Jay to the cabin. There wasn't anything I could do to help him.

Maybe a cold swim will make me feel better, I thought.

Maybe *nothing* will make me feel better, I told myself glumly.

I stared out at the other boys in the water. Larry and another counsellor were setting up a race. I could hear them discussing what kind of stroke should be used.

They all seem to be having a great time, I thought, watching them line up.

So why aren't I?

Why have I been so frightened and unhappy since I arrived here? Why don't the other campers see how weird and frightening this place is?

I shook my head, unable to answer my questions.

I need a swim, I decided.

I took a step towards the water.

But someone reached out from the bushes and grabbed me roughly from behind.

I started to scream out in protest.

But my attacker quickly clamped a hand over my mouth to silence me.

I tried to pull away, but I'd been caught off guard.

As the hands tugged me, I lost my balance and I was pulled back into the bushes.

Is this a joke? What's going on? I wondered.

Suddenly, as I tried to tug myself free, the hands let go.

I went sailing headfirst into a clump of fat green leaves.

It took me a long moment to pull myself up. Then I spun round to face my attacker.

"Dawn!" I cried.

"Ssshhhh!" She leapt forward and clamped a hand over my mouth again. "Duck down," she whispered urgently. "They'll see you."

I obediently ducked behind the low bush. She let go of me again and moved back. She was wearing a blue, one-piece bathing suit. It was wet. Her blonde hair was also wet, dripping down onto her bare shoulders.

225

"Dawn—what are you *doing* here?" I whispered, settling onto my knees.

Before Dawn could reply, another figure in a swimsuit moved quickly from the bushes, crouching low. It was Dawn's friend Dori.

"We swam over. Early this morning," Dori whispered, nervously pushing at her curly red hair. "We waited here. In the bushes."

"But it's not allowed," I said, unable to hide my confusion. "If you're caught—"

"We had to talk to you," Dawn interrupted, raising her head to peep over the top of the bushes, then quickly ducking back down.

"We decided to risk it," Dori added.

"What—what's wrong?" I stammered. A red-and-black insect crawled up my shoulder. I brushed it away.

"The girls' camp. It's a nightmare," Dori whispered.

"Everyone calls it Camp *Nightmare* instead of Camp Nightmoon," Dawn added. "Strange things have been happening."

"Huh?" I gaped at her. Not far from us in the water, I could hear the shouts and splashes of the swimming race beginning. "What kinds of strange things?"

"Scary things," Dori replied, her expression solemn.

"Girls have disappeared," Dawn told me. "Just vanished from sight."

226

"And no one seems to care," Dori added in a trembling whisper.

"I don't believe it!" I uttered. "The same thing has happened here. At the boys' camp." I swallowed hard. "Remember Mike?"

Both girls nodded.

"Mike disappeared," I told them. "They removed his stuff, and he just disappeared."

"It's unbelievable," Dori said. "Three girls have gone from our camp."

"They announced that one was attacked by a bear," Dawn whispered.

"What about the other two?" I asked.

"Just gone," Dawn replied, the words catching in her throat.

I could hear whistles blowing in the water. The race had ended. Another one was being organized.

The sun disappeared once again behind high white clouds. Shadows lengthened and grew darker.

I told them quickly about Roger and Jay and the attack at the Forbidden Cabin. They listened in open-mouthed silence. "Just like at our camp," Dawn said.

"We have to do something," Dori said heatedly.

"We have to get together. The boys and the girls," Dawn whispered, peering once again over the tops of the leaves. "We have to make a plan."

"You mean to escape?" I asked, not really understanding.

The two girls nodded. "We can't stay here," Dawn said grimly. "Every day another girl disappears. And the counsellors act as if nothing is happening."

"I think they *want* us to get killed or something," Dori added with emotion.

"Have you written to your parents?" I asked.

"We write every day," Dori replied. "But we haven't heard from them."

I suddenly realized that I hadn't received any post from my parents, either. They had both promised to write every day. But I had been at camp for nearly a week, and I hadn't received a single piece of post.

"Visitors Day is next week," I said. "Our parents will be here. We can tell them everything."

"It may be too late," Dawn said grimly.

"Everyone is so scared!" Dori declared. "I haven't slept for two nights. I hear these horrible screams outside every night."

Another whistle blew, closer to shore. I could hear the swimmers returning. Morning swim was over.

"I—I don't know what to say," I told them. "You've got to be careful. Don't get caught."

"We'll swim back to the girls' camp when everyone has left," Dawn said. "But we have to meet again, Billy. We have to get more people together. You know. Maybe if we all get organized . . ." Her voice trailed off.

"There's something bad going on at this camp," Dori said with a shiver, narrowing her eyes. "Something evil."

"I—I know," I agreed. I could hear boys' voices now. Close by. Just on the other side of the leafy bushes. "I've got to go."

"We'll try to meet here again the day after tomorrow," Dawn whispered. "Be careful, Billy."

"*You* be careful," I whispered. "Don't get caught."

They slipped back, deeper in the bushes.

Crouching low, I made my way away from the shore. When I was past the clump of bushes, I stood up and began to run. I couldn't wait to tell Colin and Jay about what the girls had said.

I felt frightened and excited at the same time. I thought maybe it would make Jay feel a bit better to know that the same kinds of horrible things were happening across the river at the girls' camp.

Halfway to the bunks, I had an idea. I stopped and turned towards the lodge.

I suddenly remembered seeing a pay phone on the wall on the side of the building. Someone had told me that phone was the only one campers were allowed to use.

I'll call Mum and Dad, I decided.

Why hadn't I thought of it before?

I can phone my parents, I realized, and tell them everything. I could ask them to come and get me. And they could get Jay, Colin, Dawn, and Dori, too.

Behind me, I saw my group heading towards the scratchball field, their swimming towels slung over their shoulders. I wondered if anyone had noticed that I was missing.

Jay and Colin were missing, too, I told myself. Larry and the others probably think I'm with them.

I watched them trooping across the tall grass in twos and threes. Then I turned and started jogging up the hill towards the lodge.

The idea of calling home had cheered me up already.

I was so eager to hear my parents' voices, so eager to tell them the strange things that were happening here.

Would they believe me?

Of *course* they would. My parents always believed me. Because they trusted me.

As I ran up the hill, the dark pay phone came into view on the white lodge wall. I started to run at full speed. I wanted to *fly* to the phone.

I hope Mum and Dad are home, I thought.

They've *got* to be home.

I was panting loudly as I reached the wall. I

lowered my hands to my knees and crouched there for a moment, waiting to catch my breath.

Then I reached up to take the receiver down.

And gasped.

The pay phone was plastic. Just a stage prop. A fake.

It was a thin sheet of moulded plastic held to the wall by a nail, made to look just like a telephone.

It wasn't real. It was a fake.

They don't want us to phone home, I thought with a sudden chill.

My heart thudding, my head spinning in bitter disappointment, I turned away from the wall—and bumped right into Uncle Al.

15

"Billy—what are you doing up here?" Uncle Al asked. He was wearing baggy green camp shorts and a sleeveless white T-shirt that revealed his meaty pink arms. He carried a brown clipboard filled with papers. "Where are you supposed to be?"

"I . . . uh . . . wanted to make a phone call," I stammered, taking a step back. "I wanted to phone my parents."

He eyed me suspiciously and fingered his yellow moustache. "Really?"

"Yeah. Just to say hi," I told him. "But the phone—"

Uncle Al followed my gaze to the plastic phone. He chuckled. "Someone put that up as a joke," he said, grinning at me. "Did it fool you?"

"Yeah," I admitted, feeling my face grow hot. I raised my eyes to his. "Where is the real phone?"

His grin faded. His expression turned serious. "No phone," he replied sharply. "Campers

232

aren't allowed to call out. It's a rule, Billy."

"Oh." I didn't know what to say.

"Are you really homesick?" Uncle Al asked softly.

I nodded.

"Well, go and write your mum and dad a long letter," he said. "It'll make you feel a lot better."

"Okay," I said. I didn't think it *would* make me feel better. But I wanted to get away from Uncle Al.

He raised his clipboard and gazed at it. "Where are you supposed to be now?" he asked.

"Scratchball, I think," I replied. "I didn't feel too well, you see. So I—"

"And when is your canoe trip?" he asked, not listening to me. He flipped through the sheets of paper on the clipboard, glancing over them quickly.

"Canoe trip?" I hadn't heard about any canoe trip.

"Tomorrow," he said, answering his own question. "Your group goes tomorrow. Are you excited?" He lowered his eyes to mine.

"I—I didn't really know about it," I confessed.

"Lots of fun!" he exclaimed enthusiastically. "The river doesn't look like much up here. But it gets pretty exciting a few kilometres down. You'll find yourself in some good rapids."

He squeezed my shoulder briefly. "You'll enjoy it," he said, grinning. "Everyone always enjoys the canoe ride."

233

"Great," I said. I tried to sound a little excited, but my voice came out flat and uncertain.

Uncle Al gave me a wave with his clipboard and headed around towards the front of the lodge, taking long strides. I stood watching him till he disappeared around the corner of the building. Then I made my way down the hill to the cabin.

I found Colin and Jay on the grass at the side of the cabin. Colin had his shirt off and was sprawled on his back, his hands behind his head. Jay sat cross-legged beside him, nervously pulling up long, slender strands of grass, then tossing them down.

"Come inside," I told them, glancing around to make sure no one else could hear.

They followed me into the cabin. I closed the door.

"What's up?" Colin asked, dropping onto a lower bunk. He picked up his red bandanna and twisted it in his hands.

I told them about Dawn and Dori and what they had reported about the girls' camp.

Colin and Jay both reacted with shock.

"They really swam over here and waited for you?" Jay asked.

I nodded. "They think we have to get organized or escape or something," I said.

"They could get into big trouble if they get caught," Jay said thoughtfully.

"We're all in big trouble," I told him. "We have to get *out*!"

"Visitors Day is next week," Colin muttered.

"I'm going to write to my parents right now," I said, pulling out the case from under my bunk, where I kept my paper and pens. "I'm going to tell them I *have* to come home on Visitors Day."

"I think I will, too," Jay said, tapping his fingers nervously against the bunk frame.

"Me, too," Colin agreed. "It's just too ... weird here!"

I pulled out a couple of sheets of paper and sat down on the bed to write. "Dawn and Dori were really scared," I told them.

"So am I," Jay admitted.

I started to write my letter. I wrote *Dear Mum and Dad, HELP!* then stopped. I raised my eyes across the cabin to Jay and Colin. "Do you two know about the canoe trip tomorrow?" I asked.

They stared back at me, their expressions surprised.

"Whoa!" Colin declared. "A five-kilometre hike this afternoon, and a canoe trip tomorrow?"

It was my turn to be surprised. "Hike? What hike?"

"Aren't you coming on it?" Jay asked.

"You know that really tall counsellor? Frank? The one who wears the yellow cap?" Colin asked. "He told Jay and me we're going on a five-kilometre hike after lunch."

"No one told me," I replied, chewing on the end of my pen.

"Maybe you're not in the hike group," Jay said.

"You'd better ask Frank at lunch," Colin suggested. "Maybe he couldn't find you. Maybe you're supposed to come, too."

I groaned. "Who wants to go on a five-kilometre hike in this heat?"

Colin and Jay both shrugged.

"Frank said we'd really like it," Colin told me, knotting and unknotting the red bandanna.

"I just want to get out of here," I said, returning to my letter.

I wrote quickly, intensely. I wanted to tell my parents all the frightening, strange things that had happened. I wanted to make them see why I couldn't stay at Camp Nightmoon.

I had written nearly a page and a half, and I was up to the part where Jay and Roger went out to explore the Forbidden Cabin, when Larry burst in. "You boys taking the day off?" he asked, his eyes going from one of us to the other. "You think this is a holiday or something?"

"Just messing about," Jay replied.

I folded up my letter and started to tuck it under my pillow. I didn't want Larry to see it. I realized I didn't trust Larry at all. I had no reason to.

"What are *you* doing, Billy?" he asked

suspiciously, his eyes stopping on the letter I was shoving under the pillow.

"Just writing home," I replied softly.

"You homesick or something?" he asked, a grin spreading across his face.

"Maybe," I muttered.

"Well, it's lunchtime, boys," he announced. "Let's go, okay?"

We all climbed out of our bunks.

"Jay and Colin are going on a hike with Frank this afternoon, I heard," Larry said. "Lucky boys." He turned and started out of the door.

"Larry!" I called to him. "Hey, Larry—what about me? Am I supposed to go on the hike, too?"

"Not today," he called back.

"But why not?" I said.

But Larry disappeared out of the door.

I turned back to my two cabin mates. "Lucky boys!" I teased them.

They both growled back at me in reply. Then we headed up the hill for lunch.

They served pizza for lunch, which is usually my favourite. But today, the pizza was cold and tasted like cardboard, and the cheese stuck to the roof of my mouth.

I wasn't really hungry.

I kept thinking about Dawn and Dori, how frightened they were, how desperate. I wondered when I'd see them again. I wondered if they would swim over and hide at the boys' camp again before Visitors Day.

After lunch, Frank came by our table to pick up Jay and Colin. I asked him if I was supposed to come, too.

"You weren't on the list, Billy," he said, scratching at a mosquito bite on his neck. "I can only take two at a time, you know? The trail gets a little dangerous."

"Dangerous?" Jay asked, climbing up from the table.

Frank grinned at him. "You're a big strong lad," he told Jay. "You'll do okay."

I watched Frank lead Colin and Jay out of the refectory. Our table was empty now, except for a couple of blond-haired boys I didn't know who were arm-wrestling down at the end near the wall.

I pushed my tray away and stood up. I wanted to go back to the cabin and finish the letter to my parents. But as I took a few steps towards the door, I felt a hand on my shoulder.

I turned to see Larry grinning down at me. "Tennis tournament," he said.

"Huh?" I reacted with surprise.

"Billy, you're representing Cabin 4 in the tennis tournament," Larry said. "Didn't you see the lineup? It was posted on the announcements board."

"But I'm a terrible tennis player!" I protested.

238

"We're counting on you," Larry replied. "Get a racquet and get your bod down to the courts!"

I spent the afternoon playing tennis. I beat a little kid in straight sets. I had the feeling he had never held a tennis racquet before. Then I lost a long, hard-fought match to one of the blond-haired boys who'd been arm-wrestling at lunch.

I was drowning in sweat, and every muscle in my body ached when the match was over. I headed to the riverbank for a refreshing swim.

Then I returned to the cabin, changed into jeans and a green-and-white Camp Nightmoon T-shirt, and finished my letter to my parents.

It was nearly dinnertime. Jay and Colin weren't back from their hike yet. I decided to go up to the lodge and post my letter. As I headed up the hill, I saw clusters of kids hurrying to their cabins to change for dinner. But no sign of my two cabin mates.

Holding the letter tightly, I headed round to the back of the lodge building where the camp office was located. The door was wide open, so I walked in. A young woman was usually behind the counter to answer questions and to take the letters to be posted.

"Anyone here?" I called, leaning over the counter and peering into the tiny back room, which was dark.

No reply.

"Hi. Anyone here?" I repeated, clutching the envelope.

No. The office was empty.

Disappointed, I started to leave. Then I glimpsed the large sack on the floor just inside the tiny back room.

The mailbag!

I decided to put my letter in the bag with the others to be posted. I slipped around the counter and into the back room and crouched down to put my envelope into the bag.

To my surprise, the mailbag was stuffed full of letters. As I pulled the bag open and started to shove my letter inside, a bunch of letters fell out onto the floor.

I started to scoop them up when a letter caught my eye.

It was one of mine. Addressed to my parents.

One I had written yesterday.

"Weird," I muttered aloud.

Bending over the bag, I reached in and pulled out a big handful of letters. I sifted through them quickly. I found a letter Colin had written.

I pulled out another pile.

And my eyes fell upon two other letters I had written nearly a week ago when I'd first arrived at camp.

I stared at them, feeling a cold chill run down my back.

All of our letters, all of the letters we had

written since the first day of camp, were here. In this mailbag.

None of them had been posted.

We couldn't phone home.

And we couldn't *write* home.

Frantically, my hands trembling, I began shoving the envelopes back into the mailbag.

What is going on here? I wondered. *What is going on?*

16

By the time I got to the refectory, Uncle Al was finishing the evening announcements. I slid into my seat, hoping I hadn't missed anything important.

I expected to see Jay and Colin opposite my place at the table. But their places were empty.

That's strange, I thought, still shaken from my discovery about the mailbag. They should be back by now.

I wanted to tell them about the post. I wanted to share the news that our parents weren't getting any of the letters we wrote.

And we weren't getting any of theirs.

The camp had to be keeping our post from us, I suddenly realized.

Colin and Jay—where are you?

The fried chicken was greasy, and the potatoes were lumpy and tasted like paste. As I forced the food down, I kept turning to glance at the refectory door, expecting to see my two cabin mates.

But they didn't show up.

A heavy feeling of dread formed in my stomach. Through the refectory window, I could see that it was already dark outside.

Where could they be?

A five-kilometre hike and back shouldn't take this many hours.

I pulled myself up and made my way to the counsellors' table in the corner. Larry was having a loud argument about sport with two of the other counsellors. They were shouting and gesturing with their hands.

Frank's chair was empty.

"Larry, did Frank get back?" I interrupted their discussion.

Larry turned, a startled expression on his face. "Frank?" He motioned to the empty chair at the table. "Suppose not."

"He took Jay and Colin on the hike," I said. "Shouldn't they be back by now?"

Larry shrugged. "Beats me." He returned to his argument, leaving me standing there staring at Frank's empty chair.

After the trays had been cleared away, we pushed the tables and benches against the wall and had indoor relay races. Everyone seemed to be having a great time. The shouts and cheers echoed off the high-raftered ceiling.

I was too worried about Jay and Colin to enjoy the games.

Maybe they decided to camp out overnight, I told myself.

But I had seen them leave, and I knew they hadn't taken any tents or sleeping bags or other overnight supplies.

So where *were* they?

The games finished a little before lights out. As I followed the crowd to the door, Larry appeared beside me. "We're leaving early tomorrow morning," he said. "First thing."

"Huh?" I didn't understand what he meant.

"The canoe trip. I'm the canoe counsellor. I'll be taking you boys," he explained, seeing my confusion.

"Oh. Okay," I replied without enthusiasm. I was so worried about Jay and Colin, I'd nearly forgotten about the canoe trip.

"Straight after breakfast," Larry said. "Wear your swimming trunks. Bring a change of clothes. Meet me at the riverbank." He hurried back to help the other counsellors pull the tables into place.

"After breakfast," I muttered. I wondered if Jay and Colin were also coming on the canoe trip. I had forgotten to ask Larry.

I headed quickly down the dark hill. The dew had already fallen, and the tall grass was slippery and wet. Halfway down, I could see the dark outline of the Forbidden Cabin, hunched forward as if preparing to strike.

Forcing myself to look away, I jogged the rest of the way to Cabin 4.

To my surprise, I could see through the window that someone was moving around inside.

Colin and Jay are back! I thought.

Eagerly, I pushed open the door and burst inside. "Hey—where've you two been?" I cried.

I stopped short. And gasped.

Two strangers stared back at me.

One was sitting on the edge of Colin's top bunk, pulling off his trainers. The other was leaning over the chest of drawers, pulling a T-shirt from one of the drawers.

"Hi. You in here?" the boy at the chest of drawers stood up straight, his eyes studying me. He had very short black hair, and a gold stud in one ear.

I swallowed hard. "Am I in the wrong cabin? Is this Cabin 4?"

They both stared at me, confused.

I saw the other boy, the one in Colin's bunk, also had black hair, but his was long and straggly and fell over his forehead. "Yeah. This is Cabin 4," he said.

"We're new," the short-haired boy added. "I'm Tommy, and he's Chris. We just started today."

"Hi," I said uncertainly. "My name's Billy." My heart was pounding like a drum in my chest. "Where are Colin and Jay?"

"Who?" Chris asked. "They told us this cabin was mostly empty."

"Well, Colin and Jay—" I started.

"We've just arrived. We don't know anyone," Tommy interrupted. He pushed the drawer shut.

"But that's Jay's drawer," I said, bewildered, pointing. "What did you do with Jay's stuff?"

Tommy gazed back at me in surprise. "The drawer was empty," he replied.

"Almost all the drawers were empty," Chris added, tossing his trainers down to the floor. "Except for the bottom two drawers."

"That's my stuff," I said, my head spinning. "But Colin and Jay—their stuff was here," I insisted.

"The whole cabin was empty," Tommy said. "Maybe your friends were moved."

"Maybe," I said weakly. I sat down on the lower bunk beneath my bed. My legs felt shaky. A million thoughts were whirring through my mind, all of them frightening.

"This is weird," I said aloud.

"It's not a bad cabin," Chris said, pulling down his blanket and settling in. "Quite cosy."

"How long are you staying at camp?" Tommy asked, pulling on a baggy white T-shirt. "All summer?"

"No!" I exclaimed with a shudder. "I'm not staying!" I spluttered. "I mean—I mean . . . I'm leaving. On...uh...I'm leaving on Visitors Day next week."

Chris flashed Tommy a surprised glance. "Huh? When are you leaving?" he asked again.

"On Visitors Day," I repeated. "When my parents come up for Visitors Day."

"But didn't you hear Uncle Al's announcement before dinner?" Tommy asked, staring hard at me. "Visitors Day has been cancelled!"

I drifted in and out of a troubled sleep that night. Even with the blanket pulled up to my chin, I felt shivery and afraid.

It felt so weird to have two strange boys in the bunk, sleeping where Jay and Colin slept. I was worried about my missing friends.

What had happened to them? Why hadn't they come back?

As I tossed restlessly in the top bunk, I heard howls in the distance. Animal cries, probably coming from the Forbidden Cabin. Long, frightening howls carried by the wind into our open cabin window.

At one point, I thought I heard kids screaming. I sat up straight, suddenly alert, and listened.

Had I dreamed the frightful shrieks? I was so scared and confused, it was impossible to tell what was real and what was a nightmare.

It took hours to get back to sleep.

I awoke to a grey, overcast morning, the air heavy and cold. Pulling on swimming trunks and a T-shirt, I raced to the lodge to find Larry. I had to find out what had happened to Jay and Colin.

I searched everywhere for him without success. Larry wasn't at breakfast. None of the other counsellors admitted to knowing anything. Frank, the counsellor who had taken my two friends on the hike, was also missing.

I finally found Larry at the riverbank, preparing a long metal canoe for our river trip. "Larry—where are they?" I cried out breathlessly.

He gazed up at me, holding an armload of canoe paddles. His expression turned to bewilderment. "Huh? Chris and Tommy? They'll be here soon."

"No!" I cried, grabbing his arm. "Jay and Colin! Where are they? What happened to them, Larry? You've *got* to tell me!"

I gripped his arm tightly. I was gasping for breath. I could feel the blood pulsing at my temples. "You've got to tell me!" I repeated shrilly.

He pulled away from me and let the paddles fall beside the canoe. "I don't know anything about them," he replied quietly.

"But Larry!"

"Really, I don't," he insisted in the same quiet voice. His expression softened. He placed a hand on my trembling shoulder. "Tell you what, Billy," he said, staring hard into my eyes. "I'll ask Uncle Al about it after our trip, okay? I'll find out for you. When we get back."

I stared back at him, trying to decide if he was being honest.

I couldn't tell. His eyes were as calm and cold as marbles.

He leaned forward and pushed the canoe into the shallow river water. "Here. Take one of those life jackets," he said, pointing to a pile behind me. "Strap it on. Then get in."

I did as he instructed. I saw that I had no choice.

Chris and Tommy came running up to us a few seconds later. They obediently followed Larry's instructions and strapped on the life-jackets.

A few minutes later, the four of us were seated cross-legged inside the long, slender canoe, drifting slowly away from the shore.

The sky was still charcoal-grey, the sun hidden behind hovering, dark clouds. The canoe bumped over the choppy river waters. The current was stronger than I had realized. We began to pick up speed. The low trees and shrubs along the riverbank slid past rapidly.

Larry sat facing us in the front of the canoe.

He demonstrated how to paddle as the river carried us away.

He watched us carefully, a tight frown on his face, as the three of us struggled to pick up the rhythm he was showing us. Then, when we finally seemed to catch on, Larry grinned and carefully turned round, gripping the sides of the canoe as he shifted his position.

"The sun is trying to come out," he said, his voice muffled in the strong breeze over the rippling water.

I glanced up. The sky looked darker than before.

He stayed with his back to us, facing forward, allowing the three of us to do the paddling. I had never paddled a canoe before. It was harder than I'd imagined. But as I fell into the rhythm of it with Tommy and Chris, I began to enjoy it.

Dark water smacked against the prow of the canoe, sending up splashes of white froth. The current grew stronger, and we picked up speed. The air was still cold, but the steady work of rowing warmed me. After a while, I realized I was sweating.

We rowed past tangles of yellow and grey-trunked trees. The river suddenly divided in two, and we shifted our paddles to take the left branch. Larry began paddling again, working to keep us off the tall rocks that jutted between the river branches.

The canoe bobbed up and slapped down. Bobbed up and slapped down. Cold water poured over the sides.

The sky darkened even more. I wondered if it was about to storm.

As the river widened, the current grew rapid and strong. I realized we didn't really need to paddle. The river current was doing most of the work.

The river sloped down. Wide swirls of frothing white water made the canoe leap and bounce.

"Here come the rapids!" Larry shouted, cupping his hands around his mouth so we could hear him. "Hang on! It gets pretty choppy!"

I felt a tremor of fear as a wave of icy water splashed over me. The canoe rose up on a shelf of white water, then hit hard as it landed.

I could hear Tommy and Chris laughing excitedly behind me.

Another icy wave rolled over the canoe, startling me. I cried out and nearly let go of my paddle.

Tommy and Chris laughed again.

I took a deep breath and held on tightly to the paddle, struggling to keep up the rhythm.

"Hey, look!" Larry cried suddenly.

To my astonishment, he climbed to his feet. He leaned forward, pointing into the swirling, white water.

"Look at those fish!" he shouted.

As he leaned down, the canoe was jarred by a powerful rush of current. The canoe spun to the right.

I saw the startled look on Larry's face as he lost his balance. His arms shot forward, and he plunged headfirst into the tossing waters.

"Noooooo!" I screamed.

I glanced back at Tommy and Chris, who had stopped paddling and were staring into the swirling, dark waters, their expressions frozen in open-mouthed horror.

"Larry! Larry!" I was screaming the name over and over without realizing it.

The canoe continued to slide rapidly down the churning waters.

Larry didn't come up.

"Larry!"

Behind me, Tommy and Chris also called out his name, their voices shrill and frightened.

Where was he? Why didn't he swim to the surface?

The canoe was drifting farther and farther downriver.

"Larrrrrry!"

"We have to stop!" I screamed. "We have to slow down!"

"We can't!" Chris shouted back. "We don't know how!"

Still no sign of Larry. I realized he must be in trouble.

Without thinking, I tossed my paddle into the river, climbed to my feet, and plunged into the dark, swirling waters to save him.

I jumped without thinking and swallowed a mouthful of the brown water as I went down.

My heart thudded in my chest as I struggled frantically to the surface, spluttering and choking.

Gasping in a deep breath, I lowered my head and tried to swim against the current. My trainers felt as if they weighed a tonne.

I realized I should have pulled them off before I jumped.

The water heaved and tossed. I moved my arms in long, desperate strokes, pulling myself towards the spot where Larry had fallen in. Glancing back, I saw the canoe, a dark blur growing smaller and smaller.

"Wait!" I wanted to shout to Tommy and Chris. "Wait for me to get Larry!"

But I knew that they didn't know how to slow down the canoe. They were helpless as the current carried them away.

Where was Larry?

I sucked in another mouthful of air—and froze as I felt a sharp cramp in my right leg.

The pain shot up through my entire right side.

I slid under the water and waited for the pain to lessen.

The cramp seemed to tighten until I could barely move the leg. Water rushed over me. I struggled to pull myself up to the surface.

As I choked in more air, I swam rapidly and hard, pulling myself up, ignoring the sharp pain in my leg.

Hey!

What was that object floating just ahead of me? A piece of driftwood being carried by the current?

Brown water washed over me, blinding me, tossing me back. Spluttering, I pulled myself back up.

Water rolled down my face. I struggled to see.

Larry!

He came floating right up to me.

"Larry! Larry!" I managed to scream.

But he didn't answer me. I could see clearly now that he was floating face down.

The leg cramp miraculously vanished as I reached out with both arms and grabbed Larry's shoulders. I pulled his head up from the water, rolled him onto his back, and wrapped my arm around his neck. I was using the lifesaving technique my parents had taught me.

Turning downriver, I searched for the canoe. But the current had carried it out of sight.

I swallowed another mouthful of icy water. Choking, I held onto Larry. I kicked hard. My right leg still felt tight and weak, but at least the pain had gone. Kicking and pulling with my free hand, I dragged Larry towards the shore.

To my relief, the current helped. It seemed to pull in the same direction.

A few seconds later, I was close enough to shore to stand. Wearily, panting like a wild animal, I tottered to my feet and dragged Larry onto the wet mud of the shore.

Was he dead? Had he drowned before I'd reached him?

I stretched him out on his back and, still panting loudly, struggling to catch my breath, to stop my whole body from trembling, I leaned over him.

And he opened his eyes.

He stared up at me blankly, as if he didn't recognize me.

Finally, he whispered my name. "Billy," he choked out, "are we okay?"

Larry and I rested for a bit. Then we walked back to camp, following the river upstream.

We were soaked through and covered in mud,

but I didn't care. We were alive. We were okay. I had saved Larry's life.

We didn't talk much all the way back. It was taking every ounce of strength we had just to walk.

I asked Larry if he thought Tommy and Chris would be okay.

"Hope so," he muttered, breathing hard. "They'll probably ride to shore and walk back like us."

I took this opportunity to ask him again about Jay and Colin. I thought maybe Larry would tell me the truth since we were completely alone and since I had just saved his life.

But he insisted he didn't know anything about my two cabin mates. As we walked, he raised one hand and swore he didn't know anything at all.

"So many frightening things have happened," I muttered.

He nodded, keeping his eyes straight ahead. "It's been strange," he agreed.

I waited for him to say more. But he walked on in silence.

It took three hours to walk back. We hadn't travelled downriver as far as I had thought, but the muddy shore kept twisting and turning, making our journey longer.

As the camp came into view, my knees buckled and my legs nearly collapsed under me.

Breathing hard, drenched in perspiration, our

clothes still damp and mud-splattered, we trudged wearily onto the riverbank.

"Hey—!" a voice called from the swimming area. Uncle Al, dressed in a baggy, green tracksuit, came hurrying across the mud to us. "What happened?" he asked Larry.

"We had an accident!" I cried before Larry had a chance to reply.

"I fell in," Larry admitted, his face reddening beneath the splattered mud. "Billy jumped in and saved me. We walked back."

"But Tommy and Chris couldn't stop the canoe. They drifted away!" I cried.

"We both nearly drowned," Larry told the frowning camp director. "But, Billy—he saved my life."

"Can you send someone to find Tommy and Chris?" I asked, suddenly starting to shake all over, from exhaustion, I suppose.

"The two boys floated on downriver?" Uncle Al asked, staring hard at Larry, scratching the back of his fringe of yellow hair.

Larry nodded.

"We have to find them!" I insisted, trembling harder.

Uncle Al continued to glare at Larry. "What about my canoe?" he demanded angrily. "That's our best canoe! How am I supposed to replace it?"

Larry shrugged unhappily.

"We'll have to go and look for that canoe tomorrow," Uncle Al snapped.

He doesn't care about the two boys, I realized. *He doesn't care about them at all.*

"Go and get into dry clothes," Uncle Al instructed Larry and me. He stormed off towards the lodge, shaking his head.

I turned and started for the cabin, feeling chilled, my body still trembling. I could feel a strong wave of anger sweep over me.

I had just saved Larry's *life*, but Uncle Al didn't care about that.

And he didn't care that two campers were lost on the river.

He didn't care that two campers and a counsellor had never returned from their hike.

He didn't care that boys were attacked by *creatures*!

He didn't care that kids disappeared and were never mentioned again.

He didn't care about any of us.

He only cared about his canoe.

My anger quickly turned to fear.

Of course, I had no way of knowing that the *scariest* part of my summer was yet to come.

260

I was all alone in the cabin that night.

I pulled an extra blanket onto my bed and slid into a tight ball beneath the covers. I wondered if I'd be able to fall asleep. Or if my frightened, angry thoughts would keep me tossing and turning for another night.

But I was so weary and exhausted, even the eerie, mournful howls from the Forbidden Cabin couldn't keep me awake.

I fell into deep blackness and didn't wake up until I felt someone shaking my shoulders.

Startled alert, I sat up straight. "Larry!" I cried, my voice still clogged with sleep. "What's happening?"

I squinted across the room. Larry's bed was rumpled, the blanket balled up at the end. He had obviously come in late and slept in the bunk.

But Tommy's and Chris's beds were still untouched from the day before.

"Special hike," Larry said, walking over to his bunk. "Hurry. Get dressed."

"Huh?" I stretched and yawned. Outside the window, it was still grey. The sun hadn't come up. "What kind of hike?"

"Uncle Al has called a special hike," Larry replied, his back to me. He grabbed the sheet and started to make his bed.

With a groan, I lowered myself to the cabin floor. It felt cold beneath my bare feet. "Don't we get to rest? I mean, after what happened yesterday?" I glanced once again at Tommy's and Chris's unused beds.

"It's not just us," Larry replied, smoothing the sheet. "It's the whole camp. Everyone's going. Uncle Al is leading it."

I pulled on a pair of jeans, stumbling across the cabin with one leg in. A sudden feeling of dread fell over me. "It wasn't scheduled," I said darkly. "Where is Uncle Al taking us?"

Larry didn't reply.

"Where?" I repeated shrilly.

He pretended he didn't hear me.

"Tommy and Chris—they didn't come back?" I asked glumly, pulling on my trainers. Luckily, I had brought two pairs. My shoes from yesterday sat in the corner, still soaked through and mud-covered.

"They'll turn up," Larry replied finally. But he didn't sound as if he meant it.

I finished getting dressed, then ran up the hill to get breakfast. It was a warm, grey morning. It must have rained during the night. The tall grass glistened wetly.

Yawning and blinking against the harsh grey light, campers headed quietly up the hill. I saw that most of them had the same confused expression I had.

Why were we going on this unscheduled hike so early in the morning? How long was it going to be? Where were we going?

I hoped that Uncle Al or one of the other counsellors would explain everything to us at breakfast, but none of them appeared in the refectory.

We ate quietly, without the usual joking around.

I found myself thinking about the terrifying canoe trip yesterday. I could almost taste the brackish brown water again. I saw Larry floating towards me, face down, floating on the churning water like a clump of seaweed.

I pictured myself trying to get him, struggling to swim, struggling to go against the current, to keep afloat in the swirls of white water.

And I saw the blur of the canoe as the strong river current carried it out of sight.

Suddenly Dawn and Dori burst into my thoughts. I wondered if they were okay. I wondered if they were going to try and meet me again by the riverbank.

Breakfast was French toast with syrup. It was usually my favourite. But this morning, I just poked at it with my fork.

"Line up outside!" a counsellor cried from the doorway.

Chairs scraped loudly. We all obediently climbed to our feet and began making our way outside.

Where were they taking us?

Why doesn't anyone tell us what this is about?

The sky had brightened to pink, but the sun still hadn't risen over the horizon.

We formed a single line along the side wall of the lodge. I was near the end of the line towards the bottom of the hill.

Some kids were cracking jokes and playfully shoving each other. But most were standing quietly or leaning against the wall, waiting to see what was going to happen.

Once the line was formed, one of the counsellors walked the length of it, pointing his finger and moving his lips in concentration as he counted us. He counted us twice to make sure he had the right number.

Then Uncle Al appeared at the front of the line. He wore a brown-and-green camouflage outfit, the kind soldiers wear in films. He had on very black sunglasses, even though the sun wasn't up yet.

He didn't say a word. He signalled to Larry and another counsellor, who were both carrying very large, heavy-looking brown bags over their shoulders. Then Uncle Al strode quickly down the hill, his eyes hidden behind the dark glasses, his features set in a tight frown.

He stopped in front of the last camper. "This way!" he announced loudly, pointing towards the riverbank.

Those were his only words. "This way!"

And we began to follow, walking at a pretty fast pace. Our trainers slid against the wet grass. A few kids were giggling about something behind me.

To my surprise, I realized I was now nearly at the front of the line. I was close enough to call out to Uncle Al. So I did. "Where are we going?" I shouted.

He quickened his pace and didn't reply.

"Uncle Al—is this a long hike?" I called.

He pretended he hadn't heard.

I decided to give up.

He led us towards the riverbank, then turned right. Thick clumps of trees stood a short way up ahead where the river narrowed.

Glancing back to the end of the line, I saw Larry and the other counsellors, bags on their shoulders, hurrying to catch up with Uncle Al.

What is this about? I wondered.

And as I stared at the clumps of low, tangled

trees up ahead, a thought pushed its way into my head.

I can escape.

The thought was so frightening—but suddenly so real—it took a long time to form.

I can escape into these trees.

I can run away from Uncle Al and this frightening camp.

The idea was so exciting, I nearly stumbled over my own feet. I bumped into the kid ahead of me, a big bruiser of a boy called Tyler, and he turned and glared at me.

Whoa, I told myself, feeling my heart start to pound in my chest. Think about this. Think carefully. . . .

I kept my eyes locked on the woods. As we drew closer, I could see that the thick trees, so close together that their branches were all intertwined, seemed to stretch on forever.

They'd never find me in there, I told myself. It would be really easy to hide in those woods.

But then what?

I couldn't stay in the woods forever.

Then what?

Staring at the trees, I forced myself to concentrate, forced myself to think clearly.

I could follow the river. Yes. Stay on the shore. Follow the river. It was bound to come to a town eventually. It *had* to come to a town.

I'd walk to the first town. Then I'd call my parents.

I can do it, I thought, so excited I could barely stay in line.

I just have to run. Make a dash for it. When no one is looking. Into the woods. Deep into the woods.

We were at the edge of the trees now. The sun had pulled itself up, brightening the rose-coloured morning sky. We stood in the shadows of the trees.

I can do it, I told myself.

Soon.

My heart thudded loudly. I was sweating even though the air was still cool.

Calm down, Billy, I warned myself. *Just calm down.*

Wait your chance.

Wait till the time is right.

Then leave Camp Nightmare behind. Forever.

Standing in the shade, I studied the trees. I spotted a narrow path into the woods a few metres up ahead.

I tried to calculate how long it would take me to reach the path. Probably ten seconds at the most. And, then, in another five seconds, I could be into the protection of the trees.

I can do it, I thought.

I can be away in less than ten seconds.

I took a deep breath. I braced myself. I tensed my leg muscles, preparing to run.

Then I glanced to the front of the line.

To my horror, Uncle Al was staring directly at me. And he held a rifle in his hands.

I cried out when I saw the rifle in his hands.

Had he read my thoughts? Did he know I was about to make a run for it?

A cold chill slid down my back as I gaped at the rifle. As I raised my eyes to Uncle Al's face, I realized he wasn't looking at me.

He had turned his attention to the two counsellors. They had lowered the bags to the ground and were bending over them, trying to get them open.

"Why did we stop?" Tyler, the kid ahead of me, asked.

"Is the hike over?" another kid joked. A few kids laughed.

"Can we go back now?" said another kid.

I stood watching in disbelief as Larry and the other counsellor began unloading rifles from the two bags.

"Line up and get one," Uncle Al instructed us, tapping the handle of his own rifle against the ground. "One rifle per boy. Come on—hurry!"

No one moved. I think everyone thought Uncle Al was kidding or something.

"What's *wrong* with you boys? I said *hurry!*" he snapped angrily. He grabbed up an armload of rifles and began moving down the line, pushing one into each boy's hands.

He pushed a rifle against my chest so hard, I staggered back a few steps. I grabbed it by the barrel before it fell to the ground.

"What's going on?" Tyler asked me.

I shrugged, studying the rifle with horror. I'd never held any kind of real gun before. My parents were both opposed to firearms of all kinds.

A few minutes later, we were all lined up in the shadow of the trees, each holding a rifle. Uncle Al stood near the middle of the line and motioned us into a tight circle so we could hear him.

"What's going on? Is this target practice?" one boy asked.

Larry and the other counsellor sniggered at that. Uncle Al's features remained hard and serious.

"Listen up!" he barked. "No more jokes. This is serious business."

The circle of campers tightened round him. We grew silent. A bird squawked noisily in a nearby tree. Somehow it reminded me of my plan to escape.

Was I about to be really sorry that I hadn't made a run for it?

"Two girls escaped from the girls' camp last night," Uncle Al announced in a flat, business-like tone. "A blonde and a redhead."

Dawn and Dori! I exclaimed to myself. I bet it was them!

"I believe," Uncle Al continued, "that these are the same two girls who sneaked over to the boys' camp and hid near the riverbank a few days ago."

Yes! I thought happily. It *is* Dawn and Dori! They escaped!

I suddenly realized a broad smile had broken out on my face. I quickly forced it away before Uncle Al could see my happy reaction to the news.

"The two girls are in these woods, boys. They're nearby," Uncle Al continued. He raised his rifle. "Your guns are loaded. Aim carefully when you see them. They won't get away from us!"

"Huh?" I gasped in disbelief. "You mean we're supposed to *shoot* them?"

I glanced around the circle of campers. They all looked as dazed and confused as I did.

"Yeah. You're supposed to shoot them," Uncle Al replied coldly. "I *told* you—they're trying to escape."

"But we can't!" I cried.

"It's easy," Uncle Al said. He raised his rifle to his shoulder and pretended to fire it. "See? Nothing to it."

"But we can't kill people!" I insisted.

"Kill?" His expression changed behind the dark glasses. "I didn't say anything about killing, did I? These guns are loaded with tranquillizer darts. We just want to stop these girls—not hurt them."

Uncle Al took two steps towards me, the rifle still in his hands. He stood over me menacingly, lowering his face close to mine.

"You got a problem with that, Billy?" he demanded.

He was challenging me.

I saw the other boys back away.

The woods grew silent. Even the birds stopped squawking.

"You got a problem with that?" Uncle Al repeated, his face so close to mine, I could smell his sour breath.

Terrified, I took a step back, then another.

Why was he doing this to me? Why was he challenging me like this?

I took a deep breath and held it. Then I screamed as loudly as I could: "I—I won't do it!"

Without completely realizing what I was doing, I raised the rifle to my shoulder and aimed the barrel at Uncle Al's chest.

"You're gonna be sorry," Uncle Al growled in a low voice. He tore off the sunglasses and heaved them into the woods. Then he narrowed his eyes furiously at me. "Drop the rifle, Billy. I'm gonna make you sorry."

"No," I told him, standing my ground. "You're not. Camp is over. You're not going to do anything."

My legs were trembling so hard, I could barely stand.

But I wasn't going to go hunting Dawn and Dori. I wasn't going to do anything else Uncle Al said. Ever.

"Give me the rifle, Billy," he said in his low, menacing voice. He reached out a hand towards my gun. "Hand it over, boy."

"No!" I cried.

"Hand it over, now," he ordered, his eyes narrowed, burning into mine. "Now!"

"No!" I cried.

He blinked once. Twice.

Then he leapt at me.

I took a step back with the rifle aimed at Uncle Al—and pulled the trigger.

The rifle emitted a soft *pop*.

Uncle Al tossed his head back and laughed. He let his rifle drop to the ground at his feet.

"Hey—!" I cried out, confused. I kept the rifle aimed at his chest.

"Congratulations, Billy," Uncle Al said, grinning warmly at me. "You passed." He stepped forward and reached out his hand to shake mine.

The other campers dropped their rifles. Glancing at them, I saw that they were all grinning, too. Larry, also grinning, flashed me a thumbs-up sign.

"What's going on?" I demanded suspiciously. I slowly lowered the rifle.

Uncle Al grabbed my hand and squeezed it hard. "Congratulations, Billy. I *knew* you'd pass."

"Huh? I don't understand!" I screamed, totally frustrated.

But instead of explaining anything to me,

Uncle Al turned to the trees and shouted, "Okay, everyone! It's over! He passed! Come out and congratulate him!"

And as I stared in disbelief, my wide-open mouth hanging down around my knees, people began stepping out from behind the trees.

First came Dawn and Dori.

"You *were* hiding in the woods!" I cried.

They laughed in response. "Congratulations!" Dawn cried.

And then others came out, grinning and congratulating me. I screamed when I recognized Mike. He was okay!

Beside him were Jay and Roger!

Colin stepped out of the woods, followed by Tommy and Chris. All smiling and happy and okay.

"What—what's going *on* here?" I stammered. I was totally stunned. I felt dizzy.

I didn't get it. I really didn't get it.

And then my mum and dad stepped out from the trees. Mum rushed up and gave me a hug. Dad patted the top of my head. "I knew you'd pass, Billy," he said. I could see happy tears in his eyes.

Finally, I couldn't take it any more. I pushed Mum gently away. "Passed *what*?" I demanded. "What *is* this? What's going on?"

Uncle Al put his arm around my shoulders and guided me away from the group of campers.

Mum and Dad followed close behind.

"This isn't really a summer camp," Uncle Al explained, still grinning at me, his face bright pink. "It's a government-testing lab."

"Huh?" I swallowed hard.

"You know your parents are scientists, Billy," Uncle Al continued. "Well, they're about to leave on a very important expedition. And this time they wanted to take you along with them."

"How come you didn't tell me?" I asked my parents.

"We couldn't!" Mum exclaimed.

"According to government rules, Billy," Uncle Al continued, "children aren't allowed to go on official expeditions unless they pass certain tests. That's what you've been doing here. You've been taking tests."

"Tests to see what?" I demanded, still dazed.

"Well, we wanted to see if you could obey orders," Uncle Al explained. "You passed when you refused to go to the Forbidden Cabin." He held up two fingers. "Second, we had to test your bravery. You demonstrated that by rescuing Larry." He held up a third finger. "Third, we had to see if you knew when *not* to follow orders. You passed that test by refusing to hunt for Dawn and Dori."

"And everyone was in on it?" I asked. "All the campers? The counsellors? Everyone? They were all actors?"

277

Uncle Al nodded. "They all work here at the testing lab." His expression turned serious. "You see, Billy, your parents want to take you to a very dangerous place, perhaps the most dangerous place in the known universe. So we had to make sure you can handle it."

The most dangerous place in the universe?

"Where?" I asked my parents. "Where are you taking me?"

"It's a very strange planet called Earth," Dad replied, glancing at Mum. "It's very far from here. But it could be exciting. The inhabitants there are weird and unpredictable, and no one has ever studied them."

Laughing, I stepped between my mum and dad and put my arms around them. "Earth?! It sounds pretty weird. But it could *never* be as dangerous or exciting as Camp Nightmoon!" I explained.

"We'll see," Mum replied quietly. "We'll see."

The Ghost Next Door

Hannah wasn't sure which had woken her—the brittle crackling sounds or the bright yellow flames.

She sat up straight in bed and stared in wide-eyed horror at the fire that surrounded her.

Flames rippled across her chest of drawers. The burning wallpaper curled and then melted. The door of the wardrobe had burned away, and she could see the fire leaping from shelf to shelf.

Even the mirror was on fire. Hannah could see her reflection, dark behind the wall of flickering flames.

The fire moved quickly to fill the room.

Hannah began to choke on the thick, sour smoke.

It was too late to scream.

But she screamed anyway.

How nice to find out it was only a dream.

Hannah sat up in bed, her heart pounding, her mouth as dry as cotton wool.

No crackling flames. No leaping swirls of yellow and orange.

No choking smoke.

All a dream, a horrible dream. So real.

But a dream.

"Wow. That was really scary," Hannah muttered to herself. She sank back on her pillow and waited for her heart to stop thudding so hard in her chest. She raised her grey-blue eyes to the ceiling, staring at the cool whiteness of it.

Hannah could still picture the black, charred ceiling, the curling wallpaper, the flames tossing in front of the mirror.

"At least my dreams aren't *boring*!" she told herself. Kicking off the light blanket, she glanced at her desk clock. Only eight-fifteen.

How can it be eight-fifteen? she wondered. I feel as if I've been sleeping forever. What day is it, anyway?

It was hard to keep track of these summer days. One seemed to melt into another.

Hannah was having a lonely summer. Most of her friends had gone away on family holidays or to camp.

There was so little for a twelve-year-old to do in a small town like Greenwood Falls. She read a lot of books and watched a lot of TV and rode her bike around town, looking for someone to hang around with.

Boring.

But today Hannah climbed out of bed with a smile on her face.

She was alive!

Her house hadn't burned down. She hadn't been trapped inside the crackling wall of flames.

Hannah pulled on a pair of fluorescent green shorts and a bright orange sleeveless top. Her parents were always teasing her about being colour blind.

"Give me a *break*! What's the big deal if I like bright colours!" she always replied.

Bright colours. Like the flames around her bed.

"Hey, dream—get *lost*!" she muttered. She ran a hairbrush quickly through her short blonde hair, then headed downstairs to the kitchen. She could smell the eggs and bacon frying on the cooker.

"Good morning, everyone!" Hannah chirped happily.

She was even happy to see Bill and Herb, her six-year-old twin brothers.

Pests. The noisiest nuisances in Greenwood Falls.

They were tossing a blue rubber ball across the breakfast table. "How many times do I have to tell you—no ball-playing in the house?" Mrs Fairchild called, turning away from the cooker to scold them.

"A million," Bill said.

Herb laughed. He thought Bill was hilarious. They both thought they were a riot.

Hannah stepped behind her mother and wrapped her up in a tight hug around the waist.

"Hannah—stop!" her mother cried. "I nearly knocked over the eggs!"

"Hannah—stop! Hannah—stop!" the twins imitated their mother.

The ball bounced off Herb's plate, rebounded off the wall, and flew onto the cooker, inches from the frying pan.

"Nice shot, ace," Hannah teased.

The twins laughed their high-pitched laughs.

Mrs Fairchild spun round, frowning. "If the ball goes in the frying pan, you're going to *eat* it with your eggs!" she threatened, shaking her fork at them.

This made the boys laugh even harder.

"They're in goofy moods today," Hannah said, smiling. She had a dimple in one cheek when she smiled.

"When are they ever in *serious* moods?" her mother demanded, tossing the ball into the hallway.

"Well, I'm in a *great* mood today!" Hannah

declared, gazing out of the window at a cloudless, blue sky.

Her mother stared at her suspiciously. "How come?"

Hannah shrugged. "I just am." She didn't feel like telling her mother about the nightmare, about how good it felt just to be alive. "Where's Dad?"

"Went to work early," Mrs Fairchild said, turning the bacon with the fork. "Some of us don't get the entire summer off," she added. "What are you going to do today, Hannah?"

Hannah opened the fridge and pulled out a carton of orange juice. "The usual, I suppose. You know. Just hang about."

"I'm sorry you're having such a boring summer," her mother said, sighing. "We just didn't have the money to send you to camp. Maybe next summer—"

"That's okay, Mum," Hannah replied brightly. "I'm having an okay summer. Really." She turned to the twins. "How'd you two like those ghost stories last night?"

"Not scary," Herb quickly replied.

"Not scary at all. Your ghost stories are pathetic," Bill added.

"You both looked pretty scared to me," Hannah insisted.

"We were pretending," Herb said.

She held up the orange juice carton. "Want some?"

"Does it have pulp in it?" Herb asked.

Hannah pretended to read the carton. "Yes. It says 'one hundred per cent pulp'."

"I hate pulp!" Herb declared.

"Me, too!" Bill agreed, making a face.

It wasn't the first time they'd had a breakfast discussion about pulp.

"Can't you buy orange juice without pulp?" Bill asked their mother.

"Can you strain it for us?" Herb asked Hannah.

"Can I have apple juice instead?" Bill asked.

"I don't want juice. I want milk," Herb decided.

Normally, this discussion would have made Hannah scream. But today, she reacted calmly. "One apple juice and one milk coming up," she said cheerfully.

"You certainly *are* in a good mood this morning," her mother commented.

Hannah handed Bill his apple juice, and he promptly spilled it.

After breakfast, Hannah helped her mother clear up the kitchen. "Nice day," Mrs Fairchild said, peering out of the window. "Not a cloud in the sky. It's supposed to go up to ninety."

Hannah laughed. Her mother was always

286

giving weather reports. "Maybe I'll go for a long bike ride before it gets really hot," Hannah told her.

She stepped out of the back door and took a deep breath. The warm air smelled sweet and fresh. She watched two yellow-and-red butterflies fluttering side by side over the flower garden.

She took a few steps across the grass towards the garage. From somewhere down the road she could hear the low drone of a lawn mower.

Hannah gazed up at the clear blue sky. The sun felt warm on her face.

"Hey—*look out!*" an alarmed voice cried.

Hannah felt a sharp pain in her back.

She uttered a frightened gasp as she fell to the ground.

Hannah landed hard on her elbows and knees. She turned quickly to see what had hit her.

A boy on a bike. "Sorry!" he called. He jumped off the bike and let it fall to the grass. "I didn't see you."

I'm wearing fluorescent green and orange, Hannah thought. Why couldn't he see me?

She climbed to her feet and rubbed the grass stains on her knees. "Ow," she muttered, frowning at him.

"I tried to stop," he said quietly.

Hannah saw that he had bright red hair, almost as orange as corn, brown eyes, and a face full of freckles.

"Why were you riding in my garden?" Hannah demanded.

"*Your* garden?" He narrowed his dark eyes at her. "Since when?"

"Since before I was born," Hannah replied sharply.

288

He pulled a leaf from her hair. "You live in that house?" he asked, pointing.

Hannah nodded. "Where do *you* live?" she demanded. She examined her elbows. They were dirty, but not bruised.

"Next door," he said, turning towards the redwood ranch-style house across the drive.

"Huh?" Hannah reacted with surprise. "You can't live there!"

"Why not?" he demanded.

"That house is empty," she told him, studying his face. "It's been empty ever since the Dodsons moved away."

"It's not empty now," he said. "I live there. With my mum."

How can that be? Hannah wondered. How could someone move in right next door without my knowing it?

I was playing with the twins back here yesterday, she thought, gazing hard at the boy. I'm sure that house was dark and empty.

"What's your name?" she asked.

"Danny. Danny Anderson."

She told him her name. "I suppose we're neighbours then," she said. "I'm twelve. How about you?"

"Me, too." He bent to examine his bike. Then he pulled out a tuft of grass that had got caught in the spokes of the back wheel. "How come I've never seen you before?" he asked suspiciously.

"How come I've never seen *you*?" she replied.

He shrugged. His eyes crinkled in the corners as a shy smile crossed his face.

"Well, have you just moved in?" Hannah asked, trying to get to the bottom of the mystery.

"Uh-uh," he replied, concentrating on the bike.

"No? How long have you lived here?" Hannah asked.

"A while."

That's impossible! Hannah thought. There's no way he could have moved in next door without me knowing it!

But before she could react, she heard a high-pitched voice calling her from the house. "Hannah! Hannah! Herb won't give back my Gameboy!" Bill stood on the back step, leaning against the open screen door.

"Where's Mum?" Hannah shouted back. "She'll get it for you."

"Okay."

The screen door slammed hard as Bill went to find Mrs Fairchild.

Hannah turned back to talk to Danny, but he had vanished into thin air.

The post usually came a little before noon. Hannah rushed eagerly down to the bottom of the drive and pulled open the postbox lid.

No letters for her. No post at all.

Disappointed, she hurried back to her room to write a scolding letter to her best friend, Janey Pace.

Dear Janey,

I hope you're having a good time at camp. But not too good—because you broke your promise. You said that you'd write to me every day, and so far, I haven't even received a crummy POSTCARD.

I am so BORED I don't know what to do! You can't imagine how little there is to do in Greenwood Falls when no one is around. It's really like DEATH!

I watch TV and I read a lot. Can you believe

I've already read ALL the books on our summer reading list? Dad promised to take us all camping in Miller Woods—BIG THRILL—but he's been working just about every weekend, so I don't think he will.

BORING!

Last night I was so bored, I marched the twins outside and built a little campfire behind the garage and pretended we were away at camp and told them a load of scary ghost stories.

The boys wouldn't admit it, of course, but I could see they enjoyed it. But you know how ghost stories freak me out. I started seeing weird shadows and things moving behind the trees. It was really kind of hilarious, I suppose. I totally scared MYSELF.

Don't laugh, Janey. You don't like ghost stories, either.

My only other news is that a new boy has moved into the Dobsons' old house next door. His name is Danny and he's our age, and he has red hair and freckles, and he's kind of cute, I think.

I've only seen him once. Maybe I'll have more to report about him later.

But now it's YOUR TURN to write. Come on, Janey. You promised. Have you met any cute boys at camp? Is THAT why you're too busy to write to me?

If I don't hear from you, I hope you get poison

ivy all over your body—especially in places where you can't scratch!

Love,
Hannah

Hannah folded the letter and stuffed it into an envelope. Her small desk stood in front of the bedroom window. Leaning over the desk, she could see the house next door.

I wonder if that's Danny's room? she thought, peering into the window just across the drive. Curtains were pulled over the window, blocking her view.

Hannah pulled herself to her feet. She ran a hairbrush through her hair, then carried the letter to the front door.

She could hear her mother scolding the twins somewhere in the back of the house. The boys were giggling as Mrs Fairchild yelled at them. Hannah heard a loud crash. Then more giggling.

"I'm going out!" she shouted, pushing open the screen door.

They probably hadn't heard her, she realized.

It was a hot afternoon, no breeze at all, the air heavy and wet. Hannah's father had mowed the front lawn the day before. The freshly cut grass smelled sweet as Hannah made her way down the drive.

She glanced over at Danny's house. No signs of life there. The front door was closed. The big living room picture window appeared bare and dark.

Hannah decided to walk the three blocks to town and post the letter at the post office. She sighed. Nothing else to do, she thought glumly. At least a walk to town will kill some time.

The pavement was covered with cut blades of grass, the green fading to brown. Humming to herself, Hannah passed Mrs Quilty's redbrick house. Mrs Quilty was bent over her garden, pulling up weeds.

"Hi, Mrs Quilty. How are you?" Hannah called.

Mrs Quilty didn't look up.

What a snob! Hannah thought angrily. I know she heard me.

Hannah crossed the street. The sound of a piano floated from the house on the corner. Someone was practising a piece of classical music, playing the same wrong note over and over, then starting the piece again.

I'm glad they're not *my* neighbours, Hannah thought, smiling.

She walked the rest of the way to town, humming to herself.

The two-storey white post office stood across the tiny town square, its flag drooping on the pole in the windless sky. Around the square stood a bank, and a barber's, a small grocery shop, and a petrol station. A few other shops,

Harder's Ice-Cream Parlour, and a diner called Diner stretched behind the square.

Two women were walking out of the grocery shop. Through the barber's window, Hannah could see Ernie, the barber, sitting in the chair, reading a magazine.

Really exciting round here, she thought, shaking her head.

Hannah crossed the small, grassy square and dropped her letter in the postbox in front of the post office door. She turned back towards home—but stopped when she heard the angry shouts.

The shouts were coming from behind the post office, Hannah realized. A man was screaming.

Hannah heard boys' voices. More shouts.

She began jogging around the side of the building, towards the angry voices.

She was nearly at the alley when she heard the shrill *yelp* of pain.

"Hey—!" Hannah called out and ran the rest of the way. "What's going on?"

A narrow alley stretched behind the post office. It was a hidden place where kids liked to hang out.

Hannah saw Mr Chesney, the post office manager. He was shaking a fist angrily at a wiry brown mutt.

There were three boys in the alley. Hannah recognized Danny. He was hanging behind the two boys she didn't recognize.

The dog had its head lowered and was whimpering softly. A tall boy, thin and lanky with straggly blond hair, grabbed the dog gently and bent down to comfort it.

"Don't throw stones at my dog!" the boy shouted at Mr Chesney.

The other boy stepped forward. He was a short, stubby kid, pretty tough-looking, with spiky black hair. He glared at Mr Chesney, his hands clenched into fists at his sides.

Danny lingered away from the others, very pale, his eyes narrowed tensely.

"Get away! Go! I warned you!" Mr Chesney snarled. He was a thin, red-faced man, totally bald, with a busy brown moustache under his pointed nose. He wore a tight-fitting grey wool suit, despite the summer heat.

"You don't have the right to hurt my dog!" the blond boy insisted, still cradling the mutt. The dog's stubby tail was wagging furiously now. The dog licked the boy's hand.

"This is government property," the post office manager replied sharply. "I'm warning you— get away from here. This isn't a hangout for you troublemakers." He took a menacing step towards the three boys.

Hannah saw Danny take a few steps back, his expression frightened. The other two boys stood their ground, staring at the red-faced post office manager defiantly. They were big, Hannah saw. Bigger than Danny. They appeared to be older than Danny.

"I'm telling my dad you hurt Rusty," the blond boy said.

"Tell your dad you were trespassing as well," Mr Chesney shot back. "And while you're at it, tell him you were rude and disrespectful. And tell him I'll file a complaint against all three of you louts if I catch you back here again."

"We're not louts!" the heavier boy shouted angrily.

Then all three boys turned and started running down the alley. The dog zigzagged excitedly at their heels, its stubby tail twitching wildly.

Mr Chesney stormed past Hannah, muttering curses to himself. He was so angry, he pushed right past her as he made his way to the front of the post office.

What a jerk, Hannah thought, shaking her head. What is his problem, anyway?

All of the kids in Greenwood Falls hated Mr Chesney. Mainly because Mr Chesney hated kids. He was always shouting at them to stop loitering in the square, or stop playing such loud music, or stop talking so loudly, or stop laughing so much, or to get out of his precious alley.

He acts as if he owns the whole town, Hannah thought.

At Hallowe'en, Hannah and a group of her friends had decided to go to Mr Chesney's house and spray-paint his windows. But to their disappointment, Chesney was prepared for any Hallowe'en trick-players. He stood at the ready in his front window, an enormous shotgun in his hand.

Hannah and her friends had gone on their way, disappointed and scared.

He knows how much we all hate him, Hannah realized.

And he doesn't care.

The alley was quiet now. Hannah headed back towards the town square, thinking about Danny. He had looked so frightened, so pale. So pale, he nearly seemed to fade away in the bright sunlight.

Danny's two friends didn't seem frightened at all, Hannah thought. They seemed angry and tough. Or maybe they were just acting tough because Mr Chesney was being so horrible to the blond boy's dog.

Crossing the square, Hannah searched for signs of life. In his brightly lit shop, Ernie was still sitting in the barber's chair, his face buried in a magazine. A blue estate car had pulled into the petrol station. A woman Hannah didn't recognize was hurrying to get to the bank before it closed.

No sign of Danny and his two friends.

I think I'll go home and watch *General Hospital*, Hannah thought with a sigh. She crossed the street and made her way slowly towards home.

Tall trees, maples and birches and sassafras, lined the pavement. The leaves were so thick, they nearly blocked the sunlight.

It was cooler under their shade, Hannah realized as she walked under them.

She was halfway down the block when the dark figure slid out from behind a tree.

At first Hannah thought it was just the shadow cast by the wide trunk. But then, as her eyes adjusted to the shade, the figure became clear.

Hannah gasped and stopped walking.

She stared hard, squinting at him, struggling to bring him into focus.

He stood in a deep blue puddle of shadow. Dressed in black, he was tall and slender, his face completely hidden in darkness.

Hannah felt a cold shiver of fear roll down her body.

Who is he? she wondered. Why is he dressed like that?

Why is he standing so still, keeping in the shadows, staring back at me from the dark shade?

Is he trying to scare me?

He slowly raised a hand, motioning for her to come nearer.

Her heart fluttering in her chest, Hannah took a step back.

Is there really someone there?

A figure dressed in black?

Or am I seeing shadows cast by the trees?

She wasn't sure—until she heard the whisper: "Hannah ... Hannah ..."

The whisper was as dry as the brush of tree

leaves, and nearly as soft.

"Hannah . . . Hannah . . ."

A slender black shadow, beckoning to her with arms as bony as twigs, whispering to her. Such a dry, inhuman whisper.

"No!" Hannah cried.

She spun round and struggled to run. Her legs felt weak. Her knees didn't want to bend.

But she forced herself to run. Faster.

Faster.

Was he following her?

Panting loudly, Hannah crossed the street without stopping to look for traffic. Her trainers pounded against the pavement as she ran.

One more block to go.

Is he following?

The shadows shifted and bent as she ran under the trees. Shadows on top of shadows, sliding over each other, grey on black, blue on grey.

"Hannah ... Hannah ..." The dry whisper.

Dry as death.

Calling to her from the shifting shadows.

He knows my name, she thought, gulping for breath, forcing her legs to keep moving.

And then she stopped.

And spun round.

"Who *are* you?" she shouted breathlessly. "What do you *want*?"

But he had vanished.

There was silence now. Except for Hannah's hard breathing.

Hannah stared into the tangle of late afternoon shadows. Her eyes darted over the shrubs and hedges of the gardens in her road. She searched the spaces between the houses, the darkness behind an open garage door, the slanting grey square beside a small shed.

Gone. Vanished.

No sign of the black-enshrouded figure that had whispered her name.

"Whoa—!" she uttered out loud.

It was an optical illusion, she decided, her eyes still warily studying the front lawns.

No way.

She argued with herself. An optical illusion doesn't call your name.

There's nothing there, Hannah, she assured herself. Her breathing returned to normal. Nothing there.

You're making up more ghost stories. You're scaring yourself again.

You're bored and lonely, and so you're letting your imagination run away with you.

Feeling only slightly better, Hannah jogged the rest of the way home.

Later, at dinner, she decided not to mention the shadow figure to her parents. They would never believe it anyway.

Instead, Hannah told them about the new family who had moved in next door.

"Huh? Someone has moved into the Dodsons' house?" Mr Fairchild put down his knife and fork and stared across the table at Hannah from behind his square-framed horn-rimmed glasses.

"There's a boy my age," Hannah reported. "His name is Danny. He has bright orange hair and freckles."

"That's nice," Mrs Fairchild replied distractedly, motioning for the twins to stop shoving each other and eat their dinners.

Hannah wasn't even sure her mother had heard her.

"How did they move in without us seeing them?" Hannah asked her father. "Did you see a removal van or anything?"

"Nope," Mr Fairchild muttered, picking up his cutlery and returning to his roast chicken.

"Well, don't you think it's *weird*?" Hannah demanded.

But before either parent could reply, Herb's chair toppled over backwards. His head hit the lino, and he began to howl.

Her mum and dad leapt off their chairs and bent to help him.

"I didn't push him!" Bill screamed shrilly. "Really. I didn't!"

Frustrated that her parents weren't interested

in her big news, Hannah carried her plate to the kitchen. Then she wandered into her bedroom.

Making her way to her desk, she pushed aside the curtains and peered out of the window.

Danny, are you in there? she wondered, staring at the curtains that covered his dark window. What are you doing right now?

The summer days seemed to float by. Hannah could barely remember how she passed the time. If only some of my friends were around, she thought wistfully.

If only *one* of my friends was around!

If only one of my friends would write.

Such a lonely summer . . .

She looked for Danny, but he never seemed to be around. When she finally saw him in his back garden one late afternoon, she hurried over to talk to him. "Hi!" she cried enthusiastically.

He was tossing a tennis ball against the back of the house and catching it. The ball made a loud *thock* each time it hit the wall.

"Hi!" Hannah called again, jogging across the grass.

Danny turned, startled. "Oh. Hi. How's it going?" He turned back to the house and tossed the ball.

He was wearing a blue T-shirt over baggy black-and-yellow-striped shorts. Hannah walked up beside him.

Thock. The ball hit the wall just below the gutter and bounced into Danny's hand.

"I haven't seen you around," Hannah said awkwardly.

"Uh-huh," was his brief reply.

Thock.

"I saw you behind the post office," she blurted out.

"Huh?" He spun the ball in his hand, but didn't throw it,

"A few days ago, I saw you in the alley. With those two boys. Mr Chesney is a real jerk, isn't he?" Hannah said.

Danny sniggered. "When he shouts, his whole head turns bright red. Just like a tomato."

"A rotten tomato," Hannah added.

"What's his problem, anyway?" Danny asked, tossing the ball. *Thock.* "My friends and I—we weren't doing anything. Just messing about."

"He thinks he's a big shot," Hannah replied. "He's always bragging about how he's a *government* employee."

"Yeah."

"What are you doing this summer?" she asked. "Just hanging around like me?"

"Kind of," he said. *Thock.* He missed the ball and had to chase it to the garage.

As he walked back towards the house, he gazed at her, as if seeing her for the first time.

Hannah suddenly felt self-conscious. She was wearing a yellow top with jam stains on the front, and her rattiest blue cotton shorts.

"Those two boys, Alan and Fred—they're the boys I usually hang around with," he told her. "Boys from school."

Thock.

How could he have friends from school? Hannah wondered. Hasn't he just moved here?

"Where do you go to school?" she asked, dodging out of the way as he backed away to catch the ball.

"Maple Avenue Middle School," he replied.

Thock.

"Hey—that's where I go!" Hannah exclaimed.

How come I've never seen him there? she wondered.

"Do you know Alan Miller?" Danny asked, turning to her, shading his eyes with one hand from the late afternoon sun.

Hannah shook her head. "No."

"Fred Drake?" he asked.

"No," she replied. "What grade are you in?"

"I'll be in the eighth this year," he said, turning back to the wall.

Thock.

"Me, too!" Hannah declared. "Do you know Janey Pace?"

"No."

"How about Josh Goodman?" Hannah asked.

Danny shook his head. "Don't know him."

"Weird," Hannah said, thinking out loud.

Danny threw the tennis ball a little too hard, and it landed on the sloping grey-tiled roof. They both watched it hit, then roll down into the gutter. Danny sighed and, staring up at the gutter, made a disgusted face.

"How can we be in the same grade and not know any of the same kids?" Hannah demanded.

He turned to her, scratching his red hair with one hand. "I don't know."

"How weird!" Hannah repeated.

Danny stepped into the deep blue shadow of the house. Hannah squinted hard. He seemed to disappear in the wide rectangle of shadow.

That's impossible! she thought.

I would have seen him at school.

If we're in the same grade, there's no way I could have missed him.

Is he lying? Is he making all this up?

He had completely vanished in the shadow. Hannah squinted hard, waiting for her eyes to adjust.

Where is he? Hannah asked herself.

He keeps disappearing.

Like a ghost.

A ghost. The word popped in and out of her mind.

When Danny came back into view, he was pulling an aluminium ladder along the back wall of the house.

"What are you going to do?" Hannah asked, moving closer.

"Get my ball," he replied, and began climbing the ladder, his white Nikes hanging over the narrow metal rungs.

Hannah moved closer. "Don't go up there," she said, suddenly gripped with a cold feeling.

"Huh?" he called down. He was already halfway up the ladder, his head nearly level with the gutter.

"Come down, Danny." Hannah felt a wave of dread sweep over her. A heavy feeling in the pit of her stomach.

"I'm a good climber," he said, pulling himself up higher. "I climb everything. My mum says I should be in a circus or something."

Before Hannah could say anything more, he had clambered off the ladder and was standing on the sloping roof, his legs spread apart, his hands stretched high in the air. "See?"

Hannah couldn't shake off the premonition, the heavy feeling of dread.

"Danny—please!"

Ignoring her shrill cry, he bent to pick the tennis ball from the gutter.

Hannah held her breath as he reached for the ball.

Suddenly, he lost his balance. His eyes went wide with surprise.

His trainers slipped on the tiles. His hands shot up as if trying to grab on to something.

Hannah gasped, staring helplessly as Danny toppled head first off the roof.

Hannah screamed and shut her eyes.

I've got to get help, she thought.

Her heart pounding, she forced herself to open her eyes, and searched the ground for Danny. But to her surprise, he was standing in front of her, a mischievous grin on his face.

"Huh?" Hannah uttered a gasp of surprise. "You—you're okay?"

Danny nodded, still grinning.

He didn't make a sound, Hannah thought, staring hard at him. He landed without making a sound.

She grabbed his shoulder. "You're okay?"

"Yeah, I'm fine," Danny said calmly. "My middle name is Daredevil. Danny Daredevil Anderson. That's what my mum always says." He tossed the ball casually from hand to hand.

"You scared me to death!" Hannah cried. Her fright was turning to anger. "Why did you do that?"

He laughed.

"You could've been killed!" she told him.

"No way," he replied quietly.

She scowled at him, staring hard into his brown eyes. "Do you do things like that all the time? Falling off roofs just to scare people?"

His grin grew wider, but he didn't say anything. He turned away from her and tossed the tennis ball at the house.

Thock.

"You were falling head first," Hannah said. "How did you land on your feet?"

Danny chuckled. "Magic," he replied slyly.

"But—but—!"

"Hannah! Hannah!" She turned to see her mother calling to her from the back door.

"What is it?" Hannah shouted.

Thock.

"I have to go out for an hour. Can you come and take care of Bill and Herb?"

Hannah turned back to Danny. "I've got to go. See you."

"See you," he replied, flashing her a freckle-faced grin.

Thock.

Hannah heard the sound of the ball against the redwood wall as she jogged across the drive to her house. Again, she pictured Danny plummeting off the roof.

How did he do it? she wondered. How did he land on his feet so silently?

"I'll only be gone an hour," her mother said, searching her bag for the car keys. "How is it out? It's supposed to cloud over and rain tonight."

Another weather report, Hannah thought, rolling her eyes.

"Don't let them kill each other, if you can help it," Mrs Fairchild said, finding the keys and shutting her bag.

"That was Danny," Hannah told her. "The new kid next door. Did you see him?"

"Uh-uh. Sorry." Mrs Fairchild hurried to the door.

"You didn't see him?" Hannah called.

The screen door slammed.

Bill and Herb appeared and pulled Hannah into their room. "Snakes and Ladders!" Bill demanded.

"Yeah. Let's play Snakes and Ladders!" Herb echoed.

Hannah rolled her eyes. She *hated* that game. It was so childish. "Okay," she agreed with a sigh. She dropped down opposite them on the rug.

"Yaaaay!" Bill cried happily, opening the gameboard. "You'll play?"

"Yeah. I'll play," Hannah told him unhappily.

"And can we cheat?" Bill asked.

"Yeah! Let's cheat!" Herb urged with grinning enthusiasm.

After dinner, the twins were upstairs, arguing with their parents over which of them got to have the *last* bath. They both hated baths and always fought to be the last.

Hannah helped clear the table, then wandered into the study. She was thinking about Danny as she made her way to the window.

Pushing aside the curtains, she pressed her forehead against the cool glass and stared across the drive to Danny's house.

The sun had lowered behind the trees. Danny's house was cast in heavy, dark shadows. The windows were covered with curtains and blinds.

Hannah realized she had never actually seen anyone inside the house. She had never seen Danny go into the house or come out of it.

She had never seen *anyone* come out of the house.

Hannah stepped back from the window, thinking hard. She remembered the morning she had met Danny, after he had run her down in the back garden. She had been talking to him— and he had *vanished* into thin air.

She thought about how he had seemed to disappear into the shadow at the side of his house, how she'd had to squint really hard to see

314

him. And she thought about how he had seemed to float to the ground, landing silently from the roof.

Silent as a ghost.

"Hannah, what are you *thinking*?" she scolded herself.

Am I making up another ghost story?

She suddenly had so many questions running through her mind. How had Danny and his family moved in without her noticing? How could he be in her school, in her *grade*, without her ever seeing him there?

How come she didn't know his friends, and he didn't know hers?

It's all so *weird*, Hannah thought.

I'm not imagining it all. I'm *not* making it up.

What if Danny really is a ghost?

If only she had someone to talk to, someone to discuss Danny with. But her friends were all away. And her parents would certainly never listen to such a crazy idea.

I'll have to prove it myself, Hannah decided. I'll study him. I'll be scientific. I'll *observe* him. I'll *spy* on him.

Yes. I'll *spy* on him.

I'll go and look in his kitchen window, she decided.

She stepped out onto the back step and pushed the screen door shut behind her. It was a warm, still night. A pale sliver of moon hung above the back garden in a royal-blue sky.

As Hannah headed across her back garden, taking long, rapid strides, crickets began to chirp loudly. Danny's house loomed in front of her, low and dark against the sky.

The ladder was still propped against the back wall.

Hannah crossed the drive that separated her garden from his. Her heart pounding, she crept across the grass and climbed the three low concrete steps onto the back porch. The kitchen door was closed.

She stepped up to the door, pressed her face close to the window, peered into the kitchen— and gasped.

Hannah gasped because Danny was staring
back at her from the other side of the
window.

"Oh!" she cried out and nearly toppled backwards off the narrow porch.

Inside the house, Danny's eyes opened wide
with surprise.

Behind him, Hannah could see a table laid
with bright yellow plates. A tall, slender, blonde-
haired woman—Danny's mum, most likely—
was pulling something out from a microwave
oven onto the worktop.

The door swung open. Danny poked his head
out, his expression still surprised. "Hi, Hannah.
What's up?"

"Nothing. I—uh—nothing, really," Hannah
stammered. She could feel her cheeks grow hot,
and knew she was blushing.

Danny's eyes burned into hers. His mouth
turned up in a grin. "Well, do you want to come in

or something?" he asked. "My mum is serving dinner, but—"

"No!" she cried, much too loudly. "I don't—I mean—I—"

I'm acting like a total jerk! she realized.

She swallowed hard, staring at his grinning face.

He's laughing at me!

"See you!" she cried, then leapt awkwardly off the porch, nearly stumbling to the ground. Without looking back, she took off, running at full speed back to her house.

I've never been so embarrassed in my entire life! she thought miserably.

Never!

When she saw Danny come out of his house the next afternoon, Hannah hid behind the garage. Watching him wheel his bike down the drive, she felt her cheeks grow hot, felt embarrassed all over again.

If I'm going to be a spy, I'm going to have to be a lot cooler, she told herself. Last night, I blew it. I panicked.

It won't happen again.

She watched him climb on his bike and, standing up, pedal to the street. Pressed against the garage wall, she waited to see which direction he turned. Then she hurried into the garage to get her bike.

He's heading into town, she saw. Probably meeting those two boys. I'll let him get a head start, then I'll follow him.

She waited at the foot of the drive, straddling her bike, watching Danny until he disappeared down the next road.

Sunlight filtered through the overhanging trees as she began pedalling, keeping a slow, steady pace as she rode after him. Mrs Quilty was out weeding her garden as usual. This time, Hannah didn't bother to call hello.

A small white terrier chased her for a while, yapping loudly with excitement, then finally giving up as Hannah pedalled away.

The school playground came into view. Several kids were playing softball on the corner diamond. Hannah looked for Danny, but he wasn't there.

She continued on into town. The sun felt warm on her face. She suddenly thought about Janey. Maybe I'll get a letter from her today, she thought.

She wished Janey were around to help spy on Danny. The two of them would be a great spy team, Hannah knew. She wouldn't have lost her cool like she had last night if Janey were around.

The town square came into view. The flag above the small, white post office was fluttering in a warm breeze. Several cars were parked in front of the grocery shop. Two women holding grocery bags were talking at the kerb.

Hannah braked her bike and lowered her feet to the ground. She shielded her eyes from the sun with one hand and searched for Danny.

Danny, where are you? she thought. Are you with your friends? Where did you go?

She pedalled across the small, grassy square towards the post office. Her bike bumped over the kerb and she kept going, around the side of the building to the alley.

But the alley was silent and empty.

"Danny, where *are* you?" she called aloud in a quiet singsong. "Where *are* you?"

He was only a block ahead of me, she thought, scratching her short hair. Has he vanished into thin air again?

She rode back to the square, then peered into Harder's Ice-Cream Parlour and the burger bar.

No sign of him.

"Hannah, you're a *great* spy!" she laughed.

With a sigh of defeat, she turned round and headed for home.

She was nearly at her house when she saw the moving shadow.

It's back! she realized.

She shifted gears and started to pedal harder.

Out of the corner of her eye, she saw the shadow sliding across Mrs Quilty's front lawn.

The dark figure floated silently over the grass towards her.

Hannah pedalled harder.

It's back. I didn't imagine it.

It's real.

But what can it be?

Standing up, she pedalled harder. Harder.

But the figure glided along with her, picking up speed, floating effortlessly.

She turned to see its arms stretch out towards her.

She gasped in terror.

Her legs suddenly felt as if they weighed a tonne.

I—I can't move! she thought.

The shadow swept over her. She could feel the sudden cold.

Sticklike black arms reached out for her from the human-shaped shadow.

Its face—why can't I see its face? Hannah wondered, struggling to keep moving.

The shadow blocked the bright sun. The whole world was blackening beneath it.

Got to keep moving. Got to move, Hannah told herself.

The dark figure floated beside her, its arms outstretched.

Gaping in horror, Hannah saw bright red eyes glowing like embers from the blackness.

"Hannah . . ." it whispered. "Hannah . . ."

What does it want from me?

She struggled to keep pedalling, but her legs wouldn't cooperate.

"Hannah . . . Hannah . . ."

The dry whisper seemed to circle her, to wrap her in terror.

"Hannah . . ."

"*No!*" she screamed as she felt herself start to fall.

She struggled to keep her balance.

Too late.

She was falling. She couldn't stop herself.

"Hannah . . . Hannah . . ."

She reached out her hands to break her fall.

"Ooof!"

She gasped in pain as she landed hard on her side.

The bike fell on top of her.

The shadow figure, its red eyes glowing, moved in to capture her.

"Hannah! Hannah!"

"Hannah! Hannah!"

Its whisper became a shout.

"Hannah!"

Her side throbbed with pain. She struggled to catch her breath.

"What do you *want*?" she managed to cry. "Leave me alone! *Please!*"

"Hannah! It's me!"

She raised her head to see Danny standing above her. He straddled his bike, gripping the handlebars, staring down at her, his features tight with concern. "Hannah—are you okay?"

"The shadow—!" she cried, feeling dazed.

Danny lowered his bike to the grass and hurried over. He lifted her bike off her and laid it down beside his. Then he reached for her hands. "Are you okay? Can you get up? I saw you fall. Did you hit a stone or something?"

"No." She shook her head, trying to clear it.

323

"The shadow—he reached for me and—"

Danny's expression changed to bewilderment. "Huh? Who reached for you?" His eyes searched all around, then returned to her.

"He knew my name," Hannah said breathlessly. "He kept calling me. He followed me."

Danny studied her, frowning. "Did you hit your head? Do you feel dizzy, Hannah? Maybe I should go and get some help."

"No . . . I . . . uh . . ." She gazed up at him. "Didn't you *see* him? He was dressed in black. He had these glowing red eyes—"

Danny shook his head, his eyes still studying her warily. "I only saw you," he said softly. "You were riding really fast. Over the grass. I saw you fall."

"You didn't see someone wearing black? A man? Chasing me?"

Danny shook his head. "There was no one else on the street, Hannah. Just me."

"Maybe I *did* bump my head," Hannah muttered, raising her hands to her short hair.

Danny reached out a hand. "Can you stand? Are you hurt?"

"I—I think I can stand." She allowed him to pull her to her feet.

Her heart was still pounding. Her entire body felt shaky. Narrowing her eyes, she searched the front gardens, her eyes lingering on the wide circles of shade from the neighbourhood's old trees.

No one in sight.

"You really didn't see anyone?" she asked in a tiny voice.

He shook his head. "Just you. I was watching from over there." He pointed to the kerb.

"But I thought . . ." Her voice trailed off. She could feel her face grow red.

This is embarrassing, she thought. He's going to think I'm a total nut case.

And then she thought, maybe I am!

"You were going so fast," he said, picking up her bike for her. "And there are so many shadows, from all the trees. And you were frightened. So maybe you imagined a man dressed in black."

"Maybe," Hannah replied weakly.

But she didn't think so. . . .

High white clouds drifted over the sun the next afternoon as Hannah jogged down the drive to the postbox. Somewhere down the road, a dog barked.

She pulled down the lid and eagerly reached inside.

Her hand slid over bare metal.

No post. Nothing.

Sighing with disappointment, she slammed the postbox lid shut. Janey had promised to write every day. She had been gone for weeks, and Hannah still hadn't received even a post-card.

None of her friends had written to her.

As she trudged back up the drive, Hannah glanced at Danny's house. The white clouds were reflected in the glass of the big living room window.

Hannah wondered if Danny was at home. She hadn't seen him since yesterday morning after falling off her bike.

My spying isn't going too well, she sighed.

Taking another glance at Danny's front window, Hannah headed back up the drive to the house.

I'll write to Janey again, she decided. I have to tell her about Danny and the frightening shadow figure and the weird things that have been happening.

She could hear the twins in the study, arguing loudly about which cartoon video they wanted to watch. Her mother was suggesting they go outside instead.

Hannah hurried to her room to get paper and a pen. The room felt hot and stuffy. She had tossed a pile of dirty clothes onto her desk. She decided to write her letter outside.

A short while later, she settled under the wide maple tree in the centre of the front garden. A blanket of high clouds had rolled over the sky.

The sun was trying to poke out from the white glare. The old, leafy tree protected her in comforting shade.

Hannah yawned. She hadn't slept well the night before. Maybe I'll have a nap later, she thought. But first, I have to write this letter.

Leaning back against the solid trunk, she began to write.

Dear Janey,

How are you? I seriously hope you've fallen in the lake and drowned. That would be the only good excuse for not writing to me in all this time!

How could you ABANDON me here like this? Next summer, one way or the other, I'm going to camp with you.

Things are definitely WEIRD around here. Do you remember I told you about that boy who moved in next door? His name is Danny Anderson, and he's kind of cute. He has red hair and freckles and SERIOUS brown eyes.

Well, don't laugh, Janey—but I think Danny is a GHOST!

I can hear you laughing. But I don't care. By the time you get back to Greenwood Falls, I'm going to have PROOF.

Please—don't tell the other girls in your cabin that your best friend has totally freaked out until you read the rest of this. Here is my evidence so far:

1. *Danny and his family suddenly appeared in the house next door. I didn't see them move in, even though I've been at home every day. Neither did my parents.*

2. *Danny says he goes to Maple Avenue, and he says he's going into eighth grade just like us. But how come we've never seen him? He hangs out with two boys I've never seen before. And he didn't know any of my friends.*

3. *Sometimes he vanishes—POOF—just like that. Don't laugh! And once he fell off the roof and landed on his feet—without making a SOUND! I'm SERIOUS, Janey.*

4. *Yesterday, I was being chased by a scary shadow, and I fell off my bike. And when I looked up, the shadow was gone, and Danny was standing in his place. And—*

Uh-oh. This is starting to sound really crazy. I wish you were here so I could explain it better. It all sounds so DUMB in a letter. Like I'm really MESSED UP or something.

I know you're laughing at me. Well, go ahead.

Maybe I won't post this letter. I mean, I don't want you to make jokes, or remind me of it for the rest of my life.

So, enough about me.

How's it going out there in the woods? I hope you were bitten by a snake and your entire body swelled up, and that's why I haven't heard from you.

Otherwise, I'm going to KILL you when you get back! Really!
WRITE!

Love,
Hannah

Yawning loudly, Hannah dropped her pen to the ground. She leaned back against the tree trunk and slowly read over the letter.

Is it too crazy to send? she wondered.

No. I *have* to send it. I *have* to tell somebody what's going on here. It's all too weird to keep to myself.

The sun had finally managed to burst through the clouds. The tree leaves above her head cast shifting shadows across the letter in her lap.

She glanced up into bright sunlight—and gasped, startled to see a face staring back at her.

"Danny—!"

"Hi, Hannah," he said quietly.

Hannah squinted up at him. His whole body was ringed by bright sunlight. He seemed to be shimmering in the light.

"I—I didn't see you," Hannah stammered. "I didn't know you were here. I—"

"Give me the letter, Hannah," Danny said softly but insistently. He reached out a hand for it.

"Huh? What did you say?"

"Give me the letter," Danny demanded, more firmly. "Give it to me now, Hannah."

She gripped the letter tightly and stared up at him. She had to shield her eyes. The bright sun seemed to shine right through him.

He hovered above her, his hand outstretched. "The letter. Hand it to me," he insisted.

"But—why?" Hannah asked in a tiny voice.

"I can't let you post it," Danny told her.

"Why, Danny? It's *my* letter. Why can't I post it to my friend?"

"Because you've found out the truth about me," he said. "And there's no way I'll let you tell anyone."

"So, I'm right," Hannah said softly. "You *are* a ghost."

She shuddered, a wave of cold fear sweeping over her.

When did you die, Danny?

Why are you here? To haunt me?

What are you going to do to me?

Questions raced through her mind. Frightening questions.

"Give me the letter, Hannah," Danny insisted. "No one will ever read it. No one can know."

"But, Danny—" She stared up at him. Stared up at a ghost.

The golden sunlight poured through him. He shimmered in and out of view.

She raised a hand to shield her eyes.

He became too bright, too bright to look at.

"What are you going to do to me, Danny?" Hannah asked, shutting her eyes tight. "What are you going to do to me now?"

He didn't reply.

When Hannah opened her eyes, she stared up into *two* faces instead of one.

Two grinning faces.

Her twin brothers pointed at her and laughed. "You were asleep," Bill said.

"You were snoring," Herb told her.

"Huh?" Hannah blinked several times, trying to clear her mind. Her neck felt stiff. Her back ached.

"Here's how you were snoring," Herb said. He performed some hideous snuffling sounds.

Both boys fell on to the grass, laughing. They rolled into each other and began an impromptu wrestling match.

"I had a bad dream," Hannah said, more to herself than to her brothers. They weren't listening to her.

She got to her feet and stretched her arms above her head, trying to stretch away her stiff neck. "Ow." Falling asleep sitting up against a tree trunk was a bad idea.

Hannah gazed towards Danny's house. That dream was so real, she thought, feeling a cold chill down her back. So frightening.

"Thanks for waking me up," she told the twins. They didn't hear her. They were racing towards the back garden.

Hannah bent down and picked up the letter. She folded it in half and made her way up the lawn to the front door.

Sometimes dreams tell the truth, she thought, her shoulders still aching. Sometimes dreams tell you things you couldn't know any other way.

I'm going to find out the truth about Danny, she vowed.

I'm going to find out the truth if it kills me.

The next evening, Hannah decided to see if Danny was at home. Maybe he'd like to walk to Harder's and buy ice-cream cones, she thought.

She told her mother where she was going and made her way across the back garden.

It had rained all day. The grass glistened wetly, and the ground beneath her shoes was soft and marshy. A pale, crescent-shaped moon rose above wisps of black cloud. The night air felt tingly and wet.

Hannah crossed the drive, then hesitated a few metres from Danny's back door. A square of dim yellow light escaped through the window of the back door.

She remembered standing at this door a few nights before and being totally embarrassed when Danny opened the door and she couldn't think of a thing to say.

At least this time I know what I'm going to say, she thought.

Taking a deep breath, Hannah stepped into the square of light on the porch. She knocked on the window of the kitchen door.

She listened. The house was silent.

She knocked again.

Silence. No footsteps to answer the door.

She leaned forward and peered into the kitchen.

"Oh!" Hannah cried out in surprise.

Danny's mother sat at the yellow kitchen table, her back to Hannah, her hair glowing in the light of a low ceiling fixture. She had both hands wrapped around a steaming white coffee mug.

Why doesn't she answer the door? Hannah wondered.

She hesitated, then raised her fist and knocked loudly on the door. Several times.

Through the window, she could see that Danny's mother didn't react to the knocking at all. She lifted the white mug to her lips and took a long sip, her back to Hannah.

"Answer the door!" Hannah cried aloud.

She knocked again. And called: "Mrs Anderson! Mrs Anderson! It's me—Hannah! From next door!"

Under the cone of light, Danny's mother put the white mug down on the yellow table. She didn't turn round. She didn't move from her chair.

"Mrs Anderson—!"

Hannah raised her hand to knock, then lowered it in defeat.

Why can't she hear me? Hannah wondered, staring at the woman's slender shoulders, at her hair gleaming down past the collar of her blouse.

Why won't she come to the door?

And then Hannah shivered with fear as she answered her own questions.

I know why she can't hear me, Hannah thought, backing away from the window.

I know why she doesn't answer the door.

Overcome with fear, Hannah uttered a low moan and backed away from the light, off the porch, into the safety of the darkness.

Trembling all over, Hannah wrapped her arms around her chest, as if shielding herself from her frightening thoughts.

Mrs Anderson can't hear me because she isn't real, Hannah realized.

She isn't real. She's a ghost.

Like Danny.

A ghost family has moved next door to me.

And here I am, standing in this dark back garden trying to spy on a boy who isn't even alive! Here I am, trembling all over, cold with fear, trying to prove what I'm already sure of. He's a ghost. His mother is a ghost.

And I—I—

The kitchen light went out. The back of Danny's house was completely dark now.

The pale light from the crescent moon trickled onto the glistening, wet grass. Hannah stood, listening to the silence, trying to force away the frightening thoughts that crowded her mind until it felt as if her head were about to burst.

Where *is* Danny? she wondered.

Crossing the drive, she headed back to her house. She could hear music and voices from the TV in the study. She could hear the twins' laughter floating out from the upstairs window of their room.

Ghosts, she thought, staring at the lighted windows, like bright eyes shining back at her.

Ghosts.

I don't *believe* in ghosts!

The thought made her feel a little less frightened. She suddenly realized her throat was dry. The night air felt hot and sticky against her skin.

She thought of ice-cream again. Going to Harder's and getting a double-scoop cone seemed an excellent idea. Cookies-and-Cream, Hannah thought. She could already taste it.

She hurried into the house to tell her parents she was walking into town. At the doorway to the dark-panelled study, she stopped. Her parents, bathed in the glow of the TV screen, turned to her expectantly.

"What's up, Hannah?"

She had a sudden impulse to tell them everything. And so she did.

"The people next door, they're not alive," she blurted out. "They're ghosts. You know Danny,

337

the boy my age? He's a ghost. I know he is! And his mother—"

"Hannah, please—we're trying to watch," her father said, pointing to the TV with a can of Diet Coke in his hand.

They don't believe me, she thought.

And then she scolded herself. Of *course* they don't believe me. Who would believe such a crazy story?

In her room, she took a five-dollar note from her wallet and shoved it into the pocket of her shorts. Then she brushed her hair, studying her face in the mirror.

I look okay, she thought. I don't *look* like a crazy person.

Her hair was damp from the wet night air. Maybe I'll let it grow, she thought, watching it fall into shape around her face. I should have *something* to show for this summer!

As she headed towards the front door, she heard loud bumping and banging above her head. The twins must be wrestling up in their room, she realized, shaking her head.

She stepped back out into the warm, wet darkness, jogged down the front lawn to the pavement, and headed towards town and Harder's Ice-Cream Parlour.

The tall, old-fashioned-looking streetlights cast circles of blue-white light along the street. The trees, trembling in soft gusts of wind, rustled over the pavement as Hannah stepped beneath them.

Ghosts on the pavement, she thought with a shiver. They seemed to reach down for her with their leafy arms.

As she neared town, a strange feeling of dread swept over her. She quickened her pace as she passed the post office, its windows as black as the sky.

The town square was deserted, she saw. It wasn't even eight o'clock, and there were no cars passing through town, no one on the streets.

"What a boring place!" she muttered under her breath.

Behind the bank, she turned onto Elm Street. Harder's Ice-Cream Parlour stood on the next corner, a large red neon ice-cream cone in its window, casting a red glow onto the pavement.

At least Harder's stays open after dark, Hannah thought.

As she walked closer, she could see the glass front door of the small shop propped open invitingly.

She stopped a few metres from the door.

The feeling of dread suddenly became overpowering. Despite the heat of the night, she felt cold all over. Her knees trembled.

What's going on? she wondered. Why do I feel so strange?

As she stared through the red glare of the neon cone into the open doorway, a figure burst out.

Followed by another. And another.

Into the light they ran, their faces twisted in fear.

Staring in surprise, she recognized Danny in front, followed by Alan and Fred.

They each held ice-cream cones in front of them.

They ran from the shop, bent forward as if straining to flee as fast as possible. Their trainers thudded against the pavement.

Hannah heard loud, angry shouts from inside the shop.

Without realizing it, she had moved close to the door.

She could still hear the three boys running away. But she could no longer see them in the darkness.

She turned—and felt something hit her hard from behind.

"Ohh!" she cried out as she was thrown heavily on to the hard pavement.

Hannah landed hard on the pavement on her elbows and knees. The fall took her breath away.

A burning pain shot through her body.

What happened?

What hit me?

Gasping for breath, she raised her head in time to see Mr Harder barrel past her. He was shouting at the top of his lungs for the boys to stop.

Hannah slowly pulled herself to her feet. *Whoa!* she thought. *Harder is really angry!*

Standing up straight, her bare knees throbbing with pain, her heart still thudding loudly, she glared after the shop owner.

He could have at least said he was sorry he knocked me over, she thought angrily.

She leaned over to examine her knees in the light from the ice-cream parlour. Were they cut?

No. Just a little bruised.

Brushing down her shorts, she glanced up to see Mr Harder hurrying back to the shop. He was a short, fat man with curls of white hair around his round, pink face. He wore a long white apron that flapped in the wind as he walked, his fists swinging at his sides.

Hannah ducked back out of the light, behind a wide tree trunk.

A few seconds later, she could hear him back behind the counter, complaining loudly to his wife. "What is wrong with these kids?" he was bellowing. "They take ice-cream and run without paying? Don't they have parents? Don't they have anyone to teach them right from wrong?"

Mrs Harder murmured something to soothe her husband. Hannah couldn't hear the words.

With Mr Harder's angry shouts filling the air, she crept out from behind the tree and hurried away, in the direction the boys had run.

Why had Danny and his friends pulled such a stupid stunt? she wondered. What if they had been caught? Was it really worth being arrested, getting a police record just for an ice-cream cone?

Halfway down the block, she could still hear Mr Harder bellowing with rage from inside his small shop. Hannah started to run, eager to get away from his angry voice. Her left knee ached.

The air suddenly felt stiflingly hot, heavy and

damp. Strands of hair were matted against her forehead from sweat.

She pictured Danny running from the shop, holding the ice-cream cone in one hand. She pictured the frightened expression on his face as he fled. She pictured Alan and Fred right behind him, their trainers thudding against the pavement as they made their getaway.

And now she was running, too. She wasn't sure why.

Her left knee still ached from her fall. She was out of the town square now, running past dark houses and lawns.

She turned a corner, the streetlight casting a cone of white light around her. More houses. A few porchlights lit. No one on the street.

Such a boring little town, she thought again.

She stopped short when she saw the three boys. They were halfway up the block, huddled behind a tall, wall-like hedge.

"Hey—you three!" Her voice came out in a whisper.

Running in the street, she made her way towards them quickly. As she came closer, she could see them laughing together, enjoying their ice-cream cones.

They hadn't seen her. Hannah made her way into the deep shadows on the other side of the street. Keeping in the dark, she crept closer, until she was in the garden across the street from them, hidden by a bushy evergreen hedge.

Fred and Alan were shoving each other playfully, enjoying their triumph over the shop owner. Danny stood by himself, behind them against the tall hedge, silently licking his cone.

"Harder's was having a special tonight," Alan declared loudly. "Free ice-cream!"

Fred hee-hawed and slapped Alan hard on the back.

Both boys turned to Danny. The glow from the streetlight made their faces look pale and green. "You looked really scared," Alan told Danny. "I thought you were going to puke your guts out."

"Hey, no way," Danny insisted. "I was the first one out of there, you know. You two were so slow, I thought I'd have to come back and rescue you."

"Yeah. Sure," Fred replied sarcastically.

Danny's acting tough, Hannah realized. He's trying to be like them.

"That was pretty exciting," Danny said, tossing the remainder of his cone into the hedge. "But maybe we'd better be careful. You know. Not hang around there for a while."

"Hey, it's not as if we robbed a bank or something," Alan said. "It was just ice-cream."

Fred said something to Alan that Hannah couldn't hear, and the two boys started wrestling around, uttering high-pitched giggles.

"Hey, boys—not so loud," Danny warned. "I mean—"

"Let's go back to Harder's," Alan suggested. "I wanted *two* scoops!"

Fred hee-hawed and slapped Alan a high-five. Danny joined in the laughter.

"Hey, come on—we should get going," Danny said.

Before his friends could reply, the street filled with light.

Hannah turned to see two bright white lights looming towards them.

Car headlights.

The police, Hannah thought.

They're caught. All three of them are caught.

The car stopped.

Hannah peered out from behind the hedge.

"Hey, you kids—" the driver called to the boys in a gruff voice. He poked his head out of the car window.

It isn't the police, Hannah realized, breathing a long sigh of relief.

The boys froze against the hedge. In the dim light from the street lamp, Hannah could see that the driver was an elderly man, white-haired, wearing glasses.

"We're not doing anything. Just talking," Fred called to the man.

"Do any of you know how to get to Route 112?" the man asked. The light went on inside the car. Hannah could see a road map in the man's hand.

Fred and Alan laughed, relieved laughter. Danny continued to stare at the driver, his expression still frightened.

"Route 112?" the man repeated.

"Main Street turns into Route 112," Alan told the man, pointing in the direction the car was heading. "Go up two streets. Then turn right."

The light went out in the car. The man thanked them and drove off.

The boys watched until the car had disappeared in the darkness. Fred and Alan slapped each other high-fives. Then Fred shoved Alan into the hedge. They all laughed giddily.

"Hey, look where we are," Alan said, surprised.

The boys turned towards the drive. From her hiding place across the street, Hannah followed their gaze.

At the end of the hedge stood a tall wooden postbox on a pole. A hand-carved swan's head perched on top of the box, which had graceful wings jutting out from its sides.

"It's Chesney's house," Alan said, making his way along the hedge towards the postbox. He grabbed the wings with both hands. "Can you *believe* this postbox?"

"Chesney carved it himself," Fred said, sniggering. "What a dork."

"It's his pride and joy," Alan sneered. He pulled open the lid and peered inside. "Empty."

"Who would write to *him*?" Danny declared, trying to sound as tough as his two friends.

"Hey, I've got an idea, Danny," Fred said. He

stepped behind Danny and started shoving him towards the postbox.

"Whoa," Danny protested.

But Fred pushed him up to the postbox. "Let's see how strong you are," Fred said.

"Hey, wait—" Danny cried.

Hannah leaned out from behind the low hedge. "Oh, wow," she muttered to herself. "*Now* what are they going to do?"

"Take the postbox," she heard Alan order Danny. "I dare you."

"We dare you," Fred added. "Remember what you told us about dares, Danny? How you never turn one down?"

"Yeah. You told us you never turn down a dare," Alan said, grinning.

Danny hesitated. "Well, I—"

A heavy feeling of dread formed in the pit of Hannah's stomach. Watching Danny step towards Mr Chesney's hand-carved postbox, she suddenly had a premonition—a feeling that something really terrible was about to happen.

I've got to stop them, she decided.

Taking a deep breath, she stepped out from behind the bush.

As she started to call to them, everything went black.

"Hey—!" she cried aloud.

What had happened?

Her first thought was that the street light had gone out.

But then Hannah saw the two red circles glowing in front of her.

The two glowing eyes surrounded by darkness.

The shadow figure rose up centimetres in front of her.

She tried to scream, but her voice was muffled in its heavy darkness.

She tried to run, but it blocked her path.

The red eyes burned into hers.

Closer. Closer.

It's got me now, Hannah knew.

"Hannah . . ." it whispered. "Hannah . . ."

So close, she could smell its hot, sour breath.

"Hannah . . . Hannah . . ." Its whisper like crackling, dead leaves.

The ruby eyes burned like fire. Hannah felt the darkness circle her, wrap around her tightly.

"Please—" was all she could manage to choke out.

"Hannah . . ."

And the light returned.

Hannah blinked, struggled to breathe.

The sour odour lingered in her nostrils. But the street was bright now.

Car headlights washed over her.

It—it's gone, Hannah realized. The lights had chased away the shadow figure.

But would it return?

As the car passed by, Hannah dropped to the ground behind the low evergreen hedge and struggled to catch her breath. When she looked up, the boys were still huddled in front of Mr Chesney's hedge.

"Let's get going," Danny urged them.

"No way. Not yet," Alan said, stepping in front of Danny to block his way. "You're forgetting about our dare."

Fred shoved Danny towards the postbox. "Go ahead. Take it."

"Hey, wait." Danny spun round. "I never said I'd do it."

"I dared you to take Chesney's postbox," Fred told him. "Remember? You told us you never turned down a dare?"

Alan laughed. "Chesney will come out tomorrow and think his swan flew away."

"No, wait—" Danny protested. "Maybe it's a stupid idea."

"It's a *cool* idea. Chesney is a creep," Alan insisted. "Everyone in Greenwood Falls hates his guts."

"Take his postbox, Danny," Fred challenged. "Pull it up. Come on. I dare you."

"No, I—" Danny tried to back away, but Fred held him from behind by the shoulders.

"You chicken?" Alan challenged.

"Look at the chicken," Fred said in a mocking, babyish voice. "Cluck cluck."

"I'm not a chicken," Danny snapped angrily.

"Prove it," Alan demanded. He grabbed Danny's hands and raised them to the carved wings that stretched from the sides of the postbox. "Go ahead. Prove it."

"What a riot!" Fred declared. "The town postmaster—his postbox flies away."

Don't do it, Danny, Hannah urged silently from her dark hiding place across the street. *Please—don't do it.*

Another set of car headlights made the three boys back away from the postbox. The car rolled past without slowing down.

"Let's go. It's getting late," Hannah heard Danny say.

But Fred and Alan insisted, teasing him, challenging him.

As Hannah stared into the white light of the street lamp, Danny stepped up to Chesney's postbox and grabbed the wings.

"Danny, wait—" Hannah cried.

He didn't seem to hear her.

With a loud groan, he began to tug.

It didn't budge.

He lowered his hands to the pole and wrapped them tightly around it just below the box.

He tugged again.

"It's in really deep," he told Alan and Fred. "I don't know if I can get it."

"Try again," Alan urged.

"We'll help you," Fred said, placing his hands above Danny's on the box.

"Let's all pull together," urged Alan. "At

the count of three."

"*I wouldn't do that if I were you!*" exclaimed a gruff voice behind them.

They all turned to see Mr Chesney glaring at them from the drive, his face knotted in a furious snarl.

Mr Chesney grabbed Danny's shoulders and pulled him away from the postbox.

One of the wooden swan wings came off in Danny's hands. As Mr Chesney wrestled him away, Danny let it drop to the ground.

"You louts!" Mr Chesney spluttered, his eyes wide with rage. "You—you—"

"Let go of him!" Hannah screamed from across the street. But fear muffled her voice. Her cry came out a whisper.

With a loud groan, Danny pulled free of the man's grasp.

Without another word, the three boys were running, running down the middle of the dark street, their trainers pounding loudly on the pavement.

"I'll remember you!" Mr Chesney called after them. "I'll remember you. I'll see you again! And next time, I'll have my shotgun!"

Hannah watched Mr Chesney bend to pick up

the broken swan's wing. He examined the wooden wing, shaking his head angrily.

Then she began running, keeping in the dark front gardens, hidden by hedges and low bushes, running in the direction Danny and his friends had taken.

She saw the boys turn a corner, and kept running. Keeping well behind, she followed them through the town square, still deserted and dark. Even Harder's ice-cream parlour was closed now, the shop dark behind the red glare of the neon window sign.

Two dogs, tall, ungainly mutts with thin, shaggy frames, crossed the street in front of them, trotting slowly, out for their evening walk. The dogs didn't look up as the boys ran past.

Halfway up the next block, she saw Fred and Alan collapse beneath a dark tree, giggling up at the sky as they sprawled on the ground.

Danny leaned against the wide tree trunk, panting loudly.

Fred and Alan couldn't stop laughing. "Did you see the look on his face when that stupid wing dropped off?" Fred cried.

"I thought his eyes were going to pop out!" Alan exclaimed gleefully. "I thought his head was going to explode!"

Danny didn't join in their laughter. He rubbed his right shoulder with one hand. "He really wrecked my shoulder when he grabbed me," he said, groaning.

"You should sue him!" Alan suggested.

He and Fred laughed uproariously, sitting up to slap each other high-fives.

"No. Really," Danny said quietly, still rubbing the shoulder. "He really hurt me. When he swung me around, I thought—"

"What a creep," Fred said, shaking his head.

"We'll have to pay him back," Alan added. "We'll have to—"

"Maybe we should stay away from there," Danny said, still breathing hard. "You heard what he said about getting his shotgun."

The other two boys laughed scornfully. "Yeah. Sure. He'd really come after us with a shotgun," Alan scoffed, brushing blades of freshly cut grass from his straggly hair.

"The respected town postmaster, shooting at innocent kids," Fred said, sniggering. "No way. He was just trying to scare us—right, Danny?"

Danny stopped rubbing his shoulder and frowned down at Alan and Fred, who were still sitting in the grass. "I don't know."

"Oooh, Danny is scared!" Fred cried.

"You're not scared of that old geek, are you?" Alan demanded. "Just because he grabbed your shoulder doesn't mean—"

"I don't know," Danny interrupted angrily. "The old man seemed pretty out of control to me. He was so angry! I mean, maybe he *would* shoot us to protect his precious postbox."

"Bet we could make him a lot angrier," Alan said quietly, climbing to his feet, staring intently at Danny.

"Yeah. Bet we could," Fred agreed, grinning.

"Unless you're chicken, Danny," Alan said, moving close to Danny, challenge in his voice.

"I—it's getting late," Danny said, trying to read his watch in the dark. "I promised my mum I'd get home."

Fred climbed to his feet and moved next to Alan. "We should teach Chesney a lesson," he said, brushing blades of grass off the back of his jeans. His eyes gleamed mischievously in the dim light. "We should teach him not to pick on innocent kids."

"Yeah, you're right," Alan agreed, his eyes on Danny. "I mean, he hurt Danny. He had no business grabbing him like that."

"I've got to get home. See you two tomorrow," Danny said, waving.

"Okay. See you," Fred called after him.

"At least we got some free ice-cream tonight!" Alan exclaimed.

As Danny walked quickly away, Hannah could hear Alan and Fred giggling their gleeful, high-pitched giggles.

Free ice-cream, she thought, frowning. Those two boys are really looking for trouble.

She couldn't help herself. She had to say something to Danny. "Hey!" she called, running to catch up with him.

He spun round, startled. "Hannah—what are *you* doing here?"

"I—I followed you. From the ice-cream parlour," she confessed.

He sniggered. "You saw everything?"

She nodded. "Why do you hang around with those two idiots?" she demanded.

He scowled, avoiding her eyes, quickening his pace. "They're okay," he muttered.

"They're going to get in big trouble one of these days," Hannah predicted. "They really are."

Danny shrugged. "They just talk tough. They think it's cool. But they're really okay."

"But they stole ice-cream cones and—" Hannah decided she'd said enough.

They crossed the street in silence.

Hannah glanced up to see the pale crescent of moon disappear behind black wisps of cloud. The street grew darker. The trees shook their leaves, sending whispers all around.

Danny kicked a stone down the pavement. It clattered softly on to the grass.

Hannah suddenly remembered going over to Danny's house earlier to get him. In all the excitement of the stolen ice-cream cones and Mr Chesney and his postbox, she had completely forgotten what had happened on his back door step.

"I—I went over to your house tonight," she started reluctantly. "Before I went into town."

Danny stopped and turned to her, his eyes studying hers. "Yeah?"

"I thought maybe you'd want to walk to town or something," Hannah continued. "Your mother was at home. In the kitchen."

He continued to stare hard at her, as if trying to read her thoughts.

"I knocked and knocked on the kitchen door," Hannah said, tugging a strand of blonde hair off her forehead. "I could see your mother at the table. She had her back to me. She didn't turn round or anything."

Danny didn't reply. He lowered his eyes to the pavement and started walking again, hands shoved in his pockets.

"It was so strange," Hannah continued. "I knocked and knocked. Really loud. But it was as if—as if your mother was in a different world or something. She didn't answer the door. She didn't even turn round."

Their houses came into view ahead of them. A porchlight sent a yellow glow over Hannah's front lawn. On the other side of the drive, Danny's house loomed in darkness.

Hannah's throat suddenly felt dry. She wished she could ask Danny what she really wanted to ask.

Are you a ghost? Is your mother a ghost, too?

That was the real question in Hannah's mind.

But it was too crazy. Too stupid.

How can you ask a person if he is real or not? If he is alive or not?

"Danny—why didn't your mother answer the door?" she asked quietly.

Danny turned at the bottom of her drive, his expression set, his eyes narrowed. His face glowed eerily in the pale yellow light from the porch.

"Why?" Hannah repeated impatiently. "Why didn't she answer the door?"

He hesitated.

"I suppose I should tell you the truth," he said finally, his voice a whisper, as soft as the whisper of the shuddering trees.

Danny leaned close to Hannah. She could see that his red hair was matted to his forehead with sweat. His eyes burned into hers.

"There's a good reason why my mother didn't answer the door," Danny told her.

Because she's a ghost, Hannah thought. She felt a cold shiver roll down her back. A tremor of fear.

She swallowed hard. *Am I afraid of Danny?* she asked herself.

Yes. A little, she realized. Her scary dream about him flashed into her mind. *Yes. A little.*

"You see," Danny started, then hesitated. He cleared his throat. He shifted his weight nervously. "You see, my mum is deaf."

"Huh?" Hannah wasn't sure she had heard correctly. It wasn't at all what she was expecting.

"She got this inner-ear infection," Danny explained in a low voice, keeping his eyes

361

trained on Hannah. "In both ears. A couple of years ago. The doctors treated it, but the infection spread. They thought they could save one ear, but they couldn't. It made her completely deaf."

"You—you mean—?" Hannah stammered.

"That's why she couldn't hear you knocking," Danny explained. "She can't hear anything at all." He lowered his eyes to the ground.

"I see," Hannah replied awkwardly. "I'm sorry, Danny. I didn't know. I thought . . . well, I didn't know *what* to think."

"Mum doesn't like people to know," Danny continued, backing towards his house. "She thinks people will feel sorry for her if they know. She hates having people feeling sorry for her. She's a really good lip-reader. She usually fools people."

"Well, I won't say anything," Hannah replied. "I mean, I won't tell anyone. I—" She suddenly felt very stupid.

Her head lowered, she made her way up the drive towards her front path.

"See you tomorrow," Danny called.

"Yeah. Okay," she replied, thinking about what he had just told her.

She looked up to wave goodnight to him.

But he had vanished.

Hannah turned and began jogging around the

side of the house towards the back door. Danny's words troubled her. She realized all of her thoughts about ghosts might have been a big mistake.

Her parents were always predicting that one day her imagination would run away with her.

Now maybe it has, Hannah though unhappily.

Maybe I've totally blown it.

She turned the corner of the house and started towards the back door, her trainers squishing on the soft, wet ground.

The light over the porch sent a narrow cone of white light on to the concrete step.

Hannah was nearly at the door when the dark figure, wrapped in black shadow, its red eyes glowing like hot coals, stepped into the light, blocking her path.

"Hannah—stay away!" it whispered, pointing menacingly at her with one long, shadowy finger.

Gripped with horror, Hannah thought she saw the shadow of an evil grin inside the deeper shadow that hovered over the step. "Hannah, stay away. Stay away from DANNY!"

"*Nooooooooooo!*"

In her panic, Hannah didn't even realize that the howl came from her own throat.

The red eyes glowed brighter in reaction to her scream. The fiery stare burned into her eyes, forcing her to shield her face with both hands.

"Hannah—listen to my warning." The dreadful dry whisper.

The whisper of death.

The sinewy black finger, outlined in the white porchlight, pointed to her, threatened her again.

And again Hannah cried out in a voice hoarse with terror: "*Nooooooooo!*"

The dark figure swept closer.

Closer.

And then the kitchen door swung open, throwing a long rectangle of light over the garden.

"Hannah—is that you? What's going on?"

Her father stepped into the light, his features knotted with concern, his eyes peering into the darkness through his square spectacles.

"Dad—!" Hannah's voice caught in her throat. "Look out, Dad—he—he—" Hannah pointed.

Pointed to empty air.

Pointed to the empty rectangle of light from the kitchen door.

Pointed to nothing.

The shadow figure had disappeared once again.

Her mind spinning in confusion, feeling dazed and terrified, she hurried past her father, into the house.

She had told her parents about the frightening dark figure with the glowing red eyes. Her father carefully searched the back garden, his torch playing over the lawn. He found no footprints in the soft, wet ground, no sign at all of an intruder.

Hannah's mother had gazed intently at her, studying her, as if trying to find some kind of answer in Hannah's eyes.

"I—I'm not crazy," Hannah stammered angrily.

Mrs Fairchild's cheeks turned pink. "I know that," she replied tensely.

"Should I call the police? There's nothing back there," Mr Fairchild said, scratching his thinning brown hair, his spectacles reflecting the light from the kitchen ceiling.

"I'll just go to bed," Hannah told them, moving abruptly to the door. "I'm really tired."

Her legs felt trembly and weak as she hurried down the hall to her room.

Sighing wearily, she pushed open her bedroom door.

The dark shadow figure was waiting for her by her bed.

Hannah gasped and started to back away.

But as the hall light fell into the bedroom, she realized she wasn't staring at the frightening figure after all.

She was staring at a longsleeved, dark sweater she had tossed over the bedpost at the foot of her bed.

Hannah gripped the sides of the doorway. She couldn't decide whether to laugh or cry.

"What a night!" she exclaimed out loud.

She clicked on the bedroom ceiling light, then closed the door behind her. As she made her way over to the bed to pull the sweater off the bedpost, she was shaking all over.

She pulled off her clothes quickly, tossing them onto the floor, and put on a nightdress. Then she climbed under the covers, eager to get to sleep.

But she couldn't stop her mind from whirring over all that had happened. She couldn't stop the frightening pictures from playing in her head, over and over.

The shadows of tree limbs from the front garden shifted and bobbed across the ceiling. Normally, she found their silent dance soothing. But tonight the moving shadows frightened her, reminded her of the menacing dark figure that had called her name.

She tried to think about Danny instead. But those thoughts were just as troubling.

Danny is a ghost. Danny is a ghost.

The phrase repeated again and again in her mind.

He *had* to be lying about his mother, Hannah decided. He made up the story about her being deaf because he doesn't want me to work out that *she's* a ghost, too.

Questions, questions.

Questions she couldn't answer.

If Danny is a ghost, what is he doing here? Why did he move in next door to me?

Why does he hang around with Alan and Fred? Are they ghosts, too?

Is that why I've never seen them at school or in town before? Is that why I've never seen any of them? They're all ghosts?

Hannah shut her eyes, trying to force all the questions from her mind. But she couldn't stop thinking about Danny—and the dark shadow figure.

Why did the dark figure tell me to stay away from Danny? Is it trying to keep me from proving that Danny is a ghost?

Finally, Hannah fell asleep. But even in sleep, her troubled thoughts pursued her.

The sinewy black shadow followed her into her dreams. In the dream, she was standing in a grey cave. A fire burned brightly, far in the distance at the mouth of the cave.

The black figure, its red eyes glowing brighter than the fire, moved towards Hannah. Closer. And closer.

And when the black figure came so close, close enough for Hannah to reach out and touch it, the shadow figure reached up with its sticklike arms and pulled itself apart.

It reached up with its ebony hands and with boney fingers, pulled away the darkness where its face should be—revealing Danny underneath.

Danny, leering at her with glowing red eyes that burned into hers—until she woke up gasping for breath.

No, she thought, staring out of the window at the grey dawn. *No. Danny isn't the black shadow.*

No way.

It isn't Danny.

It can't be Danny. The dream makes no sense.

Hannah sat up. Her bedclothes were damp

from perspiration. The air in the room hung heavy and sour.

She kicked off the covers and lowered her feet to the floor.

She knew only one thing for certain after her long night of frightening thoughts.

She had to talk to Danny.

She couldn't spend another night like this.

She had to find out the truth.

The next morning, after breakfast, she saw him kicking a football around in his back garden. She pulled open the kitchen door and ran outside. The screen door slammed loudly behind her as she began to run to him.

"Hey, Danny—" she called. "Are you a ghost?"

"Huh?" Danny glanced at her, then kicked the black-and-white football against the side of the garage. He was wearing a navy-blue T-shirt over denim shorts. He had a blue-and-red Cubs cap pulled down over his red hair.

Hannah ran full speed across the drive and stopped a few metres from him. "Are you a ghost?" she repeated breathlessly.

He wrinkled his forehead, squinting at her. The ball bounced across the grass. He stepped forward and kicked it. "Yeah. Sure," he said.

"No. Really," Hannah insisted, her heart pounding.

The ball bounced high off the garage, and he caught it against his chest. "What did you say?" He scratched the back of one knee.

He's staring at me as if I'm nuts, Hannah realized.

371

Maybe I am.

"Never mind," she said, swallowing hard. "Can I play?"

"Yeah." He dropped the ball to the grass. "How ya doing?" he asked. "You okay today?"

Hannah nodded. "Yeah, I suppose so."

"That was pretty wild last night," Danny said, kicking the ball gently to her. "I mean, at Mr Chesney's."

The ball went past Hannah. She chased after it and kicked it back. Normally, she was a good athlete. But this morning she was wearing sandals, not the best for kicking a football.

"I really got scared," Hannah admitted. "I thought that car that stopped was the police and—"

"Yeah. It was pretty scary," Danny said. He picked the ball up and hit it back to her with his head.

"Do Alan and Fred really go to Maple Avenue School?" Hannah asked. The ball hit her ankle and rolled towards the drive.

"Yeah. They're going to be in the ninth grade," Danny told her, waiting for her to kick the ball back.

"They're not new kids? How come I've never seen them?" She kicked the ball hard.

Danny moved to his right to get behind it.

He sniggered. "How come they've never seen *you*?"

He isn't giving me any straight answers, Hannah realized. I think my questions are making him nervous. He knows I'm starting to suspect the truth about him.

"Alan and Fred want to go back to Chesney's," Danny told her.

"Huh? They what?" She missed the ball and kicked up a lump of grass. "Ow. I can't play football in sandals!"

"They want to go back tonight. You know. To pay Chesney back for scaring us. He really hurt my shoulder."

"I think Alan and Fred are really looking for trouble," Hannah warned.

Danny shrugged. "Nothing *else* to do in this town," he muttered.

The ball rolled between them.

"I've got it!" they both yelled in unison.

They both chased after the ball. Danny got to it first. He tried to kick it away from her. But his foot landed on top of the ball. He stumbled over it and went sprawling onto the grass.

Hannah laughed and jumped over him to get to the ball. She kicked it against the side of the garage, then turned back to him, smiling triumphantly. "One for me!" she declared.

He sat up slowly, grass stains smearing the chest of his T-shirt. "Help me up." He reached up his hands to hers.

Hannah reached to pull Danny up—and her hands went right through him!

They both uttered startled cries.

"Hey, come on! Help me up," Danny said.

Her heart pounding, Hannah tried to grab his hands again.

But again her hands went right through his.

"Hey—!" Danny cried, his eyes wide with alarm. He jumped to his feet, staring at her hard.

"I knew it," Hannah said softly, raising her hands to her cheeks. She took a step back, away from him.

"Knew it? Knew *what*?" He continued to stare at her, his face filled with confusion. "What's going on, Hannah?"

"Stop pretending," Hannah told him, suddenly feeling cold all over despite the bright morning sunshine. "I know the truth, Danny. You're a ghost."

"Huh?" His mouth dropped open in disbelief.

He pulled off his Cubs cap and scratched his hair, staring hard at her all the while.

"You're a ghost," she repeated, her voice trembling.

"Me?" he cried. "No way! Are you *crazy*? I'm not a ghost!"

Without warning, he stepped in front of her and shot his hand out at her chest.

Hannah gasped as his hand went right through her body.

She didn't feel a thing. It was as if she weren't there.

Danny cried out and jerked his hand back as if he had burned it. He swallowed hard, his expression tight with horror. "Y-you—" he stammered.

Hannah tried to reply, but the words caught in her throat.

Giving her one last horrified glance, Danny turned and began running at full speed towards his house.

Hannah stared helplessly after him until he disappeared through the back door. The door slammed hard behind him.

Dazed, Hannah turned and began to run home.

She felt dizzy. The ground seemed to spin beneath her. The blue sky shimmered and became blindingly bright. Her house tilted and swayed.

"Danny's not the ghost," Hannah said out loud. "I finally know the truth. Danny's not the ghost. *I am!*"

Hannah stepped up to the back door, then hesitated.

I can't go back in now, she thought. I have to think.

Maybe I'll go for a walk or something.

She closed her eyes, trying to force her dizziness away. When she opened them, everything seemed brighter, too bright to bear.

Stepping carefully off the back step, she headed towards the front, her head spinning.

I'm a ghost.

I'm not a real person any more.

I'm a ghost.

Voices broke into Hannah's confused thoughts. Someone was approaching.

She ducked out of sight behind the big maple tree and listened.

"It's a perfectly lovely house." Hannah recognized Mrs Quilty's voice.

"My cousin from Detroit looked at it last

week," another woman said. Hannah didn't recognize her. Peering out from behind the tree trunk, Hannah saw that it was a thin, haggard-looking woman wearing a yellow sundress. She and Mrs Quilty were standing halfway up the drive, admiring Hannah's house.

Afraid she might be seen, Hannah ducked back behind the tree.

"Did your cousin like the house?" Mrs Quilty asked her companion.

"Too small," was the curt reply.

"What a shame," Mrs Quilty said with a loud sigh. "I just hate having an empty house on the block."

But it's not empty! Hannah thought angrily. I live here! My whole family lives here—don't we?

"How long has it been vacant?" the other woman asked.

"Ever since it was rebuilt," Hannah heard Mrs Quilty reply. "You know. After that dreadful fire. I suppose it must have been five years ago."

"Fire?" Mrs Quilty's friend asked. "That was before I moved here. Did the whole house burn down?"

"Pretty much," Mrs Quilty told her. "It was so dreadful, Beth. Such a tragedy. The family trapped inside. Such a beautiful family. A young girl. Two little boys. They all died that night."

My dream! Hannah thought, gripping the tree trunk to hold herself up. *It wasn't a dream. It was a real fire. I really died that night.*

Tears streamed down Hannah's face. Her legs felt weak and trembly. She leaned against the rough bark of the tree and listened.

"How did it happen?" Beth, Mrs Quilty's friend, asked. "Do they know what started the fire?"

"Yes. The kids had some kind of campfire out the back. Behind the garage," Mrs Quilty continued. "When they went inside, they didn't put it out completely. The house caught fire after they'd gone to sleep. It spread so quickly."

Hannah saw the two women peering thoughtfully at the house from their position on the drive. They were shaking their heads.

"The house was gutted, then completely rebuilt," Mrs Quilty was saying. "But no one ever moved in. It's been five years. Can you imagine?"

I've been dead for five years, Hannah thought, letting the tears roll down her cheeks. No wonder I didn't know Danny or his friends.

No wonder I haven't received any letters from Janey. No wonder I haven't heard from any of my friends.

I've been dead for five years.

Now, Hannah understood why sometimes time seemed to stand still, and sometimes it floated by so quickly.

Ghosts come and go, she thought sadly. Sometimes I'm solid enough to ride a bike or kick a soccer ball. And sometimes I'm so flimsy, someone's hand goes right through me.

Hannah watched the two women make their way down the road until they disappeared from view. Clinging to the tree trunk, she made no attempt to move.

It was all beginning to make sense to Hannah. The dream-like summer days. The loneliness. The feeling that something wasn't right.

But what about Mum and Dad? she asked herself, pushing herself away from the tree. What about the twins? Do they *know*? Do they know that we're all ghosts?

"Mum!" she shouted, running to the front door. "Mum!"

She burst into the house and ran through the hall to the kitchen. "Mum! Mum! Where *are* you? Bill? Herb?"

Silence.

No one there.

They had all gone.

"Where *are* you?" Hannah cried aloud. "Mum! Bill! Herb!"

Had they gone *forever*?

We're *all* ghosts, she thought miserably. *All.*

And now they've left me here by myself.

Her heart pounding, she gazed around the kitchen.

It was bare. Empty.

No cereal boxes on the worktop where they were usually kept. No funny magnets on the fridge. No curtains at the window. No clock on the wall. No kitchen table.

"Where *are* you?" Hannah called desperately.

She pushed away from the worktop and went running through the house.

All empty. All bare.

No clothing. No furniture. No lamps or posters on the wall or books in the bookshelves.

Gone. Everything gone.

They've left me here. A ghost. A ghost all by myself.

"I've got to talk to someone," she said aloud. "Anyone!"

She searched desperately for a telephone until she found a red one on the bare kitchen wall.

Who can I call? Who?

No one.

I'm dead.

I've been dead for five years.

She picked up the receiver and brought it to her ear.

Silence. The phone was dead, too.

With a hopeless cry, Hannah let the receiver fall to the floor. Her heart thudding, tears once again rolling down her cheeks, she flung herself down onto the bare floor.

Sobbing softly to herself, she buried her head in her arms and let the darkness sweep over her.

When she opened her eyes, the darkness remained.

She pulled herself up, not sure at first where she was. Feeling shaky and tense, she raised her eyes to the kitchen window. Outside, the sky was blue-black.

Night.

Time floats in and out when you're a ghost, Hannah realized. That's why the summer has seemed so short and so endless at the same time. She stretched her arms towards the ceiling, then wandered from the kitchen.

"Anyone home?" she called.

She wasn't surprised by the silence that greeted her question.

Her family had gone.

But where?

As she made her way through the dark, empty hallway towards the front of the house, she had another premonition. Another feeling of dread.

Something bad was going to happen.

Now? Tonight?

She stopped at the open front door and peered through the screen door. "Hey—!" Danny was on his bike, pedalling slowly down his drive.

Impulsively, Hannah pushed open the screen door and ran outside. "Hey—Danny!"

He slowed his bike and turned to her.

"Danny—wait!" she called, running across her garden towards him.

"No—please!" His face filled with fright. He raised both hands as if to shield himself.

"Danny—?"

"*Go away!*" he screamed, his voice shrill from terror. "*Please—stay away!*" He gripped the handlebars and began pedalling furiously away.

Hannah jumped back, stunned and hurt.
"Don't be afraid of me!" she shouted after him,
cupping her hands around her mouth to be
heard. "Danny, please—don't be afraid!"

Leaning over the handlebars, he rode away
without looking back.

Hannah uttered a hurt cry.

As Danny disappeared down the block, the
feeling of dread swept over her.

I know where he's going, she thought.

He's meeting Alan and Fred, and they're
going to Mr Chesney's house. They're going to
get their revenge on Mr Chesney.

And something very bad is going to happen.

I'm going there, too, Hannah decided.

I *have* to go, too.

She hurried to the garage to get her bike.

Mr Chesney had repaired his postbox, Hannah
saw. The hand-carved swan wings floated out
from the pole, which had been returned to its
erect position.

Crouching behind the same low evergreen,
Hannah watched the three boys across the
street. They hesitated at the edge of Mr
Chesney's garden, hidden from the house by the
tall hedge.

In the pale white light of the street lamp,
Hannah could see them grinning and joking.

Then she saw Fred shove Danny towards the postbox.

Hannah raised her gaze beyond the hedge to Mr Chesney's small house. Orange light glowed dimly from the living room window. The porchlight was on. The rest of the house sat in darkness.

Was Mr Chesney home? Hannah couldn't tell.

His battered old car wasn't in the drive.

Hannah crouched behind the evergreen. Its prickly branches bobbed in a light breeze.

She watched Danny struggle to pull up the postbox. Alan and Fred were standing behind him, urging him on.

Danny gripped both jutting wings and pulled.

Fred slapped him on the back. "Harder!" he cried.

"What a wimp!" Alan declared, laughing.

Hannah kept glancing nervously up to the house. The boys were so noisy. What made them so sure that Mr Chesney wasn't home?

What made them so sure that Chesney wouldn't keep his promise and come after them with his shotgun?

Hannah shuddered. She felt a trickle of perspiration slide down her forehead.

She watched Danny tug furiously at the postbox. With a hard pull, he tilted it at an angle.

Fred and Alan cheered gleefully.

Danny began to rock the postbox, pushing it with his shoulder, then pulling it back. It was coming loose, tilting farther with each push, each pull.

Hannah heard Danny's loud groan as he gave it a final strong push—and the postbox fell onto its side on the ground. He backed away, a triumphant smile on his face.

Fred and Alan cheered again and slapped him high-fives.

Fred picked up the postbox, hoisted it onto his shoulder, and paraded back and forth in front of the hedge with it, as if it were an enemy flag.

As they celebrated their triumph, Hannah again glanced over the hedge to the dimly lit house.

No sign of Mr Chesney.

Maybe he wasn't there. Maybe the boys would get away without getting caught.

But why did Hannah still have the heavy feeling of dread weighing her down, chilling her body?

She gasped as she saw a shadow slide past the corner of the house.

Mr Chesney?

No.

Squinting hard into the dim light, Hannah felt her heart begin to thud against her chest.

No one there. But what was that shadow?

She had definitely seen it, a shape darker than the long night shadows, slithering against the greyness of the house.

The boys' loud voices interrupted her thoughts, drawing her attention away from the house.

Fred had tossed the postbox into the hedge. Now they had moved towards the drive. They were discussing something, arguing loudly. Alan laughed. Fred gave Alan a playful shove. Danny was saying something, but Hannah couldn't hear his words.

Get away, Hannah urged them in her mind. *Get away from there. You've pulled your stupid prank, had your stupid revenge.*

Now get away—before you get caught.

The evergreen limbs bobbed silently in a gust of hot wind. Hannah stepped back into the darkness, her eyes on the boys.

They were huddled together at the bottom of the drive. They were talking excitedly, all three at once. Then Hannah saw a flicker of light. It glowed for a moment, then went out.

It was a match, Hannah realized.

Alan was holding a large box of kitchen matches.

Hannah glanced nervously at the house. All was still. No Mr Chesney. No shadows slithering across the wall.

Go home. Please, go home, she silently urged the boys.

But to her dismay, they turned and began jogging up the gravel drive. They ducked low as they ran, trying not to be seen from the house.

What are they doing? Hannah wondered, feeling all of her muscles tighten in dread. A shiver of fear ran down her back as she stepped out from behind the evergreen.

What are they going to do?

She made her way quickly across the street and ducked in front of the hedge, her heart pounding.

She couldn't hear them. They must be nearly up to the house by now.

Should she follow them?

She stood up slowly and raised herself on tiptoes to see over the hedge.

The three boys, Alan in the lead, followed by Danny and Fred, were bent low, running rapidly across the front of the house. Caught in the dim orange glow of light from the window, Hannah could see their determined expressions.

Where are they going? What are they planning?

Hannah watched them run into the darkness around the side of the house.

Still no sign of Mr Chesney.

Keeping close to the hedge, Hannah made her way to the drive. Then, without thinking about it, without even realizing it, she was running, too.

She stopped short as she saw Alan shoving Danny up into an open window. Then Fred stepped forward, lifted his hands to the window ledge, and allowed Alan to give him a boost.

No—please! Hannah wanted to cry.

Don't go into the house! Don't go in there!

But she was too late.

All three of them had climbed into the house.

Breathing hard, Hannah began to creep towards the window.

But halfway there, she felt something grab her leg and hold her in place.

Hannah uttered a silent cry.

She struggled to free her leg—and quickly realized she had stepped into a coiled garden hose.

Exhaling loudly, she lifted her foot out of it and crept the rest of the way to the open window.

This side of the house was covered in darkness. The window was too high for Hannah to see into the room.

Standing beneath the window, Hannah could hear the boys' trainers thudding on bare floorboards. She could hear whispering voices and high-pitched, muffled laughter.

What are they doing in there? she wondered, her whole body tight with fear.

Don't they realize how much trouble they could get into?

Bright lights against the side of the house made Hannah jump back with a startled cry.

She dropped to the ground and spun round. And saw headlights through the tall hedge. Car headlights floating towards the drive.

Mr Chesney?

Was he returning home? Returning home in time to catch the three intruders in his house?

Hannah opened her mouth to call out a warning to the boys. But her voice caught in her throat.

The headlights floated past. The darkness rolled back over the garden.

The car rumbled silently on.

It wasn't Mr Chesney, Hannah realized.

She struggled to her feet and returned to her place below the window. She decided she had to let the boys know she was there. She had to get them *out* of there!

"Danny!" she called, wrapping her hands around her mouth as a megaphone. "Get out! Come on—get out *now*!"

The feeling of dread weighed her down. She shouted up to the window again. "Come out. Hurry—please!"

She could hear their muffled voices inside. And she could hear the scrape of trainers on the floor.

Staring up at the window, she saw a light come on. Orange light, dim at first, then brighter.

"Are you *crazy*?" she shouted in to them. "Turn off the lights!"

Why on earth were they turning on lights?

Did they *want* to get caught?

"Turn off the lights!" she repeated in a high, shrill, frightened voice.

But the orange light grew brighter, became a bright yellow.

And as she stared in horror, Hannah realized the light was flickering.

Not lamp light.

Fire light.

Fire!

They had started a fire!

"No!" she screamed, raising her hands to the sides of her face. "No! Get out! Get out of there!"

She could smell smoke now. She could see the reflection of the leaping flames in the window glass.

She started to shout to them again—but stopped when she saw the shadow move towards her on the wall of the house.

Hannah stopped and turned to stare.

And saw the dark figure, blacker than the night, its red eyes glowing brightly from the blackness of its face.

It stepped silently towards her, floating rapidly over the tall, weed-strewn grass. Its red eyes appeared to light up as it neared.

"Hannah—stay away!" the moving shadow called in a voice as dry as dead leaves.

"Hannah—stay away."

"Nooooo!" Hannah uttered a frightened wail as it moved towards her. A burst of frigid air encircled her body. "Noooo!"

"Hannah . . . Hannah . . ."

"Who are you?" she demanded. "What do you want?"

Behind her, she could hear the crackle of flames now. Yellow light flickered behind choking waves of black smoke from the open window.

Its fiery eyes glowing brighter, the shadow figure raised itself up, hovered closer, closer, stretching out its arms, preparing to pull her in.

Gripped with fear, Hannah raised her hands in front of her as if trying to shield herself.

She heard a sudden scrabbling at the window. A muffled cry above her head.

The shadow figure vanished.

And then she felt someone topple onto her.

They both fell in a heap to the ground.

"Alan!" she cried.

He struggled to his feet, his eyes wide with panic. "The matches!" he cried. "The matches! We—we didn't mean to. We—"

Another figure came diving out of the window as the crackle of flames grew to a roar. Fred landed hard on his elbows and knees.

Hannah stared at his dazed face in the darting orange light. "Fred—are you okay?"

"Danny," he muttered, gazing at her with horror. "Danny's in there. He can't get out."

"Huh?" Hannah leapt to her feet.

"Danny's trapped in the fire. He's going to burn!" Alan cried.

"We have to get help!" Fred said, shouting over the roar of the flames. He pulled Alan by the arm. The two boys took off, running unsteadily across the garden towards the house next door.

Bright orange-and-yellow flames licked at the windowsill above Hannah's head.

I have to save Danny, she thought.

She took a deep breath, gazing up at the flickering, flashing light of the fire. Then she started towards the open window.

But before she could take a step, the light from the window disappeared. The shadow rose in front of her.

"Hannah—go away." Its frightening, harsh whisper was so close to her face. "Go away."

"No!" Hannah screamed, forgetting her fear. "I have to save Danny."

"Hannah . . . you will not save him!" came the raspy reply.

The dark figure, eyes afire, hovered over her, blocking Hannah's path to the window.

"Let me go!" she screamed. "I have to save him!"

The red eyes loomed closer. The darkness fell heavier around her.

"Who *are* you?" Hannah shrieked. "*What* are you? What do you *want*?"

The dark figure didn't reply. The glowing eyes burned into hers.

Danny is trapped in there, Hannah thought. I *have* to get in through that window.

"*Move out of my way!*" she screamed. And in her desperation, she reached out with both hands—grabbed the dark figure by the shoulders—and tried to shove it out of the way.

To Hannah's shock, the figure felt solid. With a determined cry, she raised her hands to its face—and tugged.

The darkness that cloaked its face fell away— and beneath the darkness, *Danny's face* was revealed!

Hannah stared in horror and disbelief, struggling to breathe. The sour odour stopped her. The darkness continued to wrap around her, holding her prisoner.

Danny grinned back at her, with the same glowing red eyes as before he'd been unmasked.

"No!" Hannah cried, her voice a hoarse whisper, tight with fear. "It isn't you, Danny. It isn't!"

A cruel smile played over the figure's glowing face. "I am Danny's ghost!" he declared.

"Ghost?" Hannah tried to pull back. But the darkness held her tightly.

"I am Danny's ghost. When he dies in the fire, I will no longer be a shadow. I will be BORN— and Danny will go to the shadow world in my place!"

"No! No!" Hannah shrieked, raising her fists in front of her. "No! Danny will not die! I won't let him!"

Danny's ghost opened his mouth and uttered a foul-smelling laugh. "You're too late, Hannah!" he sneered. "Too late."

25

"Nooooooo!"

Hannah's wail echoed in the darkness that surrounded her.

The ghost-Danny's red eyes flared angrily as Hannah burst right through him.

A second later, she was raising her hands to the window ledge. "Oh!" The sill was hot from the fire.

Using all her strength, she pulled herself up towards the darting flames—and into the house. A curtain of thick, sour smoke rose up to greet her.

Ignoring the smoke and the bright wall of fire, Hannah lowered herself heavily onto the floor.

I'm a ghost, she told herself, stepping into the blazing room.

I'm a ghost. I can't die again.

She rubbed her eyes with the sleeve of her T-shirt, struggling to see. "Danny?" she called, shouting as loudly as she could. "Danny—I can't see you! Where are you?"

Shielding her eyes with one hand, Hannah took another step into the room. Flames shot up like bright geysers. Wallpaper on one wall had curled down, the blackened corner covered with leaping flames.

"Danny—where are you?"

She heard a muffled shout from the next room. Dashing through the flame-encircled doorway, she saw him—trapped behind a tall wall of flames.

"Danny—!"

He was backed into a corner, his hands raised together in front of him, shielding his face from the smoke.

I can't get through those thick flames, Hannah realized to her horror.

She took another step into the room, then held back.

No way.

No way I can save him.

But once again, she reminded herself: *I am a ghost. I can do things that living people cannot do.*

"Help me! Help me!"

Danny's voice sounded tiny and far away behind the leaping waves of flame.

Without another second's hesitation, Hannah

sucked in a deep breath, held it—and leapt into the flames.

"Help me!" He stared at her, his eyes blank. He didn't seem to see her. "Help!"

"Come on!" She grabbed his hand and tugged. "Let's go!"

The flames bent towards them, like fiery arms reaching to grab them.

"Come *on!*"

She tugged again, but he held back. "We can't make it!"

"Yes—we *have* to!" she shouted.

The heat burned her nostrils. She shut her eyes against the blinding yellow brightness. "We *have* to!"

She grabbed his hand with both of hers and pulled.

Black smoke swirled around them. Choking, she shut her eyes and pulled him, pulled him into the searing, blistering heat of the flames.

Into the flames.

Through them.

Coughing and choking. Dripping with perspiration from the furnace-like heat.

Pulled him. Pulled blindly. Pulled with all her might.

She didn't open her eyes until they were at the window.

She didn't breathe until they had tumbled to the cool darkness of the ground.

Then, on her hands and knees, panting so loudly, gasping for clean air, she gazed up.

There was the shadow figure near the house, twisting in flames. As the fire consumed it, it raised its dark arms towards the sky—and vanished without making a sound.

With a relieved sigh, Hannah lowered her gaze to Danny.

He was lying sprawled on his back, a dazed expression on his face. "Hannah," he whispered hoarsely. "Hannah, thanks."

She felt a smile start to cross her face.

Everything turned bright, as bright as the wall of flames.

Then everything went black.

Danny's mother leaned over him, pulling the light blanket up to his chest. "How are you feeling?" she asked softly.

It was two hours later. Danny had been treated by the ambulance men who arrived shortly after the firefighters. They told his worried mother that he was suffering from smoke inhalation and had a few minor burns.

After treating the burns, they drove Danny and Mrs Anderson home in an ambulance.

Now Danny lay in bed, staring up at her, still feeling groggy and dazed. Mrs Quilty stood anxiously in the corner, her arms clasped tensely in front of her, looking on in silence. She had hurried over to see what the commotion was.

"I—I'm okay, I suppose," Danny said, pulling himself up a bit on the pillow. "I'm just a little tired."

His mother pushed a lock of blonde hair off her

forehead as she stared down at him, reading his lips. "How did you ever get out? How did you get out of the house?"

"It was Hannah," Danny told her. "Hannah pulled me out."

"Who?" Mrs Anderson knotted her face in confusion. "Who is Hannah?"

"You know," Danny replied impatiently. "The girl next door."

"There's no girl next door," his mother said. "Is there, Molly?" She turned to read Mrs Quilty's lips.

Mrs Quilty shook her head. "The house is empty."

Danny sat up straight. "Her name is Hannah Fairchild. She saved my life, Mum."

Mrs Quilty tutted sympathetically. "Hannah Fairchild is the girl who died five years ago," she said quietly. "Poor Danny is a bit delirious, I'm afraid."

"Just lie back," Danny's mother said, gently pushing him back onto the pillow. "Get some rest. You'll be fine."

"But where is Hannah? Hannah is my friend!" Danny insisted.

Hannah watched the scene from the doorway.

The three people in the room couldn't see her, she realized.

She had saved Danny's life, and now the room

and the people in it were growing faint, fading to grey.

Maybe that's why my family and I came back after five years, Hannah thought. Maybe we came back to save Danny from dying in a fire as we did.

"Hannah...Hannah..." A voice called to her. A sweet, familiar voice from far away.

"Is that you, Mum?" Hannah called.

"Time to come back," Mrs Fairchild whispered. "You must leave now, Hannah. It's time to come back."

"Okay, Mum."

She gazed into the bedroom at Danny, lying peacefully on his pillow. He was fading away now, fading to grey.

Hannah squinted into the solid greyness. The house, she knew, was fading. The earth was fading from her sight.

"Come back, Hannah," her mother whispered. "Come back to us now."

Hannah could feel herself floating now. And as she floated, she gazed down—her last look at earth.

"I can see him, Mum," she said excitedly, brushing the tears off her cheeks. "I can see Danny. In his room. But the light is getting faint. So faint."

"Hannah, come back. Come back to us," her mother whispered, calling her home.

"Danny—remember me!" Hannah cried as Danny's face appeared clearly in the misty grey.

Could he hear her?

Could he hear her calling to him?

She hoped so.

R.L.Stine

Reader beware, you're in for a scare!
These terrifying tales will send shivers up your spine:

HIPPO FANTASY

Lose yourself in a whole new world, a world where anything is possible – from wizards and dragons, to time travel and new civilizations... Gripping, thrilling, scary and funny by turns, these Hippo Fantasy titles will hold you captivated to the very last page.

The Night of Wishes
Michael Ende

Malcolm and the Cloud-Stealer
Douglas Hill

The Crystal Keeper
James Jauncey

The Wednesday Wizard
Sherryl Jordan

Ratspell
Paddy Mounter

Rowan of Rin
Rowan and the Travellers
Emily Rodda

The Practical Princess
Jay Williams

*If you like animals, then you'll love
Hippo Animal Stories!*

Thunderfoot

Deborah van der Beek

When Mel finds the enormous, neglected horse
Thunderfoot, she doesn't know it will change her
life for ever...

Vanilla Fudge

Deborah van der Beek

When Lizzie and Hannah fall in love with the same dog,
neither of them will give up without a fight...

A Foxcub Named Freedom

Brenda Jobling

An injured vixen nudges her young son away from her.
She can sense danger and cares nothing for herself – only
for her son's freedom...

Pirate the Seal

Brenda Jobling

Ryan's always been lonely - but then he meets Pirate
and at last he has a real friend...

Animal Rescue

Bette Paul

Can Tessa help save the badgers of Delves Wood
from destruction?